No Harm Done

Jean McGarry

NO HARM DONE

DALKEY ARCHIVE PRESS

Library of Congress Cataloging-in-Publication Data
Names: McGarry, Jean, author.
Title: No harm done / Jean McGarry.
Description: First Dalkey Archive edition. | Victoria, TX : Dalkey
   Archive Press, 2017.
Identifiers: LCCN 2016054352 | ISBN 9781943150076 (paperback :
   alk. paper)
Classification: LCC PS3563.C3636 A6 2017 | DDC 813/.54--dc23
LC record available at https://lccn.loc.gov/2016054352

www.dalkeyarchive.com
Victoria, TX / McLean, IL / Dublin

Dalkey Archive Press publications are, in part, made possible through
the support of the University of Houston-Victoria and its programs in
creative writing, publishing, and translation.

Printed on permanent/durable acid-free paper

And the Little One Said

The day Mom made me a maple-walnut cake and threw it in my face, you stood there watching it chunk down onto my shoes. My eyes burned for days, and I couldn't get the sweet smell out of my nose. You made her do it.

My mom—our mom—was a fifty-year-old widow with a widow's peak, dark blonde hair, and a toothy smile. The day my dad died, she had a date with my uncle, and had ditched him by the time we put Dad in the ground. Give her time, people said, she's grieving.

She was grieving, but it was because her forties (called her thirties) had become her fifties (still called her thirties), and no one thought she had us at nine or ten. Dad was a pharmacist— he loathed the word druggist, but we insisted, and called his shop the drugstore. There had been three, and his was last choice, because no soda fountain, no liquor rack, no dirty magazines. Mom's dad had the best drugstore with racks of nylons and socks, tee shirts, and books with strippers and gunmen on the covers. I was in there all the time, mixing up shakes, and selling cigs and rubbers.

Mom had always thought I was the loser, because I was tall and gawky like Dad—smart, too, and a born goody-goody, while you were the type to win a prize in the turkey raffle, just the first stroke in landing you in clover.

More came along after the two of us, Frankie and Eddie, twins, living to butt heads and vie for Mom's attention, of which she had almost none, being absorbed with little Millie, Doug, and Princess, who all came after, and none of them Dad's—at least, that's what he thought. Little Millie is still only four feet tall, but she has all her marbles, and is a real pet. Mom had tried an abortion, but the doctor was a quack, and poor Millie came out too early and half baked. She's the most human of us all, the most reliable. She's the one who wiped my face that day, and cleaned out my ears. It was gloopy stuff, and to that I attribute my on-again, off-again hearing.

We admired your straight shot, first out of the house, then out of the neighborhood—our city being a place with nothing for anyone, and yet no one but you ever left, or even thought about it.

Dad died of the usual causes: drinking, heart trouble, diabetes, cancer, and the war, where—although a supply sergeant—he lost an eye and his left thumb. He wouldn't talk about it, so there had to be a story and no glory, as we liked to say about anything that went wrong. Not that we said it to his face. He had a bad temper, and kept the strap looped over the kitchen door, and we learned to run like rabbits, leaving little Millie to take the heat. And he wouldn't smack a midget, so all that rage was stored up and killed him in the end, because the one who really yanked his chain was Mom, but she was a sprinter in school, and first up the stairs and into the bathroom, door locked. (The others didn't lock, but pounding up the stairs, Dad lost his breath and his balance. We always found him sitting there, or looking out the window, gasping. If looks could kill, we'd all be long gone.)

Maple walnut was my favorite, and that meant we never got it—not in ice cream, not in cake, not even in pancake syrup. For that, we had Karo or molasses, which wrecked whatever was drowned under it, plus left a taste in your mouth for days. Mom hated cooking, so unless Dad had had a few, but not too many, and got up the dinner (beans and franks, fried eggs, or shit on a shingle—his specialties from the service—our meals were—. Well, better not say, except she could always throw together a mix cake, if she used a mix that called for water (we didn't always have milk or the egg).

I haven't mentioned Doug or Princess, but they entered the picture later, although they were there the day the cake was hurled. It was just the four of us. Dad was dead one week, and his old mother living with us, as she'd always wanted to, but waited until there was a spare bedroom. We all wanted that bedroom, but the old lady was there before we even knew it. She'd left the cemetery early, jumped into a cab and whipped past the Y to get her bag. When we got home, eyes dripping and snotty noses, she was installed, and stirring Ritz crackers into a cup of warm milk. The neighbors had brought by casseroles and baked goods, and even thought to stock the fridge (empty, except for beer and fruit Jell-O—Mom lived on fruit Jell-O, but never shared) with a quart of milk, margarine, hot dogs, hamburger, eggs, and someone had thought to make up a pitcher of Kool-Aid, and even supplied the pitcher. We sat down and gobbled. We didn't even heat up the macaroni and cheese. We cut the meat loaf right on the Reynolds' wrap. I've never been so hungry in my life—not before, or after. We ate a cake, a dozen doughnuts, the casserole and loaf, and were starting on the Hydrox cookies and Fig Newtons, when the old lady came downstairs to surprise us. First thing she did was heat the milk for her cracker soup. It was one bully taking over for another in a single day. Even Mom was crying, and it had nothing to do with the druggist. I missed him. We had the same name, Eddy. He was Eddy, too, and for gas—because we got along once in a blue moon—he called me Eddy-wood. I loved it, and it stuck.

"Hey, Eddy-wood," he'd say. "How's tricks?"

"Fine, Eddy, and you?"

"Fine and dandy," he'd say. Then, I wouldn't hear from him for a month, but I was the only one he talked to. The rest, he beat—if he could catch them—or ignored, smoking cigs and reading the funny papers. He liked the fights, too. In our city, the fights were an industry, that and cheap jewelry and bed sheets. Mom had worked in a mill and her girlfriends gave her twelve sheets and twelve pillowcases for a wedding present.

They were seconds, but didn't fall apart right away. They were yellow rags by the time the kids came along. We stripped the beds and played ghost when no one was home. For us, ghost was a fresh way to beat on each other, and scare the girls.

All the other wedding presents we'd wrecked—the candlesticks were dented, knick-knacks chipped with their heads snapped off, blankets frayed with burn holes. No cup with a handle, tables banged up, writing all over and under them, and on the walls. We'd thrown things down the toilet, bones were broken and joints dislocated.

The cops came, and the parish priest; the nuns sent home a weekly note, and prayers were offered when punishment, detentions, demerits, and demotions went unremarked.

Those were the good old days. Once Grams was unleashed, a different kind of bedlam broke out, because she despised her daughter-in-law, and blamed us for Big Eddie's croaking before his time, even though she got something out of it—a room with a view—and never paid a dime in rent, or bought, with her own money, a stick of celery or a can of beans. She cashed her social security, divvying it up between St. Vincent de Paul's and gambling. She'd been an orphan and cried to see the conditions the babies lived in, packed in together like sardines, in the home at the foot of our street. She helped them out, scrubbing their floors and washing their windows (she was a scrubwoman by trade, and had confiscated tools from every place of hire). Dad's room was packed with old brooms and dusters, gallon upon gallon of suds, bleach, scrub brushes, and mops of every kind. She'd been socking it away for years, stored in Eddie's garage. We had no car.

So, how did a person like me, a lambkin, a pushover, Mr. Clean, bust into that crowd? People wanted to know and weren't afraid to ask, when they had me cornered. I was an altar boy, a choir boy, a Boy Scout, the top of my class (not saying much), a sodalist, valedictorian, seminarian, and then—whammo, but I'll save that for later.

I was destined for Rome, where they send the pick of the litter to be near the pope, and take courses in Latin, reading the books on the Index to get a taste of what we couldn't have, or what we'd hear about in the confessional. Know thyself—they never put it that way, but that was the gist; get a blueprint of the world, flesh, and devil, and be shut of it. For me, it would have been a breeze. I never felt so much as a twit of temptation. My soul was ready, at all times, for judgment.

One thing I loved—just to get them going—was to parade around the house, upstairs and down, in my cassock and collar. I was a pipsqueak, but I had the full rig. I gave the rest of the crew my blessing, whenever I could catch them, until I had them blacking their souls with cursing, taking God's name in vain, and calling Him down to kill me dead.

Little Mill was the only one to take an interest. She had sewed on the hundred black buttons, and hemmed the surplice, shined my wingtips, and made sure I had a week's worth of skivvies, because I was bunking at the Sem, bussing out on weekends to lord it over them.

I wasn't just a holy Joe, I was set to be apostolic delegate, if they'd consider a peon from the colonies. Rome is an old place with a lot of layers; our town doesn't even have one. It was one remove from the caves, and that's why everyone loved it.

One day, after tipping my hat to Grams, en route to bingo, and making three crosses—forehead, lips, and heart—in front of the church, finishing a couple of decades of the rosary, with an ejaculation on the tip of my tongue (for speedy release from Purgatory), and reading my breviary first thing in the morning, when the house was quiet, seven o'clock mass and communion—I served—and a visit to the Blessed Sacrament, plus half a dozen stations, I was kneeling in front of the Fatima shrine when the Dooley twins—they were an Eddie and Frank, too—pranced by, on their way to the cigar store, where they clerked for the bookie. It was early, and I wasn't in my full rig, just a black shirt and collar.

"Faker," was the first thing out of Frankie's hole.

"Stool pigeon," the other one said. They took after their father and talked out of one side of their mouth.

"Wha'd you call me, punks?" I said, running over to put my face into Eddie's.

"I didn't say nothin'. He said it."

"Thin-skinned, aren't you, Eddie boy?" They were bobbing and weaving because I had a fist ready to swing.

"What of it?" I said.

"Let's make him commit a big, fat sin, Franks. See if you can."

"Go ahead," I said. "Just try."

So they started mouthing off—profanity, obscenity—I smiled at the wit, because Eddie was a card—then, I gave them my blessing. They turned their backs, and would have mooned me, if Msgr. Reilly hadn't stuck his head out that minute, to see what business the undertaker had. They were cronies, and stiffs collected on one side were fair game for the other.

The Dooleys made tracks, each in a different direction. I stood my ground, doffing my hat (porkpie with a ribbon), and saluted the priest.

"Those bums pickin' on you, Ed?"

"No way, Father."

"Good. Got a minute?"

"Anytime, Father."

He wanted me to run up to Tally's, and pick up a box of candles and some incense. He had his own blend, along with a better cut of altar wine.

"Sure, why not?"

"Take the car," he said. (I wasn't quite fifteen, but I'd had my permit since age twelve.)

But the car wasn't there (the nuns had it, and left a note on the dash), so I hoofed it. The monsignor had a running tab at Tally's, and they knew me, but I got to thinking about my own needs, and was eyeballing what they had in the shantung line in chasubles and dalmatics, with matching stoles and maniples. These were pricey, but I tried on a few. They kept a spare cassock in the dressing room. I was a string bean, so the chasuble—one size—hung on me like a curtain, and I looked about ten. No matter. I bowed and blessed the curate in the mirror, joined my hands in front of my lips, the way I'd seen the young clerics do it, with their eyes wide open. I ran through the Ordinary of the mass right there in the fitting room, with myself as altar boy.

"Okay, son," I heard. "That's enough now." It was old Mr. Tally, and he was beating on the door. "Come on out of there now, and put it up."

"Hang on," I said, holding my hands up, palms out, kissing the altar stone, picking up the cup, genuflecting, "*Corpus domine nostrum, Jesu Christi.* Take this, and eat," I said. "And drink."

"I'm calling the cops if you don't get the hell out of there!" This was Tally Jr. speaking. "I've got the stuff for O'Reilly all bagged and ready. What are you doing in there, you little creep?" He was talking big, but had the voice of a fairy. They were both there, banging on the door.

"Body of Christ," I said, raising up the sacred host, and breaking it in half (the big one that people could see way in the back), and eating it. Bowing, chewing the other half, lowering the cup, and covering it with the patten and the cloth.

"Get out of there, you moron," said the older one. "Who does he think he is?" I heard.

"I am the way, the truth, and the life," I said, and in they both came, knocking me right over and into the mirror, which cracked.

But then, I refused to step into the paddy wagon. How could I jump in there, even with a cop under each arm? It was just a squad car, but I was cuffed and ankled. I was full in my dreams, as I always am when I'm having a ball by myself.

I'd been veering into the Proper of the mass, the *Segreto* and the *Agnus Dei,* "*qui tollis peccata mundi,*" and "*misere nobis,*" I answered. The cop sitting next to me was squeezing my arm to get me to shut my trap. They'd stripped the royal-purple chasuble from me, just like Jesus was stripped by the centurions, but I still had *on* the Tally's cassock, torn a little from the struggle.

"What the heck's eatin' ya, kid?" the one next to me said.

"*Misere nobis*," I said.

"Have it your way, but if I were you, I'd be saying my prayers."

"*Quod erat demonstrandum*," I said.

"Button it, punk, or I'll *smack* you one," he snarled, but I could tell they liked me, thought I was some kind of harmless nut. The backseat flatfoot unlocked the anklets, but my hands were still crossed behind my back.

It turned out the driver, a rookie, had gone to my school, and had some of the same crones in first, second, and third. "They still kickin'?" he said. "Tell me their kooky names, I forget."

"Fidelis, Annunciata, Perpetua, Magdalen Joseph, Delores, Agatha." I could've gone on, but we were at the station, in one of the bays. Too bad they didn't run the siren, but it was an uncomplicated case of destruction of property, loitering, assuming a false identity (that one came later), when the two Tallys hauled me out, and I claimed one of them as my father.

They wrestled me to the floor—a wood floor, with splinters, which is how their private property (the purple silk) was wrecked. Not wrecked, really, but full of runs and snags. Something tarry stuck to the embroidery cross.

Was I getting too big for my britches? was the thought aired out by the police chief, Frank O'Mara, friend of my father's, but not one of them on the take. They'd flushed out those palookas—not fast enough, though, for my dad to lose his shirt in kickbacks and just poor business sense. A crabby druggist is a liability; it doesn't matter how good you are at counting pills, or—more important, in our town—stretching one prescription to last a lifetime. Frank had done what he could for Dad, including pulling out the parking meters in front of the store, and getting him the police and fire contracts for knockout drops, sedatives, pep pills and antacids. Was the trade going on under the table? In our town, no would even think to ask.

"So," said the chief, "what's up? Why are you aggravatin' the Tallys? What's it to ya?"

When I didn't answer, they shut me up in the one cell next to the john. It was just a room with a lock, where they stored the brooms and riot gear.

"Cool your heels, son," he said. "Maybe you'd like your poor mum to know what you're up to? Think about it. Hasn't she had enough grief without you pulling a stunt like this?"

There was an old day bed in there, so I lay down. I was still saying mass, the *Regina Coeli*, if you have to know. Was I a real stuntman, or a just a rope-a-dope? I hadn't even thought to collect the goods O'Reilly had sent me to get. What was I trying to prove?

I lay back, telling myself they'd be sending me to the chair, but no dice, they must've put in a call, because Mom showed up with Millie in tow, carrying Princess, with little Doug in a stroller.

"I'll take over from here," she told the chief. "I'll return these," she said, nabbing me by the bracelets still dangling from one hand. She snapped the free one to the stroller bar, and now we were five.

It was a pleasant walk, five blocks, past the school and church. (I used the wrong hand to bless myself.) "Where's Frankie?" I said. But, that's when things went sour.

"What are you jabbering about, numbskull?"

Then, I remembered—as I always do, at the last minute, never saved by the bell—that Frankie was you, my alter ego. You were the bad and I was the good. You were the left, and I the right, for strait is the gate and narrow the way and, although we'd been twins, you died squeezing yourself out first, making way for the lord. This was the sad fact. Even mentioning you made Mom go mental, although she'd made it up to herself with the stream of kids that followed. Why she tried to off

Millie, we'll never know. I should add that she almost left me in there, expecting only you.

"Poor Frankie," I said.

"If I told you once," she said, "I told you a thousand times! And why are you wearing that dress?"

"It isn't a dress."

"I can see it isn't a dress. Why are you wearing it?"

"It's a long story. I think I lost my vocation," I mumbled.

"What?"

"You heard me."

"Don't talk to me that way, sonny boy."

Then, I was crying. Was I crying because I was thinking of you, or was I thinking of you because I was crying?

"Poor Frankie," I bawled.

"What did I just say to you!"

Little Millie slipped her sticky paw into mine, swinging it to give me courage.

"Take it off before you trip and crack your skull," Mom said, and then I noticed she was all dolled up, with a rhinestone brooch and dangly earrings. "Hey, you look like a million dollars."

"Thanks," she said, because we could be pals, if she didn't have to claim me as a child, boosting her to the henny age, where she wasn't, by God, going any time soon.

"Where ya goin'?"

"None of your beeswax, jailbird," she said, but she winked at me, cuffing me on the back of the head. "I need you to babysit. Your Grams won't be back till midnight. And, you lucked out, buddy boy, because the Tallys had insurance. They can replace the merchandise—that's what they called it—and fix the one you wrecked, so they're ahead of the game by one."

To make a long story short, her date was with junior, the one who'd kneed me to the floor. They were going nightclubbing, although she wasn't "putting out" (I blocked my ears) for that twerp. The sacrifice of precious time was made entirely for me, and did I get it?

I did. It wasn't the first, and wouldn't be the last time Mom saved my bacon. Family was family, even for a stinker like me. I'd been man of the house for a total of two weeks—not even— and I was already more trouble than the druggist.

Next day (did she stay out all night? Millie said she did, Grams said she didn't. How could they know? They both slept like logs. We all did. At night, you could get away with murder), Mom was in a beaut of a mood, singing, cracking wise, yucking up a storm. This set us all back, because all we knew, at this hour, was bellyache, gripes, and even fisticuffs if so much as a glass went overboard, or the toast was too black. I looked at Millie, and she looked at me. Grams cooked up a crock of milk crackers, then scrammed. Stop, look, and listen was the byword, until we knew the name of the game.

"Eddie?" she said.

"Call me Eddy-wood." This just shot out of my mouth, but she ignored it.

"What you don't know is today is your real birthday, not any Monday in May."

I'd always had a movable birthday, because she'd said (and Big Ed, the druggist, never crossed her) the exact date had slipped her mind. I had a birth certificate somewhere, but she claimed the date was never filled in, or there was an inkblot, or they erased it and the paper wore away. Tough luck. So, my birthday was always a Monday, but it could be any Monday in May.

I ran to the calendar and saw that the day, a Saturday, was April 1. "Very funny," I said. "So funny, I forgot to laugh."

We sat down and had our breakfast tea. "No, I mean it. You were born on April 1. Your dad wanted to change the day, and I wanted to keep it, so we made it Mayday, except I wanted some leeway, too, first Monday of May, or thereabouts. Did you ever get gypped of a birthday? Did you? Well, don't give me any lip, then."

"And April Fool's—that's Frankie's birthday, too, or did you make that up?"

"Don't you dare," she said, in the fighting tone.

"Well, if it's Eddie's birthday," Millie piped up, "make him a cake."

"*You* make him a cake, if you're so smart and full of beans," she said to the midget, in a tone never used on Shorty. "Sorry," she said.

But, poor Millie, treated with kid gloves by one and all, was already in tears.

"Okay, I get it," said our beautiful mother—and she *was* beautiful, a skinny Marilyn Monroe, if you want to know, but quicker on the uptake.

And then, Mom, remembering her widowhood, started sniveling. At that point, we all missed the druggist. In fact, nothing was ever the same. Every family needs a straight man, someone to absorb the blows, take the heat. He didn't offer, but he did it, and up to then, all hell didn't break loose the way it was starting to. You had to appreciate that, even if we never threw the guy a bone, or gave him a minute's peace.

Mom went to get the mix. Our grub was in a cabinet on the cellar stairs, with the bag of potatoes and onions, although who ever needed them, or for what, I never knew. We were box and can people. "Scratch," in our house, meant boiling a hotdog to go with the pork and beans.

There wasn't a cake mix, so tough patooties, birthday boy, she was fixing to say, when I piped up that I had enough saved in my mission box from Lent (I was the only one who saved the dimes and pennies for the African babies, but people were known to shake out what they needed, so it was almost always empty).

But, I had tucked away, and rolled up, a batch of quarters, five bucks' worth, and kept it in the duster bag, where no one would think to look, or even go near.

I filched it out to round eyes, and to the tune of snitch,

scrooge, pig, rat, and ingrate.

Slipping the roll in my pocket, and giving them all a bow and a blessing, I hoofed it to the A&P, and bought—not chocolate for Mom, not yellow for Millie, marble for Princess, or cupcake for Doug, but maple-walnut batter and maple-walnut frosting. I picked up walnuts, jimmies, and maple-walnut ice cream. I had an extra dollar from my paper route, so it panned out.

Home I went. Mom was in her apron, pre-heating the oven that hadn't been fired up since last Thanksgiving. Soon the kitchen was filled with smoke, and everyone choking and coughing. Someone had left a pan of peanut brittle or rice krispie treats, leftover from the funeral meats.

We raced out to the porch, waving off the smoke.

"Go on in there now, smarty pants," Mom said, "and crack the windows."

I was still dangling the cuffs (no key), but in I went. Our windows were forever jammed, so it took me an hour to find the hammer and screwdriver to jimmy and pound them, propping them with the sticks kept in the windowsills. In some ways, we were as prepared as a person could be.

In they came, sniffing the air. Mom said she was pooped, didn't have the oomph to lift a finger, so would I get it started, while she took a nap?

To make a long story short, after setting my sleeve on fire, and burning my eyelashes, I had that baby in the oven. We didn't have cake pans, so I used a pot with no handle. I knew, from reading the directions, not to fill it to the top. Millie helped with the substitutes for eggs and milk. (I'd gotten the wrong box.) She suggested creamed corn, and if the niblets made it through, think of them as walnuts, or walnut skins. We were laughing, as we always did, when we took over the kitchen and started to ad lib. We decided the cake should be blue, so in went the food coloring. In place of milk, we found an old quart of Narragansett lager, flat, and measured it out with a teacup. In it went. Doug was in his high chair, and Princess chained to the doorknob with her harness. They wanted to help, and were screeching, but nosireebob.

About an hour later, after three games of pinochle, we opened the oven to a sky-blue bomb, bubbling away and spitting. We had no temp gauge, so we'd turned it up all the way. No potholders, so back to the duster bag for a pair of the druggist's work pants, but still so burning hot, that I was swearing to high heaven, and blowing on my hands when Mom walked in with her hair up in curlers. "Holy cow!"

"Can you give us a hand," I said. Mill had pushed me over to the sink and was running the tap over my flaming hands.

"Jesus Marian Joseph!" we heard.

Next thing, the pot on the floor, where she dropped it, and now two of us were crying, and the little kids followed suit. Only Millie still had her thinking cap on, and ran for the afghan that hung, raggedy and dusty, on the back of the couch. With that wrapped around both arms, she hoisted the steaming pot onto the table.

"How come," Mom said, when the dust settled, "it's blue?" Then, she started to laugh. She couldn't help it. That's how funny the gunky mess looked, especially when its peak collapsed into a puddle of batter. "Do I smell beer?" she said.

"Happy birthday to me," I said, using the church key to pry off the lid on the frosting. "Mm-Mm good," I said.

"You have to wait till it cools," Millie said, but, by then, we were all sitting at the table, Princess unhooked from the doorknob, perched on Mom's lap.

"I can't wait forever," I said.

"You have to get it out of the pot first, dodo," Mom said. "How do you plan to do that?"

Well, by and by, when the cake fell out in five melting icebergs on the turkey platter (our only good dish), it was such a pity and such a shame; and after all I'd been through, at Tally's, but even before that, I burst into tears again, not the first, but not the last time either, cross my heart and hope to die.

"Crybaby!" Mom said, but she got me a dishcloth, and even said in my ear: "Are you still my baby boy, or what?"

I cried harder to hear the first kind words of my life.

"Don't overdo it," I heard, but that only made me cry harder.

Millie came to comfort me, and so did Princess, with the harness hanging from her waist. They adored me. I was their only friend. Little Dougie started crying and held out his baby arms to be lifted. I got up and grabbed him. All the kids were strung on me like the birdies on St. Francis. It was so beautiful, I couldn't stop blubbering, and neither could they, and now Mom was bawling.

"What are we crying about?" she said, first to shake herself clear. "Frost the cake, get on with it. I don't have all day."

So, I did, and it was easy living for the first time in months. But, what was I supposed to frost—and where?

I coated the blue icebergs on all sides, and the frosting melted in, disappearing.

"Boo!" Mom was saying, pinching her nose. "You know, Eddie, everything you do is like that," she said in the most thoughtful tone I'd ever heard. She was thinking. "I can never figure it out, because you're smart. What do you think's wrong with you?"

"What do you mean *everything*?" I said. I sounded like the druggist, peeved, petulant, picking at scabs.

"You know."

"Don't pick on him," said Millie. "It's his birthday."

"Who wants a piece?" I said.

"No, thanks," Mom said, "but I could use a drink, after this production." She was off to find the whisky bottle to make her favorite toddy: milk, whisky, and coffee syrup.

"What's that mess?" Grams said, appearing on the scene with her eyes bleary from her nap.

"It's my birthday," I said.

"No, it isn't," she said, always the contrarian. She sat on the chair Mom had left, so when Mom returned, after warming the milk, she sat on the stool.

What were they all waiting for? I knew the kids were waiting for cake, so I carved the bergs and flopped them on saucers. The forks were dirty, so I handed out spoons.

"Don't I get any?" the old lady said. "And what about your own mother?"

"Sure," I said. "My pleasure." But there were no more saucers, so I dished up, and dropped the chunks in teacups.

I put out an extra cup and dumped in a whole berg. Then, I licked the knife.

"Who's that one for?" Grams asked.

"Happy birthday to you!" I sang. "Happy birthday, dear Frankie, Happy—."

That's when I got the cake—what was left on the turkey platter—right in the puss, followed by the chunk in Mom's teacup, and what she could grab from the plates around her. A saucer was flung, too, and hit me over the eyes.

"Madelyn!" Grams screamed. "Madelyn Grady O'Hara, you are the limit!"

I got stitches for my head, but the burn in my eyes and the ear infection lasted a month. I can still taste it. I think it was the corn that wrecked it, although the little kids ate theirs fine. I sat there, stinging eyes glaring. Millie got up to wipe me off, but I pushed her away.

Then, I closed my eyes tight, and there on the back of my head, upside down like inside a camera, was you, Frank, and you were laughing. Your whole face was filled in, and—surprise!— you looked nothing like me, or the like rest of that crew. Then, you got small and slipped through the pinhole.

No Harm Done

I

DOLLY WAS BORN first, then Joan, Claire, John, Mary Madeline, and Francis, all in ten years, and starting not even one year after Ellen and Frank were married. They celebrated their cloth anniversary in the second-floor flat with their whole brood in attendance, Francis still in arms, and the older girls in charge of little John and Mary Mad, getting them dressed in the bedroom they'd shared with the "half-pints." The full-pints, all girls, moved to the big bedroom when Ma and Dad transferred to the parlor couch, where Francis was conceived; dividing up, shortly after, with Ma joining the half-pints on a rollaway bed near the cribs, and Frank left to the couch. Ellen and Frank loved kids, they loved each other, but they had enough now, and had learned how one thing led to another.

The tenth was a grand celebration: cases of beer standing in a cold bath, chips and dip, pot-luck casseroles, hamburgers and hotdogs on the grill, lemonade, and a big pink bakery cake— Frank and Ellen, June 14, 1948. And no neighbors to complain about the racket of the all-day affair, because the neighbors were there, as the party spread from the Halloran's tenement to the Reilly's and over to the McDevitt's, even lapping onto the immaculate white gravel yard of the Corselli's, the one Italian family. It would have spread further if the Corselli's hadn't abutted the avenue, with the rectory and church just across the way. Father Walsh, St. T's curate, had said the anniversary mass and was sitting on the porch steps with a cold one in his hand and another beside him. He'd been in school—the school behind the rectory—with Ellen (Frank was from St. Pius's, half a mile away). Ellen's father, the old undertaker, had lent the limousine for his ordination twelve years ago June. Fr. Joe had baptized each child and given the last rites to Ellen's ailing mother, now deceased. They were all up in the Mt. Carmel Cemetery with a patch of high ground reserved for the religious order who taught at St. T's Grammar.

It was a hot day, not a cloud in the sky, but none of the babies napped for the noise, and the toddlers got loose when Dolly and her sisters cut down the clothesline for a game of Double Dutch. John, three, broke his arm toppling off the rock wall onto the sidewalk, and Mary Mad swallowed a diaper pin. Two runs were made to the emergency room but only one, for the broken arm, was really necessary. The pin had been closed and would come out in a day or two, as did everything that Mary Mad swallowed: the pennies, jacks, marbles, and crackerjack prizes. No harm done was the order of the day, as it was the order for every day in the life of this easy-going couple, married ten years that Saturday.

While they were all having a hell of a time in the kitchen, parlor, and backyard, Joannie was under the porch, nursing a doll. The rest of the kids had formed an army for games and foolishness; Dolly was supposed to be in charge of the brats, Claire was spinning her hoop for the eyes of Fr. Joe, so Joannie made her way to her favorite spot, where she could see but not be seen. She had her baby doll, Ruth—Baby Ruth, as her father called her—a deck of cards, a pink ball, and a book about flowers. She'd hauled it all out while the adults were filling the bathtub and setting out plates and cups—slapping faces, too, as olives, nuts, and chips were snuck by grubby fingers. Claire saw her go, but no one else. She even had a dishcloth to sit on, to preserve the party dress from the dirt. There was a good smell down there and a thousand spy holes. But, once under, with her cloth spread and herself on it, she felt funny. Party sounds were everywhere, and a girl screaming, "Old mother witch, are you ready?" She was missing something. No one was in the front of the house; it was just a hot summer day with a raft of clouds sailing in from the bay. She came out and sat down on the step. Next, she was crying.

Why did a party make her sad? That's what Dolly asked her that night, when they'd finally climbed into bed around midnight—that's how long the cleanup had taken, and the kitchen was still lined with bags stuffed with mustardy rolls, butts, and empties, enough to make the whole house stink. That could be one reason. Why was she forever thinking ahead, or thinking back? Joannie had wrapped her sister Dolly's arm around her neck and was ready to say more, but Dolly had fallen asleep. In the meanwhile, Claire had traipsed into the full-pints' room and onto the double bed; she had her arm around Dolly's waist. Joannie tried to peel the arm off, but Claire was strong—a year younger, but twice as strong as Joannie. Daddy and Ma were on the couch tonight with the parlor door shut.

Why was a party so sad, and everything else, too? Joannie lay awake, too steeped in the sound of breathing and the smell of beer, to think why. Dolly had the black hair and blue eyes of the Burkes, Claire was fair as dandelion fluff, Mary Mad's face was never quiet enough to see who she took after, and the little kids were just freckled midgets. Joannie was different. She felt different, and the cracked mirror over the bathroom sink said it, too. She had carroty hair, and eyes yellow as a cat's, although they never had a cat or a dog. No turtle, fish, or bird, either. Their house was nothing but people, people everywhere, and bedlam from morning till night with the yelling, crying, bellyaching, singing (their father had a fresh song for every day), squawking, fussing, and taking the name of God in vain. Joannie was quiet as a mouse and kept her thoughts to herself unless she had the ear of her big sister, whom she adored. But, all the rest of them did, too. The little kids hung off Dolly's arms and tagged after her all the livelong day. She had her father's disposition, Claire had her mother's green Irish eyes, and Mary

Mad, her earsplitting laugh, without the rasp. What did Joannie have? She was Thursday's child, her Dad said, full of woe. Once he said it, no one forgot: she was pegged—sourpuss, face a mile long, party pooper, killjoy. When he said it, pulling a face and drooping his shoulders and boohooing like a baby, it was funny, and he made mock of them all: that was his way. It bothered Joannie more because she was the kind that always took things too hard.

Once these words were rolling in her head, she'd never get to sleep, so out of the bed she fell, listening as the two girls spread themselves out. The room was pitch black with the shades pulled, the tan one and the green one, but she knew where the crib was, the toy box, the bassinet, and chest of drawers, and she was skinny enough to slide through without making a peep. She pushed out the door over the linoleum hump and crept down into the hallway, so narrow, she could touch each wall.

The streetlight shone into the parlor, falling on the opened-out couch where there were two heads and a hump under the old satin puff. Joannie held her nose and proceeded to the kitchen, the biggest room, whose windows overlooked the dirt yard and garages. She listened to the clock. Down there was nothing: not a cat, not a dog. She smelled the smell of night: damp and sweet like nuts and rotten apples, with a coal smell mixed in, and, of course, the cloud of beer fumes all around her. She counted the ticks of the clock, then she got up and started tonguing the burning dregs from each of the brown bottles. She emptied them one by one, three bags full, although not more than a sprinkle in each. She waited a minute to see what would happen, then sprawled on the cold floor, where she could see the sky and stars, and fell dead asleep.

II

HER BIRTHDAY FELL in December, but so did Claire's, Daddy's, Mary Mad's, and there was Christmas and New Year's, so where was the extra cash coming from to throw a party for each? That year, Daddy turned thirty-five and a big bash—a surprise—was planned for December 26, to coincide with the annual open house. To save money, each of the birthday kids' big present from Santa would include the birthday; and cake, ice cream, favors, and games would be folded into the grand December 26 blowout. Joannie—who preferred Joan to "boney Joannie" or "Toni Joanie," a label applied after her permanent turned her hair into a "maroon haystack," passed her birthday, the Friday before the long holiday weekend, in the garage, crying on the backseat of the car. She wasn't a brain like Claire, or a living saint like Dolly, a boy like John, a brat like Mary Mad, in detention four days out of five, or a baby like Francis, the last of the Hallorans, after Ma lost number eight falling down the back stairs. Joannie had tried for a vocation, but was discouraged by the vocation nun, who liked to make her own pick and had singled out Mary Ellen Gray, the doctor's daughter, who allowed herself to be counseled, but was going next year to Classical High School. What was left? Joannie wasn't a bookworm, a tomboy, teacher's pet, mother's helper, boy crazy, or dedicated to Mary and wearing blue and white. What was left? she asked herself with her nose flat on the scratchy seat, wetting it with tears, and biting it with the two front teeth that needed braces, the dentist had said—but nothing doing in a family scrambling to pay the rent, put food on the table, and still shelling out for Ma's operation, Francis's bad leg, Daddy's pleurisy, and Dolly's bleeding ulcer. That one tooth lapped over the other, giving Joannie's baby face a "demented" look, was just something she'd have to lump. So she used those yellowish, sharp, lapped-over teeth to bite: biting the tops off pens and pencils, her fingernails, corners of books and, at night, her tongue, leaving blood stains impossible to bleach out, and shame on her for wrecking the only good things Ma had left from her hope chest, now used as a hassock and to hold those last few things—a bureau scarf, a crocheted potholder, two silver spoons and a fork, which the

half-pints used to play house, sitting under the kitchen table.
Joannie was a dreamer and would be one, no matter how hard
the nuns tried to knock some sense into her head.

She'd been in Daddy's car for an hour. She knew because
there was a ticking clock on the dashboard. She was fourteen
today and fourteen was just the kind of nothing year that suited
a nothing like herself. She was "developing," but who cared?
The tender new areas, "doorknobs," the boys called them, did
nothing for a figure swaddled in the heavy blue uniform, itchy
sweaters, and a hand-me-down coat from Dolly, miles too big.

She liked boys, but was afraid of them—their wildness, and
how much trouble they could lead to, then run off scot-free.
She didn't like school, even the classes where she was a brain:
English and History, because she had a good memory, and could
make a story out of a few facts. She never finished reading her
books: she could guess the ending after a few pages.

Daddy had taken a swing at her for badmouthing the nuns,
the school, the church, her brothers and sisters. About them,
she wouldn't dare speak a word, but everyone else was fair game
for a mentality like hers—ungrateful, faultfinding, miserable.
Look to yourself, girlie-girl, he liked to say, grabbing her collar
to give her a shake. She received the belt in the kisser, and the
inside of her mouth was ragged; a welt was growing on her
cheek, but she didn't cry. One time, she'd socked him right back
and gotten shaken until her teeth rattled and one eye rolled
up and stayed there. She and her father were forever at each
other. She was the birthday girl today, but what difference did it
make? And now she was crying sticky tears that wet the car seat
and burned her sore face.

She let herself out into the cold, slamming the door shut,
cracking open the garage door, and squeezing through. Mary
Mad spotted her from the window, and a minute later, that
window flew up. "Get in here," she heard her mother yell, "if
you know what's good for you!" But Joan kept walking—to the
edge of the lot and across the street, down the hill, along the

avenue, and on, until she'd walked all the way downtown—
with her nightie on underneath Dolly's coat and just boots, no
socks. She hadn't even washed her face. Seeing it in Woolworths'
windows, "ragamuffin," she said out loud, and grinned, because
that's what she looked like. She ended up, that day, in the police
station, with hell to pay at home, where they were worried sick,
and on the day before the day before Christmas. "You stupid,
stupid, stupid." Thoughtless, too, forever thinking only of
herself.

And down for Christmas and the blowout with the grippe,
watching it all happen from her bed, where treats were brought
in, hot cocoa with floating marshmallows, until the crowd
arrived, and flung their coats on the bed and on the floor next
to it. She watched from there until her burning hot eyes closed
over gritty eyeballs, and no Dolly, with a face cloth dipped in
witch hazel. Then, Joan fell asleep, hot and raving, but no one
in that racket to hear.

Around her, the singing, laughing, and drinking. "Thanks
for the Memory" and "Auld Lang Syne," but that was New
Year's and she was still laid up, with pneumonia in both lungs,
limp as a doll, coughing so to choke.

III

THEN, SHE BLOOMED, and everyone could see it on the day they
waked her father, fallen off a ladder painting the only house
they ever owned, breaking his neck, but it was the concussion
that killed him. He was still young, not fifty, and finally with
a union job and benefits, although only baby Francis at home.

He'd gotten the best of care for the neck, but his brain had
swelled from the blow and he was gone before nightfall the
same day. Ma was put to bed with knockout drops, and it was
Dolly and Joannie at the head of the casket that first night, to
receive friends and relatives, and an endless string of buddies
from every chapter of his life, starting with grade school, all

the way to the war, the wedding, and the twenty or thirty jobs that lasted no more than a few months, just long enough to make a lifelong friend. Had he been drinking the beer up on that ladder? Joannie heard said in one tone, and then another, during the talks and toasts at the house, when Ma managed to pull herself together to sit in a chair and weep, with her arms around Mary Mad, a housekeeper at the rectory, or baby brother, who'd never left home.

Joannie, staying with Dolly in Olneyville, had let her heavy red hair grow to her shoulders in waves and ringlets, bright and shiny in the light. She was a practical nurse and the bed making and lugging of patients kept her strong and slim. A late growth spurt made her tower over her pint-sized mother and look her father straight in the eye. They didn't get along, and right up to the end, had nothing good to say about each other. Why was it that Joannie, of all the kids, cried the hardest, seeing him in his box dropped into the hole—sobbed even harder when Mary Mad jabbed her in the ribs ("I thought you hated his guts?"). "Don't be an actress," her mother said, back at the dinky little house he'd killed himself trying to keep up.

That was the day their old paperboy, now on the police force, clapped eyes on Joannie, with the stunning figure packed into a black knit suit. He brought over two glasses of the hard stuff, although he'd taken the pledge for the fourth or fifth time that Christmas. Her face was puffy and blotched with the crying, but you could see it was a nice face, and Joannie still a nice girl. She had big hands and he held one of them in both of his, when she started up again at the sound of the old songs. But, he liked the older one, too, bustling around with a tray of sandwiches and Danish, and ended up asking the kid sister he'd gone to school with to a dinner dance at the Friendly Sons. Joannie was a cold fish—that's what her sister said—when he asked what she'd been doing all these years and what made her leave the old neighborhood.

"We don't ask," she also said, rolling her eyes, but they did know because they'd wormed it out of Dolly. Joan was now working at a ritzy girls' school in New Hampshire and living on the grounds for free. She'd taken a few courses; she was a dietician, and no longer emptied bedpans. Did the sister put it that way, the cop wondered, because she was still changing the priests' sheets and scrubbing their floors?

Did it matter what a person did to keep body and soul together? No one thought it did until Joannie came back to see her father into his grave. She wasn't going to give a cop walking the beat a tumble—that was clear—even one as sharp and on the ball as Jimmy Ahern. But, he was good enough for Mary, who married him a year later in her Ma's backyard. Joannie came down again, but not as a bridesmaid, because her sister wouldn't think to ask, with how they'd all been snubbed in a thousand ways.

By then, she had a room over the infirmary with a kitchen and little backyard, but no one invited up to see it—not even their Ma, who needed a change of scene after the year she'd had. They all chipped in to take care of their mother: there was no insurance, and the father's union job too recent for vesting. Dolly wanted to take her in, but Ma wasn't budging. This was her home and she'd earned it. She had six grown children, big and strong, and it was the least they could do for one who'd killed herself to keep them fed and clothed, no questions asked. Joannie had no car, no family, no obligations, so it was no wonder she gave the most, paying the mortgage, taxes, and utilities. Mary Mad, who still had the rectory job, cooked a little extra for the fathers and trotted over with it after supper. The priests had plenty, and wasn't it the Hallorans supporting them with their weekly offerings at Mass? So, Ma stayed put and got old and frail, with no Frank or kids to look after. She ate like a horse, according to Baby Brother—a delivery boy for the drugstore, who shared the fathers' suppers and Sunday roasts.

Ma still fit into her wedding dress—ivory satin with sweetheart neckline—and wore it, shortened, to Mary Mad's wedding. It would have been her silver anniversary: there was that for an excuse, plus her daughter had chosen to get married in a pants suit, as mannish as can be. The policeman's suit was the exact same color, so didn't they look a pair with their matching boutonnieres. Dolly stood up for her sister in a strapless gown with matching shoes. They were a sight to behold, piling into the old beach wagon with cracked windshield, and muffler dragging on the ground. Joannie was crushed in the back seat between Francis and the flowers. Marching up the aisle on the arms of her two brothers, Mary Mad was met by the bridegroom and his four—including the retarded one, still living at home.

After that, and never forgetting that Jimmy Ahern had picked Joannie first, then Dolly, only settling for Mary Mad, the family saw even less of Joan. She was training to teach grade school, taking night courses here and there; became a reading specialist, and then headmistress. This, they heard through Dolly, who was working the late shift at Cumberland Farms, when she was held up, refused to open the cash drawer, and was beaten senseless, left for dead, and then, up at Roger Williams for a month recovering from broken ribs, a concussion, and ruptured spleen. She couldn't live alone after that, and moved in with her mother and brother. It was Dolly who was invited, after she got back on her feet, to go up and visit the school, and the tale she brought back was still making the rounds of the Hanrahan clan, the church, and the rectory. She grew her own food, made her own bread, she sewed and knitted, and refinished old furniture. She looked like a nun without the wimple—no makeup, long hair streaked with gray, and kept stray cats in a barn on the property. No TV, no car, she rode a bike to the school, where she was in charge of everything—and bossy! Dolly had seen it with her own eyes. Everything just so in the house, not a dish, not a rag out of place, and cold it was, even in summer, heated only by a wood stove, and guess who chops the wood!

Dolly didn't know what to think. That anyone would want to live in the sticks was itself a mystery, and then—she said this in a whisper, a whisper of outrage—she'd lost her faith. Joannie didn't say as much, but Sunday rolled around, and were the two of them going to ride the bike into Kingston, where the only Catholic church (a puny one made of wood like the Protestants) was to be found? Dolly said not a word, but she would have to confess it on Saturday, although it was no fault of hers. And, what did Joannie do with herself when she wasn't teaching or running the show from an office that looked like the mayor's or the bishop's, with a dictionary on its own altar? She hiked up the mountains, she went to concerts (for that, of course, there was transportation!), she went to the theater. What did they talk about up there?—for Dolly had been away from Monday to Monday, gone up and back on the Greyhound bus. Nothing much. Joannie never let her hair down; it was please and thank you and cloth napkins on the table, but Dolly hadn't been bored, not at all, just amazed, and a little shocked because Joannie didn't seem like family anymore. Everything she said was dry, or in a know-it-all tone; specifically, what each of them had wrong with them and why, where they got it from and how hopeless it all was. Easy enough now to laugh, sitting in the attic on Regent Avenue with Mary Mad and Jim. But eating the meatballs and spaghetti cooked for last night's supper at the rectory, and not one fork to match another, with no napkins, just a bare table with the pot standing on it; and with the cop drinking from a can and her sister from a jelly glass, and the TV blaring ("Wheel of Fortune," or whatever it was. "You know what it is!" Mary'd said to Dolly, who looked like she'd been hit by a lead pipe just because she'd been up to New Hampshire and back), was it really so easy to laugh?

Her mother didn't want to talk about it at all; she was only interested in her boy, her Franny, who'd been picked to be Eucharistic minister at church, by the very fathers Mary Mad cooked and cleaned for. Mary Mad had worked for it, but Ma only heard that her pride and joy would read the prayer and pass out the hosts at the children's Mass. He'd lost his job, when the drugstore eliminated home deliveries, but he was still collecting unemployment and disability for the gimpy leg. Her Franny was, she claimed, the spittin' image of his dad which, as anyone with eyes could see—fat and slovenly—he wasn't, but they played along because she was daft and he'd gone to sixth grade and no farther. Joannie had said (and Dolly tried to imitate her fruity accent) that this was likely the case of a woman bearing children beyond her time, and that drinking didn't help. She had a remark like this for everything, and it was never what you wanted to hear. How did someone so critical succeed at anything in life? This question Dolly asked Mary Mad—Claire was there, too, eager to get the dirt straight from the horse's mouth—went unanswered.

Dolly tried again: if you have nothing good to say, isn't it better to say nothing? The thought had occurred to her—and the other two were quick to see the point—that the girl might have taken something belonging to all of them; in other words, more than her share. Did that ring a bell?

Jimmy Ahern was feeling no pain that night and added his two cents: namely, weren't we all the same in the eyes of God, so why not let up on the girl. This stopped everyone in their tracks.

No, we certainly are not, Dolly was thinking. The Aherns, who lived in a basement hovel and couldn't scrape together the few hundred bucks to send their kids to Catholic school, were not the same at all. There were nine of them and, if the uncle hadn't been on the force, the cops would never have taken Jimmy; and the rest of them had gotten nowhere: one was even doing time for breaking into a neighbor's house; two had enlisted; one was selling candy bars in the cigar store; one was in the hospital laundry, where the father had worked when he wasn't up at Wallem Lake with TB. Was Joannie, in other words, as different from the rest of the Hallorans as the Halloran family was from the Ahern tribe? Could that be? Wasn't it time to go home? It was time to go home and Dolly made Claire drive her.

IV

MA DIED ON Easter Saturday, sitting in front of the TV, and the day being what it was, no undertaker free to pick up the body, so the cops came from Jimmy's precinct and delivered it, no charge. Dolly and Francis went along for the ride. Was it a paddy wagon they were in? Mary Mad asked her husband, because that's what the vehicle looked like, with the black windows and chains on the door. You had to laugh, but it was hard to, in the shock of the moment. One minute, Ma was watching Wiley Coyote, as alive as can be; next, she was dead on the floor. Dolly was on the phone when she heard the thump that could mean only one thing, because Francis was forever falling, sometimes on his face, which was how she found her mother, with Francis already kneeling beside her, stroking her head.

At her last birthday, she was only sixty-eight, but she looked ninety. Would they put her in her wedding dress? John asked. His wife worked for the undertaker and would do the makeup, when the embalmers were finished. If she wore the gown, maybe a white casket, although it cost a little more. She'd always liked to dress up for a party. The sister-in-law could get them a markdown, and there was a showroom model with a few nicks no one would see in the gloom of the funeral parlor.

V

JOANNIE GOT THE news after dark, and a friend drove her to the bus station, where she caught a ride to the airport. Looking out onto the snowy valleys and lurching up the steep passes, Joannie tried to suck into herself, as much as she could, the atmosphere of the clattering, rumbling, smelly bus. It was the only way she could think of to block out everything else. She was afraid for her legs—that they might not carry her all the way out of the noxious cone into the slick terminal, to be shot through space and pulverized. The bus kept pushing, and soon, spreading its apron of icy blue lights, the airport rose up from the fields.

Only a few years back, there was no airport, no way up the mountains of New Hampshire except by rolling the four-lane highways to two lanes, coiling along the country roads to the gravel roads and across the trackless acreage where she'd built a house from her own drawing and simple needs. It was windy and the small plane she'd boarded with two other passengers was punched and bumped and rolled in the gusts. She watched the wing lights sizzle, drawing small comfort from the warmth and softness of her knitted hat and mittens, legwarmers and wristbands, the mohair coat with thick shawl wrapped around her neck. She'd swallowed all her tonics and herbals for today and for tomorrow, and packed a hot water bottle and sleeping pills. She'd reserved a room in a Japanese-run hotel famous for its cleanliness and customer satisfaction, and had hired a car to take her there.

The local airport was deserted, but the driver's bluff friendliness and accent, his eagerness to tell some of his stories and a few jokes to this "Eskimo," without pausing for breath or a word of reply, was just what Joannie needed. When he pulled up to the hotel, and saw her red eyes—although she'd laughed the whole way up 95—he carried her backpack to the desk, squeezing her arm through the thick layers. He waited while she presented her card at the desk (he knew the name, and maybe even a brother or cousin), then offered to stand her a beer or a coffee, extend a friendly ear, and who is it, dearie, who passed on? The hotel clerk offered his condolences, too; the bar, he said, was across the street. Joannie laughed again, but no, thank you, and she required no help with the bag. The driver wouldn't accept a tip, and he and the clerk were still looking as the elevator door closed. What exactly was so funny? They didn't know—but for her, the ice was broken. And weren't those the words her mother used to send Francis in to sleep on her father's rollaway, before poor Dad was even cold in the ground. Where did all the ice come from? she wondered. There was a knock and a pink slip was handed in, from earlier in the day. Before there was time to turn on the light, the phone rang.

It was Dolly, who'd called earlier, and was calling again just to make sure her sister would be ready tomorrow morning, and that she had arrived safely. Claire was picking her up early. They would gather at the funeral home for a last goodbye. The Mass was at nine. Do you have what you need there? her sister asked, and asked again. What she meant was: why hadn't she stayed with one of them? She and Franny had the extra room—Ma's. John and Kathleen, too, even Mary Mad and her husband could afford to put a person up. I'm fine where I am, Joannie said.

She turned on the light. And, she added, I've got two big beds. Maybe you'll come back here tomorrow and stay with me.

There was a pause, followed by the screech. "At Gladding's! You think I'm going to Gladding's?"

So far out of reach was the Hotel Gladding from a family like the Hallorans that "going to Gladdings" was short for a one-way trip to the nuthouse.

"Come to Gladding's," Joannie whispered.

VI

IN THE LIMOUSINE following their mother's hearse, they were all six of them together; the wives, husbands, and kids packed in the cars just behind. Female relatives were now welcome as pallbearers, so there were enough of them to carry their mother on their shoulders. Each of them was handed a pair of white gloves. They were fat and thin, tall and short; Dolly, Claire, and Mary had heads of black, blonde, and brown curled and sprayed into place, Joannie's hair was salt-and-pepper like her brother's. The years had exaggerated points of resemblance: Claire and John had their father's mobile face and toothy grin; Mary Mad, his stiff, belligerent jaw; Francis looked like his father asleep with slack skin and deep eye sockets; Dolly made you think that Ma had come back to life as a fat woman.

It was Joannie's eyes making the connections, because the rest of them were still bickering about the "collation" (a word Joannie hadn't heard in ages, and then only on the lips of the nuns, forbidden to eat in public, but with their own special terms for meals light and heavy, ferial and festal), and whether drinks should be offered. She was the only one in black, so removed from "reality," she didn't realize that only the Italian crones still wore weeds. The rest were in all colors of the rainbow—Claire in black and tan houndstooth, Dolly in aqua, John in a maroon parka and Francis, a purplish plaid from a trip to Ireland. It had been decided to have the two quarts of Johnny Jameson—which no one was known to drink—and shot glasses borrowed from the funeral home. It was Mary Mad's choice, "to impress the yokels," she said, and that became the word of the day, and a way of bringing their dad back into the party, once the business was done.

Now, they were driving up to the old three-decker, spotting the dirt driveway and stone wall John used as a diving board, and how, Mary Mad said, could that dump have been the site of so many good times? Dolly was offended. She had spent the most time there, and happy years they were, too, when she, and she alone was the "pride and joy." And now, of course, they had to hear about the portrait album, made by an uncle with a fancy camera, of number one, wearing her father's christening gown, which they'd all worn, although no more portrait albums followed, nothing but a snapshot or two of the party that followed. Baby Dolly was shot in her bassinet from every angle; she was still in a ball with feet and hands clenched, a familiar face of fury and concentration—and what was it they liked to say, each of them, to the one just following behind by a year, or less? "And then, *you* came along to wreck it!"

That line landed, of course, on Francis, with no one to pass it on to. And with no Ma now to protect him, and they were starting up again, chanting it, and singing it louder, right to his face.

Was it funny? Not so much, Joannie thought, when Ma got wind of it, and started shouting it at Dolly, with the thinnest skin of them all. Did it still hurt? Just look at Baby Brother with the tears welling in his eyes.

They were still in the pod, these Hallorans, although the pod had burst open years ago and was now withered, soon to be dust. They had stuck to it, but why? Joannie leaned forward on the jump seat, where she and Francis were sitting side by side, facing the others. Her face came to life, as it always did when she was thinking hard.

"You know what?" she said.

"Say what it is you have to say," Mary Mad said. "Spit it out." And all eyes were on her.

Just then, though, the limo driver slammed on the brakes. Joannie was jerked off her seat and Francis's head struck the door handle. He was left sitting on the floor, stunned. Looking out the window, Mary Mad spotted the old dog, a collie, who'd been sitting, the driver explaining, turning back to them, in the middle of the road.

"Let me see it now," Dolly said to Francis, trying to peel the hand away from his hurt, but his hand stayed put. Now, everyone was mad—mad, hurt, fed up, at the end of their rope. But, thank goodness, they were there. The driver got out to open the door. As soon as he did, you could smell the flowers, the fresh dirt, and the sharp, wintry air.

Just a few feet more they had to carry their mother on their backs. The hole itself was covered over with a tarp, and the white casket, set down next to it, heaped with flowers, including the "blanket" whose satin ribbon spelled out "Children." Already down there were their father, his folks, a bachelor uncle, a great aunt and her husband, and the seven empty shelves. Francis had had his name carved on the stone when their mother added hers, next to their father's. Dolly and Claire had added theirs, with their birthdays, and a dash. They were all out of order, leaving no open space on the stone for the missing names, but

Francis had started that business, putting his first.

The priest read from the office of the dead, but the wind swallowing most of his words. He was a newcomer to Mary Mad's rectory, just ordained in Ireland, where most of their priests now came from. Dolly wound her arm through Joannie's, and Francis, seeing it, linked himself up to her other side. Mary Mad shook her head, but a minute later, linked arms with Claire. There was space for John, who was still standing back, beside his wife with their two children tucked between. Claire beckoned to him; there was room; come and grab hold.

Father McIntyre shook holy water first over the blanket, then up at the head, and down to the feet—absolving their mother's body of trespasses on earth. Their brother came up to join them—on Francis's side, for Franny was starting to give way, as they knew he would, when it dawned on him that, when all was said and done, he was going home and Ma was staying here.

Before leaving, the priest came over to shake each of their hands, and the Halloran children plucked flowers from their mother's blanket, to wear all that day, white for the girls, and red for the boys. The big sister pinned a flower on Francis's coat, and he sniffed it. They gave him a real seat in the limo, and he bent over in grief, his head nearly touching his knees.

"Come on, Franny boy," Claire said, "pull yourself together."

"Act your age," Mary Mad added, which made Francis sink lower.

"Leave the boy alone!" Joannie heard herself say. Everyone looked. The note was struck.

"Don't you get started," Johnnie said, and, at hearing the note, everyone laughed.

"You always overdo it," Dolly said, stretching it further.

"Are you talking to me!" How much farther could it go?

"You stay out of it!" they heard.

When they arrived at the funeral home—in stitches—the whole gang was there.

Last Rites

ONCE THE MOTHER was dead, the children gone, the dog sent back, and the husband moonlighting, or in his basement cubby, Eenie stood still in her kitchen. Everything was wrong. It was a dark house, the window glass scaled and scratched, the woodwork thin and rotting, the ceiling low, the furniture ugly at purchase, the plants and flowers fake, and the wrong things on show: canned goods and soda bottles, the open tray of forks and knives; and a dripping sink. There was noise (buzzing, ticking, whirring), and there was also the empty air.

What next? she wondered, but the inside was the very image of the outside. And she couldn't escape the squalor by a sudden dive into sleep; the memory of the departed bulked up wherever she looked, so she wasn't free, or even alone.

She sunk into the chair upon which the dead mother had spent her days, but jumped right up, because that zone, carpet to ceiling, was heavy with the mother's air: stagnant, fetid, almost a color of its own, as the mother's skin had become a floury white, pierced by eyes of blue glass. Sitting there, she *was* her mother; and jumping up, she still was, so she sat again, closing her eyes, letting the tears flow. What did they mean?

They were a relief. She let her body relax, feeling what her mother had felt, for her mother's thighs and back had turned the softness of filling and fabric into a shell. Her own thighs and back were bigger, but the narrow grooves held their shape against hers, and she felt that shape with a thrill, the first she'd felt since the night her second child was born.

She closed her eyes, and the mother was back, standing over her, watching. How dare she come back at the first free hour

Eenie had had since graduating from high school, and traveling
by bus to the beach to live for a short week with a group of
boys and girls. That week was as vivid as anything in the last
thirty years—the smell of hamburger grease sizzling on glowing
charcoal, the musty towels, and day after day of humid heat
and late-afternoon thunder, the slick sheets and smell of beer,
with beer bottles heaped everywhere, even in the bathroom sink
and bedroom closets. There were two small bedrooms for the
ten of them, with a couch, cot, and rollaway bed. By morning,
five, mix and match, were under the chenille spread, sandy arms
and scratchy legs, and that pungent smell of sweat and semen,
suntan lotion and cheap cologne. Wake me when it's over, she
said out loud, and the phone rang.

It was her husband, Tony, who instructed her in his day and
evening docket. She didn't care; she knew already, and was short
with him. He heard, and hung up. She liked to hurt him, when
she was hurt, because she was (this was her thought of so many
years) the maypole around which he revolved; wrapping and
unwrapping the pole was his greatest joy and satisfaction, when
he wasn't watching baseball, hockey, basketball, and golf, which
took up most of his free time, meaning she got little of it, and
really didn't care. Her life was somewhere else, but now that the
lifetime jobs were done, where?

Sitting back down—this time in his chair, stiff and reeking
of the shaving lotion or deodorant, whatever it was he doused
himself with, night and day—she worked her way back to that
graduation week. She was there with Sally, but really with Frank
and Ed, who'd been waiting for this week for a year, since they'd
started dating Eenie, queen of the prom, head cheerleader, the
girl who'd put the lay teacher into the hospital, and got the gym
teacher fired for slapping a girl student. (The complaint said
"punching," but she'd thrown the punch.) The woman teacher
she'd spat at, hitting her right in the eye, at the moment when
her glasses were off to wipe away the first spit. Miss Hendricks,
a former nun and nervous Nellie, had called her a tramp for

what she'd seen in the cloakroom with Eddie—nothing, really, some tongue kissing and rubbing, and other kids were there. They were supposed to be watching the door, flung open by the teacher, when an enemy had squealed. That girl wouldn't have lived to see her eighteenth birthday, if Eenie had ever caught her outside the schoolyard without her older brother. Eenie had fists, and she had nails and teeth, and used them when she needed to.

So, why was she crying again? She wasn't crying; she was laughing, but no one was home to hear. No one would ever be home again, except as a guest, although she already missed her children, so adorable they were as babies, toddlers, and first-graders. After that, they had their own lives and routines, and Tony was grooming them for pitching, batting, fielding, running, skating, blocking, and stick work—they were on the short side, as was he, so no need to mount a net over the garage door.

They'd been beautiful babies, especially Leanne, perfect as a little god. Aaron was never as strong, but she and Aaron were twinned, as she and Leanne had never been. Leanne was always walking away, as soon as she could walk, but Aaron never left her side, except to go to practice with his father, who coached all their sports, before handing them over to high-school varsity.

The children had set themselves free, after saddling their parents with a lifetime of debt. When Leanne had insisted on a private college, Aaron had to go there, too, although he'd never finished.

Tears dry on her face made two lines of sparkly salt, trailing from her magnified blue eyes (just like her mother's) to her girlish lips, a perfect bow. She was studying her face in a bit of broken mirror, still on her mother's table, with a box of powder and emery board. She opened the box to dust the lines, laughing to see how the rust-colored streaks created a clown, on a face still soft and unlined. There was so much life left, but it had to start, she thought, from that week at Conimicut Beach, during that wonderful (dangerous?) summer, when she still lived here with her ma and daddy, and all the battling siblings were gone (or almost gone), and everything hers.

The phone rang again. He had altered an item in his day, and wanted a list for the grocery shopping he loved to do, but she liked to do it, too: the quiet of the smooth aisles, the passing parade of cans and sacks; of bins loaded with dewy apples and peppers, richly colored greens, and filthy mushrooms— she hated mushrooms, with their skin like human skin. The frozen ranks were boring, but much of her shopping was there, to supply his simple needs—frozen pancakes and doughnuts, greasy beef dishes in tins, with a hard crust of frosty cheese. She preferred live food: delicacies of sugar and butter, food coloring, chocolate, vanilla, and coffee, lavished with frosting. She could also taste the Crisco, the fake flavorings, but the keenness of sugar, the density of flour and oil, sated her craving, until she felt drunk with pleasure. Not pleasure, really—but filled, finally, replete.

He loved to buy her food, but she liked to reserve a trip for herself, and was queen of her kitchen, so bought him the frozen, waxy boxes, and herself, the breads and pastries, along with the bright fruit and pale green balls of lettuce, tomatoes lined up single file and wrapped in plastic, onions as big as grapefruits. No, she told him, I'm going myself, so just come home. He wouldn't hear, and would go anyway. It'd be fine, so long as their visits didn't overlap, spoiling it.

Why did it spoil it, just to see him, hauling through the aisles, dumping things in his cart? Because he was hasty, greedy. Did he think he was at the rink, spinning, speeding, crashing, and toppling in a pile of blades like knives, and the wet smack of flesh, or sweat-soaked cloth on ice? She could smell it, just thinking about it—the way the heat lamps sizzled and snapped, and the gas-driven Zamboni ribboning the gouged, crusty ice. She loved to close her eyes high up in the bleachers, inhaling a full delivery of smells in a rainbow of heats and colds, breezes and blasts, as the fans and heaters turned on their screws.

The thought of it made her smile, because she loved being alive. No one knew this, because you had to keep something to and for yourself, or they'd rob you blind, as she and her sisters and brother had robbed the dead mother of time, money, sleep, space, clothes—anything she had to call her own. They sucked her dry, as did the dad, long gone. If Eenie was the maypole for her mate, her own mother had been raw meat for the fire. (She was laughing to think this). Or, a delicious drink, a tub of rich ice cream, with nothing artificial or skimmed. It was a miracle the woman had lived to be ninety. Where was she re-charging, and with what?

But, this was a dead end—not sad, and Eenie wouldn't shed any tears—but a waste, since the mother was gone, and not a minute too soon, for she'd so failed, that the rot was already noticeable in the smell of the house; and just looking at her gave you a fright, because she'd lost control of her face, and stared, with open mouth; or grimaced, when spoken to in a harsh—or, really, any tone. Where are you? Eenie wanted to ask her. Are you in there some place? Knock-knock—but she didn't like the mockery in what should be a time devoted to saying goodbye and storing up memories.

To ask who the mother was raised a question closer to home: who am I, and where? This felt like whiplash, so Eenie stood, cracking her back, left and right; then, stepped into the kitchen to plan the next minute of the new life.

She had wanted to live through her kids, but their lives bored her—Leanne's, a replica of her own early marriage (without the marriage!), and Aaron's, the same, stuck, as she was, in a laboring job with an hourly wage. Their boats had not lifted, because hers and Tony's had sunk—not all the way—but to the gunwales. (She knew a bit about boats.) Where was that socket her mother had found to buzz herself through the disasters and calamities (a fire, two car accidents, unemployment, fights, and the sizzling contempt of a malcontent husband, who lived to smoke and drink; and, to the day of his death, regretted marrying "down"). She had kept her own four kids from death's door, battling teachers, neighbors, boyfriends and girlfriends, spouses, making them snap to attention. She was fearless, that old, rotting brood hen; she was the youngest in her family, but top dog. She could make them all cry to this day—or the day when, a collection of brainless, brittle bones and dripping skin, she'd willed herself to live years beyond her time, in addled contentment. Not even a vegetable, as they said, but a fungus or mold. She'd wrecked Eenie's home, stinking up each room, breaking every good dish and glass, burning out appliances, scorching and smoking walls and ceiling. She laughed—how could you not laugh?—to think of the pure destructive power. Where had she gotten it?

She didn't have to ask. She knew where the grandmother, villainous, got it—from her mother, a master of pain and humiliation. There was a falling off, a dilution, as the root stock was grafted with weak, sickly ghosts of people, the poorest stock, who should have died out, but instead had drifted across the sea, and trickled down to their city, in time to sap a hero's race of fierce peasant farmers. Where had she read this, or did she dream it? This was the knowledge that came with age, and welcome to it.

Eenie was rubbing the frazzled glass with a rag dipped in a basin of warm water, vinegar, and ammonia, using a section of today's paper to wipe it clean, if not clear. This was her mother's way. Nothing in their broom closet or sink cabinet was a finished product, something with a fancy name and ad budget. They did all their cleaning with the basics: scouring soap, linseed oil, turps, lye, and Lava soap. That's why her pretty hands were clothed in such polished and shiny skin, skin that sucked in the cheap oils and lotions, and were satin-smooth.

She had been beautiful.

Maybe no one knew this (no one who counted), but that face, thin, sly—a beautiful face—had been spotted by a magazine photographer, and it turned up in ads for angora caps and sweaters, exactly the thing her mother couldn't afford. She contained, as she grew, everything within herself, and needed them for nothing but barest sustenance and shelter. She had chums, teachers, scout leaders, swim coaches (especially if they were men), at her fingertips, eager to do her bidding. There were two more, at home, older and younger, but it pleased her to ignore them, as well as the parents, and the selfish grandmother, and plot her own course. That was the question so hard to answer, looking back over the battleground of work, marriage, caring for children, and aging parents, an endless string of tasks and reminders of tasks still undone—some never done. The battleground was strewn with debris and dead soldiers. Don't look, so back she went to the glorious beginning.

She was beautiful; and then, what? Courted and idolized, adored, with boyfriends up the wazoo, as her friend, Sheila, liked to say, although neither knew what a wazoo was. There was cheap makeup to buy at the drugstore, pretty blouses and short skirts, and whatever the latest shoe fashion was: squashed heel, French heel, stacked heel, cloth Mary Janes, red Keds, saddle shoes and loafers, and spikes. Spikes were the best. She graduated, wearing a thin, cherry-red gown with white spikes. Her hair was bleached yellow as a dandelion. Her life was her own, entirely hers, and she savored, sucked it, and held it off from grabbing hands, and the cloying attachment and fiery scolding of her mother, always denied, snubbed. Of all the children, Eenie was the favorite, Daddy's girl, Mamma's pet. Even the sourpuss of a grandmother favored the middle child— beautiful, sassy, bold, and elusive. The boys and girls, too—they had their mitts out to grab the prize of a minute or two of the beauty's flushes and spurts of attention. Rare enough.

The phone rang, and there he was again. The undertaker was trying to reach her, and reached him, but he didn't know, he couldn't remember the drill. Would she please call him back. He'd already called twice; the second time, Tony hadn't picked up.

Eenie rose from the kitchen chair, perched next to the glass door she'd been stroking with a wad of newsprint. Did it look any better? Outside, across the scraggly lawn, was a woebegone cemetery, a few acres of lopsided stones, small flags, and pots of faded, plastic blooms, ugly ones. There were few trees, and the ground parched and grassless. She'd never ventured into this graveyard, although it wasn't so bad to look at—better than some other bathroom window, or junky backyard, of which they had plenty, her own included, with its falling-down fence, wild bushes, and a big, bare spot where the plastic pool had sat, and collapsed that one July, with a birthday-party full of kids in it. She laughed, although it wasn't funny: the screaming, choking, sobbing little boys, all five, stuck in a watery tangle of plastic.

The old pools were more substantial, propped on metal struts, and made of solid rubber. They lasted forever, and forever intact. They had to be dragged away, even after a lifetime exposure to rain, heat, and snow. All the old things lasted forever, or long after you needed them, or knew where to put them. Her father had dragged the black pool to the front of the house with the "tins," but the trashman refused to take it; and, only after half a year, did the ragman hoist it onto his heap of old clothes and ratty sheets. His horse hauled the wagon to wherever the ragman lived, and where he stored what he collected on rag Saturday.

She shook her head hard (her hair needed washing, and a shower would help snap her out of this fog). She was normally brisk and cheery, not someone who sunk into such memories as the ragman and the black pool. What could matter less than these?

What did matter? She was in the bedroom, having caught her robe and the side of her head in the bureau mirror. She stood dead center and finger-combed the still-thick, almost bristly hair, hair like her mother's, dense, wavy, the kind of hair you could do anything with. The old lady had torched hers with cheap perms and dye; but the hair, like a live sponge, gave not an inch. It was stronger than ever, even as the skull beneath it had shrunk; and the skin so slack, it seemed melted. The undertaker's wife had worked on the awful hair, curling and spraying it into a tidy bundle that would fit into the casket's white-satin pocket. (They didn't use pillows anymore, she'd said, at the second meeting: things were simplified, and that satin lining that looked so soft, hid a net of sharp wire.) There was nothing soft about it, but the undertaker's wife had succeeded where Eenie and her mother—when it was her mother's job— had failed, and the vicious (that was the right word for it) hair grew at least an inch a month.

Eenie had that same hair, but was patient, and cared—in a way her mother hadn't, after the third child was born in five years of marriage—about her appearance, so what had been wild was tamed, and even turned to effect: now, when Eenie was bigger than she'd ever been, the curly, shiny crown was higher and fluffier, and as flattering as ever. Her face, full but not round, was unlined, with a rich, healthy color, even these days, when her spirits were so low, and the only comfort in life, a sweet, creamy treat—each week, a different one. She smiled at her own youthful face, and it smiled back.

The wake was tomorrow, a Saturday. Tony was never home weekends; his odd jobs (so, why were they always broke, if he works all the time?—this line of attack the demented mother never forgot, or forgot to say) took him out at dawn, but he swung back to check in, and pop a frozen dish in the microwave. He ate down in his basement, where all his needs were met. The death notice had run in the paper, but no one had called. The out-of-towners would be in (not here, with her, but nested all together in the mall hotel, popular with visiting cheerleaders, square dancers, fast-pitch softball players, families on a budget). They might be there already, wondering where to go next. They'd all want to take over in some way, but she was boss. She'd kept the old lady for almost a decade, skimming bit by bit her car keys, her mail, her bank account, and managing doctors, tests, meds, food, drink, and even her religious duties, as her daily life was reduced to five items: sleep, food, TV, buckets and buckets of Tang-mix. The fifth was delivery to mass on Sunday. She always sat in the same place, dropped at the door, and picked up an hour later, because Eenie would have no more to do with church, priests, parish, diocese—father, son, and holy ghost. She'd christened her children, and sent them for instructions before confession and first communion, things that couldn't be avoided in a town like theirs, if you didn't want to be an outcast. She did all that, now done. She was really done, although Ma would have her mass of Christian burial, and be buried—not in Eenie's backyard—but in the Catholic graveyard where all the Quinns and Devlins, and even the Mottas and DelGiudices, were buried (in different plots, of course, with the micks separate from the wops they'd lived next door to for ages, and married).

The phone rang. The undertaker needed a payment, and now, before the first night's wake, the "viewing," as he called it. He couldn't be local, if that's how he said it. Okay, okay, she said to herself, but promised to drop by a few minutes before seven, with a check. The undertaker hesitated—so insulting these jerks could be—but agreed, muttering to his sidekick (his kid brother) some crack, before cutting the connection. Eenie had salvaged a portion of her mother's savings for just this expense, but she'd tapped into it, when the ratty carpet needed replacing, along with the dishwasher, broken for a year, and a cracked bathroom sink, leaking water into a cabinet, and who knew where else. Where does money go, anyway? She'd have to take a loan to pay off the funeral home, the ambulance trips (not covered), and the church. The plot at St. Francis was all theirs and she planned to go there herself, and get in last. She'd seen the plan of where everyone was, and there was a spot, top-right of a double row of ten. Of course, that would put her next to her mother for eternity, but you can't worry about everything. When the plot was paid for, things must have been a lot cheaper. She cried out loud—that minute—because the cemetery was the only decent piece of property, not a wreck, a shame, or a horror. She sniffed up the brief bubble of tears, recalling an ugly phrase of the dead mother's: if the truth hurts, let it. True enough, but why did it have to hurt?

She had a beautiful black blouse for the first night. People didn't wear black anymore; they wore anything short of a bathing suit and flip-flops. Her brother had worn a Hawaiian shirt to their father's wake. His week's cruise was interrupted, and he got right back on the boat. She could have used a break like that, but there was never any cash for anything that wasn't Tony's pick—a baseball or hockey game, a trip to Cooperstown or to Fenway—she went, yes, but how romantic was it to sit in the bleachers and be fried in the sun, or frozen to death. How much fun was that?

The blouse was steaming over the bathtub, because it'd slipped off a hanger in the chaos of her closet, and been trampled underfoot. When she found it again, it was twisted in a rope of clothes waiting to be dry-cleaned, stored in the only place she could store things, and remember why they were there. Well, she hadn't remembered, and they were still there, with the black silk blouse: a bargain—she was good at knowing which of the discount outlets was flush with new merchandise, marked down multiple times. It was the kind of thing her sister, the oldest and a snob (she could afford to be), would pick for herself, new and full-price. Well, Eenie had one, too, and she'd wear it, and stand first in the line, marching up the center aisle of the old church.

***

But, as they walked down this aisle, partnering their mother's box, a dusky metal, a cheap model—and she was lucky to have it—Eenie was second in line. The cheapest casket was the particle pine, but no one wanted to be seen in that, rolling up into that big, empty church, with the few elderly souls who remembered Mrs. Hanify. The pallbearers were all the same height, but Alice, as usual, was first, alongside the brother; and Eenie, second in line, with Aaron; Leanne following, with a cousin. The old organ up in the choir had a loop of music, programmed for just this kind of service; too much for a live organist, especially given the tuneless hymns of today, plainer than plain, with a message, stupider than the stupidest sympathy card. They stepped together, left-right, each with a hand on the rolling cart, draped in white. The priest (no one they knew) was waiting at the altar steps with his bucket of holy water, flanked by an altar boy—actually, it was a girl. How things had changed.

But, there wasn't a wrinkle or smutch on the black blouse, and the black pants were only a shade or two lighter. No black pumps, but silver sandals, worn to the last real party she'd attended, were even better, and showed a slice of creamy flesh and red nails. Alice had worn a stiff-looking suit, flats, and no jewelry. She'd let her hair go white, as Eenie's would be, if gold hadn't been the better choice. Alice had lost weight and looked haggard as ever. The brother had gained, and was in a polo shirt and leather jacket—expensive-looking, and not long enough to cover the gut now spread above the belted chinos. The cousin, with no family but theirs, was huge, with a beaming smile, and—this was a surprise—beautiful, plump Leanne was sobbing.

Eenie removed herself from her place in the middle (always in the middle!), and went to stand by her daughter, picking up her hand and kissing the knuckles. "I love you, baby girl," she said, "and Grandma loved you best."

Leanne shook her head no, and leaped ahead to take her mother's place, sticking her tongue out to make sure her mother got the message.

Eenie was cut, as she had been time and again, by the one *she* loved best. And wasn't that the point of family life: you only hurt the one you love; or, for their family, you hurt the ones you can, as Leanne had learned from the source; and that source, Eenie, learned it from the demented mother; and so on into eternity. Now, Eenie was weeping, and that set the big sister off. She turned back to walk beside Eenie, offering an ironed hankie, just as nice as can be, but Eenie had a balled-up Kleenex of her own, and pulled it out, pushing her sister's hand away. Why was she so enraged? Who had done it to her?

Now, Tony was there beside her, and who invited him? She elbowed her husband, and so hard, he fell against the arm of the pew—clumsy as he was, when not on blades; and, of course, he just took it, wheeled around, and walked out. Watching him, she fell out of step, colliding into Leanne, trampling her heels, causing her child to stumble and nearly fall, if Alice hadn't steadied her, in a sharp move that sent the gurney spinning down the aisle. And, it would have kept going, if the priest hadn't rushed up to stop it with a foot, causing Mamma's box to pitch forward—the ass of an undertaker failing to latch it, or tie it down. It was hanging off the cart, all tilted, with the cloth bunched up, showing the spindly metal shelf and fold-up legs.

How could you not laugh? No one had the oomph to get the casket back on its shelf, so they left it where it was, the demented mother resting on her head. They'd heard the body clunk, that bucket of bones and hard skull. Would the thing open up? You had to laugh, if only to keep yourself from crying, or screaming.

How could there be a God if this is what happens on a person's last day? And, a person like their mother, so devout, with a lifetime's store of masses, novenas, benedictions, holy hours, first Fridays, missions, and rosaries? That was always the question Eenie asked. Out loud, if she had the chance.

But, the priest was saying (was that a stain on his chasuble, or a rip?), dumb cluck that he was, that this might demonstrate to them, the faithful, how life and death are linked. How, exactly, through a practical joke? Eenie was standing in the middle of the aisle, the only one still there, behind the upended casket, with the priest dead ahead. They were face-to-face, eye-to-eye, and the man couldn't stop blathering about the divine connection between life and death, before and after, until Eenie slowed him down and stopped him, with a look so evil, that he turned tail, and hustled up the altar steps, to continue his palaver from there.

But, Eenie, ignoring it, turned to face the music. She saw the faces, shocked and blank—how could they be both?—of family, and those who should be gone already. She had a few things to say—for her, it was a mouthful—and her face shone, burned with rage and shame for all the things gone wrong, the cheap and second-rate junk, life and death, if you will. It was time to release it, but what came forth was more like a squeak than a torrent, because she was choked by the sheer flood of thought, every bit of it important, rushing up to get there first, and be gone. She raised her fist (she had small hands and feet) and rammed it down on the pew back; raised it, and rammed it, pounding on the sticky wood, and keen to the shock of pain firing fist to elbow, elbow to neck, and back again. She pounded until the faces blurred in a watery web, until—well, there was no end, because when she woke up, in her own bedroom, there was her mother, hanging over her with those curious eyes, judging, evaluating.

So, what happens next? That's what she wanted to know. But, the demented mother was in the ground, and the family (what was left) dispersed, and Eenie, alone again, glaring out the window at the clutter of stones, mangy grass, immature trees. There was all the time in the world now to think, but think what? What was next? It had to be asked, but who would answer, and what was there to offer, with only herself to fall back on?

Tower of Ivory, House of Gold

THE TWINS WERE ten when their big sister, Ann Mary, decided to enter the convent. Of the three Flynn girls, Ann Mary, not yet sixteen, was the beauty. She did the family cooking and most of the shopping, taking the twins along to haul the groceries home in their brother's old wagon. Jimmy Flynn had died when the twins were just five. He was born with a hole in his heart that grew faster than he did. Their mother, Eileen, was known to spend the afternoons lying on the couch with her face to the crack while Ann Mary crept around boiling the potatoes and frying the pork chops. She took so much cash every Friday when Dad got paid, and slipped the fives and tens into envelopes marked rent, food, gas and electric. These envelopes were stored in a shoebox kept in the bedroom, where the twins shared a double bed and Ann Mary opened up the rollaway with the bedclothes stuffed into it.

Ann Mary was going to the Passionists, the only order that took them in so young. She would finish high school at the motherhouse in Canada, where the underage postulants were driven to an all-girls' academy, to be taught by the Mercies. The Passionists didn't teach, and they weren't contemplative either. Had they been cloistered, Mr. Flynn would really have hit the roof. As it was, he hated the whole, sickening idea and fought it by vows, oaths, threats, by crying, and finally by spending every weekday night sitting at the bar at Reilly's. He hadn't given up but, for now, left the whole business to Eileen. Let her take a turn.

Ann Mary had been a calendar baby with a face like a fresh peach. She was the Flynns' first born, although Brother came

along less than a year later. Ann Mary had been his babysitter
from the time she was five and a half, when the twins were born.
She rocked him in the rocker, fed him from his bottle, burped
him, and would have changed his diaper if her hands were up
to the task of springing the safety pins. The infant twins, too,
were fed and burped by Ann Mary, when mother was too sick
to get up. That didn't happen often, but it happened in the
weeks before their aunt Marge came for a visit and stayed for
a month, making sure everyone was fed, dishes washed, and a
diaper service hired. Eileen was Marge's baby sister and Eileen
liked nothing better than to cry on her big shoulder and blame
it all on the mister. Baby Girl was still a beauty, although her
black hair had turned white, her figure was gone, and there
would be no more babies for the damage done when the twin
girls fought their way out. Eileen was never strong and was now
a wreck. Little did they know how hard she'd take it when she
lost her only boy.

Ann Mary didn't start out so holy. When sent to the nuns
after a rambunctious year in kindergarten, she refused to unfist
her hands from the baby carriage. When they pried her off, she
slid under the carriage. She made her mother sit with her in the
back of the classroom with the two babies screaming their heads
off. Mother Anna, familiar with this problem, took her by the
hand and sat her in a chair right next to the big desk, where
Ann Mary spent that day, and the day after. After a week of
clinging close to the nun's skirts, Ann Mary was a changed girl,
or so everyone said. She walked Mother Anna to school and
back, carrying her bag and umbrella. If Mother Anna was with
Mother Barbara, who taught the other first grade, Ann Mary
tucked herself in between.

She loved school: Morning Prayer, pledge, numbers and
letters, art, recess, bible history, and the day was over. She
learned how to do a basting stitch and made her mother a
pen wiper. She helped when Brother started school, holding
his hand to cross the streets, and watching for him when the

schoolyard lines dispersed. He was a blue baby, but Ann Mary kept that secret, as she'd been told, and prayed for him at the children's mass, but his first year at St. Ann's was also his last. Right after Christmas, he sickened, and was gone by the feast of the epiphany, only six days into the new year. Ann Mary went to the wake and funeral, a high requiem with the boys' choir singing their hearts out, and all the priests in black. She went with her dad, because her mother was "prostrate." The two of them stopped for a quick one at Reilly's to buck him up for the sandwiches and coffee, the family and friends waiting at home.

The twins were just babies then, but they knew why at Christmas, everywhere you turned—whether you were snitching a cookie or washing a baby doll—someone was always crying in the broom closet, and someone else cursing in the den. It was the worst time of year. Accidents happened and trips were made to the emergency room to set bones, sew up a puncture wound, or take rusty nails out of little feet.

Although accident-prone, the twins were strong as oxes. If their big sister was a skinnymalink, their dungarees and jerseys always came in the X sizes. They wore the same size and only the family could tell them apart. For Halloween, they were hula girls, porky Cinderellas, or witches, but Ann Mary, leading them up and down the dusky streets, rain or shine, simply wore her toggle coat and held their bags. "What's wrong with her?" was something they learned not to ask. Plus, she was nice to them, helping them with long division, and reading them their favorite stories about student nurses and girl detectives. She was different, an "authority," something their father told them never to be.

By eighth grade, Ann Mary was going to daily mass and communion, although first she'd wake them up and prepare their breakfast, reminding them to get their mother up. Sometimes they didn't, and there'd be hell to pay if their father arrived home and found his wife still "dead to the world." The twins were supposed to come home for lunch and their sister would leave out bread and bologna in case Eileen wasn't up to the task of boiling them a hotdog. But, the twins didn't like coming home by themselves and often didn't, saying they'd gone to the noon mass and shared a candy treat. At the end of the day, their mother would be asked to report, but often forgot, saying they were there when they weren't. Ann Mary always knew, though, and lit into them for abusing their poor Ma and insulting the baby Jesus with their lies. She could be scary, but even they knew that the baby Jesus didn't care what they ate for lunch. He cared about some things, but not all things.

How could someone so good be so bad—or, put it another way, so holy be so mean? Did these things go together? The twins figured this out almost from birth. Did Ann Mary get it? She could see through walls and read the sins right off their black souls, but there were things she didn't know, or didn't want to know, and even their father—who killed the pain, and the knowledge that went with it, with quarts of beer—was getting wise to his favorite.

Their dad drove a bakery truck, delivering sandwich bread and pastries to out-of-the-way country stores. His day started early and ended early, so their mother knew to be out of her bathrobe by noon, come hell or high water. That's when her big sister Marge would call, letting the phone ring. Marge still called their mother Baby Girl because Eileen had been the youngest of nine and Marge had fed, bathed, and babied her up to the day of her wedding. Aunt Marge still lived in the old Lynch house, a three-decker, with Granddad and the tenants. She prayed to St. Jude for Baby Girl to get well and stay well. Jude, the mister liked to point out, was the patron of lost causes, but Marge ignored that dig and everything else the husband had to say.

To the twins, Ann Mary and Aunt Marge were peas in a pod, except that Aunt Marge was a "horror," as their dad liked to say, with a face to stop a clock, and Ann Mary prettier by the day. Her hair was down to her waist and the twins liked to play with it, when she let them. They'd climb up on the bureau to study themselves in the mirror. Then, paint Ann Mary's Cupid's bow with a tiny sample from the drugstore, perfume her ears from an old bottle of My Sin, and rouge her pure white cheeks. Jean would take the brush, Doreen the comb and they'd divide the stream, and comb and brush it until the mane looked like a mink cape.

Aunt Marge had a mink, too, brown with button eyes, which she wore to sponsor Ann Mary at confirmation, steadying the girl at the moment when the bishop clipped her on the jaw. For that day, their sister's hair was braided and tucked under the netting the nuns supplied for girls without the "means" to buy a veil.

Aunt Marge had had a vocation, which she sacrificed for the sake of her family, because charity, she told them, begins at home. And girls especially should learn never to put themselves first. But Ann Mary, come rain or come shine, still planned to go to God.

The twins were a different case: they were never growing up. They didn't have to, and no one was going to make them. They were almost one person: they looked alike, talked alike, and usually had the same bright idea. But even put together, they knew they didn't add up to an Ann Mary, even on a bad day. Only to their mother were they something special. She preferred them. They knew by heart the whole story of her love life, starting from the first date with the paperboy, to the wedding night, when the newlyweds broke the brass bed up in the Lynch attic, Dad had been a boxer and their mother was just a peanut. She was still a peanut, but nowadays Dad slept on the couch so their mother could have the sickroom. Her love life had three episodes: the paperboy, the ex-seminarian, and her wedding to Dad. She never worked a day in her life, and went straight from high school to the altar rail.

The twins liked nothing better than to haul out the old wedding gown, kept under a sheet in the closet. "Try it on, dollies," she'd call from her bed. Doreen would swing it over her head with Jean ready to pull it down. They played wedding day the whole summer Ann Mary was taking sewing lessons. One day, though, she got home early, and heard the commotion. How many times did she have to tell them to keep it down! That their mother needed peace and quiet if she were ever going to get better! Ann Mary yanked the gown up over Doreen's head. They all heard it rip. It was supposed to be hers—whether she took her vows alone, or with a man standing next to her—and just look what they'd done!

Ann Mary was entering on August 1, three months to the day. She X'd out numbers on the calendar, which hung above their May altar. It was Ann Mary's May altar, but the twins used it. They took down the blue and pink statue and walked it along the floor and up the wall. They stuffed messages and candy papers into the slot on the bottom. (Once Doreen got her tongue stuck in the slot, just as they heard their sister on the stairs. They managed to get Our Lady back on the shelf, with the paper crown hanging over her eyes.) Ann Mary always stopped in their mother's room first, even if she weren't coughing and choking. The twins waited for her to X out that day, genuflecting in front of her altar, making the sign of the cross, and kissing her thumb, just the way the Italians did it. This was something new and the twins copied it.

The father, once he started going to Reilly's, was never home till late, so they kept his plate warm in the oven. Their mother ate like a bird, crying over the baked beans when something said hit a tender spot, whether it was a memory, a dig, or just a paper napkin folded the wrong way. She didn't care for lager and ale, so Ann Mary kept the fridge stocked with porter, which their father could also drink, if he felt like it. The twins liked milk drawn through a flavored straw—chocolate in winter, strawberry in summer. Ann Mary preferred golden ginger ale. She said the grace and kept her eyes on the clock to make it on time for Benediction and be back to help the twins with their homework. On a good night, their father would be home by then, with his paper spread out on the kitchen table and the twins buzzing around him like flies. They loved their dada, and love meant kisses on his whiskery cheeks, scratches on his back with their ragged fingernails (Doreen bit hers, Jean clipped hers into points), and piling up on his lap to tuck their heads into his neck. He carried them together into the parlor to sit on the arms of his chair. They ran in and out to refill his glass. After he read them the funnies, the sports page, and the obits, he'd be on the lookout for his big girl, who'd dash in breathless, with her chapel veil still bobby-pinned to her head. Even Ann Mary liked to listen to Dada's stories and jokes. He had tricks, too, hiding a quarter in the cuff of their dungarees, in a seat cushion, or behind his ear. It was the only time their oldest sister was known to crack a smile. He called it leaving them in "stitches."

On a bad night, he wouldn't get home until they were in bed with the lights out. They could hear him, of course, cursing and swearing as he crashed into things. Ann Mary would get up to close their mother's door. A few times, she had to push him out the back door, locking it behind him. And was all this just because of a goddamned vocation to the Passionists! Was that possible?

Not just possible, their mother liked to say, but the only explanation. But would Ann Mary back down even an inch? She'd made her promise—not just to God—but to the nun at the retreat house run by the Sisters of the Cross and Passion. And no sideshow by Dada, Ma, or the brats would talk her down, or get her back out once she was in, because, as she liked to tell them, once "in," there was no coming out. Once taking her postulant's veil, she couldn't so much as step foot on their porch. Even if one of them croaked, she wasn't allowed to come to the funeral. She would never see her home again! The first time, the twins cried to hear it, and Ann Mary cried, too. She was only fifteen, after all, with a birthday in December. Maybe you'll change her mind? her mother would plead. Or have it changed for you! their father would snap back.

And it wasn't just the family. Their own parish nuns, the Faithful Friends of Jesus, who'd taught several generations of Lynches and Flynns, and were forever harping on the subject of "callings," had had a conniption when they heard where Ann Mary Flynn thought she was going. They'd had the monopoly on vocations since moving in to staff the school, but lately, were only getting a handful. They were an Irish order, semi-cloistered, with a swaddling habit of black serge, but all that didn't seem to matter. Up to then, they had claimed every parish girl with a yen for something different from what she saw at home. What the mysterious life behind the wall might consist of was vague until a couple of girls who'd been all the way "in" with the black veil on their heads, came out again to live among the laity. What goes on in there? was a question no one got tired of asking. When the twins asked Ann Mary, she pretended not to know, to be above curiosity about particulars, such as: what kind of rigging went under the serge to flatten them out, or what they ate when they ate, how bad were the duties, devotions, penances, prostrations, and mortifications of the flesh? And so on. They knew something, because they'd gone to see *The Nun's Story* and Ann Mary owned the book. But only as the day of decision approached did their sister say why these answers were so hard to come by—even after those ex-nuns were set free (or freed themselves) to live among the laity; namely, that they had to take one final vow to breathe not a word on pain of death about what went on. The upshot: before going in, you knew nothing, and coming out, you couldn't say. Did anyone really believe that?

All they knew was when their own nuns found out that the girl with this year's vocation was going somewhere else, they were fit to be tied. The twins got an earful at school, and brought it home. Ann Mary blocked her ears, but Dada was interested in anything said about his family, especially by the "cloth." Some days, he'd blow his stack; other times, he'd laugh. To hell with them! he'd say. But, wasn't that a sacrilege, given who they were?

Ann Mary held out. She started to pin a black heart with a cross through it on her clothes. The pin was the official Passionist badge, although the real badges were made of leather and hung over the heart. Ann Mary's pin was little and she could easily have hidden it, but no—she flaunted it, moving it from her toggle coat and sticking it on her bow tie, big as life.

She'd toyed with the idea of joining their own nuns, or signing on with the Mercies, but she'd have to wait the extra year or two, and she was ready to go now. Her advisor, Sister Clement, had given her the Passionists' manual so she could prepare. The manual looked like a missal and contained a page for every step in the story of Jesus's death. Each stab and insult, each slap and scourging got its own section. There was also a sentence reminding the Passionist whose fault it was and what it would take in prayer, meditation, and self-sacrifice to cancel out the wrongs done to Our Savior in the long and ongoing story of redemption. Ann Mary was in church every day working her way through the manual.

"Do you *have* to go back down there this minute? Haven't you already been there today? Give it a rest, for God's sake," she heard as she slipped out the door.

"Mind your own beeswax," she'd say if a twin were speaking the line.

She didn't mind, though, if they came along, bouncing the basketball down the hill or pushing each other into trees. Ann Mary kept a rosary in her pocket and fingered the beads to work in a mystery or two: joyful mysteries, because it was that time of year. The twins mostly stayed outside, sitting on the steps to play jacks, or "destroy church property" with a sliver of chalk. If they went in, they'd spend the time whipping their fingers across a candle flame to see who got burnt first.

Their big sister knelt at the altar rail in front of the big, wooden cross. They knew her whole routine. She'd start with the bleeding feet, crisscrossed and pinned by a single nail, then meditate her way up to the hole in the side, which a soldier pierced with his sword to make sure He was good and dead. Up to the arms, stretched to their limit on the crossbeam with a nail in each palm, then up higher to the thorn crown, rammed onto the head, taking a minute to ponder the taste of that spongeful of gall that He was forced to drink. When she got to the crown, she would start down again; or, for variety, go straight back to the feet, and start over. After she'd gone up and down, up and down—if there was still time—she was free to turn to the page on the pain of slow strangulation, which was why it took Him three hours to die. You weren't supposed to go on for too long, or risk the sin of prideful bloatation. The final pages had to do with the wrongs of the disciples. Or the trek through the dusty streets of Jerusalem, lugging the heavy lumber behind Him, until Joseph of Arimathea, converted en route, picked up the big piece. Peter the apostle, of course, stood helpless at the fountain, denying Our Lord three times until the cock crowed. He was a jerk, Ann Mary had said, and the worst of all. Why? Because he should've known better.

Ann Mary didn't care whether the twins sat around and waited, or marched up to the statue of the Little Flower to kiss the plaster roses scattered on her pedestal. Ann Mary, who was planning to take the name Teresa, often joined them there. It was immature, but they'd always liked doing it, even when the statue was gray with soot. Afterward, they'd stop for a popsicle to get the taste out of their mouths. Toward the end, though, the twins couldn't even get Ann Mary to get up and kiss the roses. She stayed put in front of the cross until, eyes wide open, tears began to roll down her cheeks. They saw it.

The question Ann Mary was asking herself, kneeling there, was: what's wrong? Was she too bloated with pride? Wouldn't this praying kill the pride and the doubts that went with it? This she asked the priest in confession. "Don't worry about it," he said. "There'll be plenty more where that comes from. They'll think of things to make you do. You won't have to lift a finger." He had told Ann Mary she was awfully young—and, now, was he trying to scare her? Becoming a nun—becoming a Passionist—meant harder penances, but Sister Clement had said that on entering, she would become "like a little child," placing herself in the hands of God. But, Ann Mary had only a couple of months to go, and things were happening beyond her control: first, she'd upped her rosaries per day, her meditations in front of the cross, her morning and nightly prayers. She was discovering new corporal and spiritual works of mercy, benedictions, litanies, weekly confession, and, always on the tip of her tongue, an ejaculation ("Jesus, Mary, and Joseph!" "Lord have mercy!"), each one absolving so many hours or days in Purgatory, while others were said to be able to wipe the entire slate clean.

It didn't matter. The calling was so weak in her heart that sometimes she could scarcely feel it. Very little homework was getting done and she had no patience for the "rogues," as their father called his twins. Her suppers were too salty or burned; she was forever scorching or cutting a finger. "O my God, I am heartily sorry for having offended Thee," bubbled out of her mouth, if you caught her by surprise. She was losing weight and her pretty face had no color at all. Did anyone notice? If they did, no one could stop her. "Through my fault," she hissed at the bus driver, dropping a coin into machine.

The doubt—the germ or acid that had eaten through the vocations of those ex-FFJs—was killing Ann Mary's calling, and she hadn't gotten out of the house yet. Where did it come from? She was an emptiness: an emptiness and a craving to do whatever it took to bring it back. She was crying so much of the time, her uniform collars were wrinkled from dampness. The twins could hear her sobbing at night and had to stick their heads under the pillow to drown out that hopeless sound.

Then, as they say to each other to this day, they reached the limit. Night before the twins' eleventh birthday, Doreen (older by a minute) piped up: "What the hell's the matter with you,

Ann Mary?" And then, the other one: "Stop your blubbering
for a minute and spit it out."

It took a while to worm it out of her, but eventually Ann
Mary spilled the beans: the vocation was gone.

Gone where? they didn't ask. They were too shocked and
sad. It was something having a sister going into the Passionists
before she even turned sixteen. At first, they just lay there,
silently breathing. Then, Doreen got up and grabbed the brush.
It was the first thing she thought of. But when she touched her
sister's hair, it was too snarly and greasy. Had the girl washed it
in the last century? She pulled the light cord to see. By then,
Jean was up, holding her nose. They looked at each other, then
Jean peeled the bedspread down and they saw. All her clothes
were on: the school sweater, the dungarees, socks, and even her
shoes. And lying there, shivering with fever. They looked at each
other, then Jean went to the dresser for one of the new nighties,
a birthday present opened that day. Doreen was unbuttoning
her sister's sweater, so Jean yanked off the dungarees. The
girl just lay there, limp as a ribbon. It was when they had her
stripped down to her skivvies that they saw what they saw. The
looney had wound half a mile of their father's garden twine
around her middle, tying it so tight they could see puffy rolls of
strangulated fat, and Ann Mary had no fat. Stuffed under the
twine were scraps of their father's sandpaper with the gravelly
side toward the skin. It was too gross to scream. They tried
untying the knots but that only made it worse, so Jean ran for
the scissors. Ann Mary had stopped crying, but her head was
cocked back and eyes rolling up. They worked hard, cursing and
sometimes gagging. When the twine was unwound, they saw
what was underneath. Doreen ran to the bathroom. A bubbly-
looking rash had spread all over Ann Mary's bony chest and
belly. The smell could almost make you throw up, but Doreen
didn't have time; she was out running a bath. Ann Mary needed
to go to the hospital, but when Jean whispered this softly, the
girl started to shriek, until a hand slapped over her mouth. "It's

okay, my girl," Doreen said, "settle down."

They could hear water splashing into the tub, and then the flowery smell of bath oil. Jean knew what was next: she pulled Ann Mary, limp and lifeless, out of bed. Once she got her in the bathroom, she locked the door behind them. "Don't say a word," she said to her sisters.

After filling the bath with a high dome of steaming pink bubbles, they stripped off their own nightgowns. This was not a plan, because there was no plan. They guided the sick girl— itching and peeling skin and bones—into the deep, soothing water—just hot enough, and then got in after her, one on each side. Using their hands and a bar of Ivory, they gently, gently soaped Ann Mary, avoiding the sorest places. She winced and cried at the touch. It was too tender to touch with soap or hands, so they cupped the warm water and rinsed her from the shoulders. They washed her face using the tips of their fingers. They washed her feet and hands. Then, Doreen jumped out and poured baby shampoo over the greasy mop and scrubbed her head. They had to practically lift her to stand her up. They couldn't towel her dry, so they just waited for the air to do it. She was shivering, even though the house was warm. She couldn't stop shivering, even when they had the nightgown over her head and a bathrobe tied around her waist. When she'd finally stopped the raspy weeping, but looked as if she could still start up again, they took her downstairs and made her drink two full cups of hot milk mixed with vanilla and sugar.

They got through that night, but no one was sure what would happen next. Would the vocation come back if she eased up and just let it?

It did come back, but not for long. There were two reasons and they had nothing to do with Ann Mary. First, their aunt Marge noticed—once the twins had her all cleaned up and back into a routine—how sick she looked. She might need something above and beyond what the family could do—and had done— in the bedlam they lived in, so the aunt moved Ann Mary in with herself and the granddad, leaving the twins in charge at home. That didn't last. Soon, Aunt Marge arranged for Baby Sister to spend a couple of months up at the state hospital for her poor lungs to dry out. That more than the lungs needed drying came as a shock only to Marge, because the granddad had gotten an inkling from his son-in-law. They found the empty jugs of kosher wine and cheap whisky under the bed and dresser and in the closet. When exactly did she get out to buy it all? was the question. She didn't get out, of course, and the mister's excuse—because he'd done all the buying—was he was afraid not to. Did they have any idea, he sobbed, how bad she could get without it? Marge felt she had to ask Ann Mary just the once. "Did you know about this, my girl?" The granddad heard it and told her to leave it alone.

By the time the great day arrived, August 15, feast of the Assumption, the day when the Blessed Mother was called to heaven before her body was corrupted or buried in the earth, the Passionists had changed their rule. Before receiving Sister Teresa into their own, a decree had come from the motherhouse, per a liberalized Vatican, to terminate teenage enlistments. The Passionists, like so many others, had lost in one blow the right to rule their own, unconditionally, and per their ancient monastic code, immutable, but eternal no longer.

They were sure to have sent her home anyway, the aunt said: her health, even after a month resting at Aunt Marge's, was too poor. The nuns had their standards, too. At that point, the aunt decided to keep Ann Mary with her. She took in the twins, too, for the two weeks when the Lynches rented their beach house. They were all three kept on a tight leash those few summers, when the skinny redhead and blonde cuties caught the eye not just of the lifeguards, but of the fathers and uncles playing catch on the beach. Ann Mary was a different girl; you'd hardly recognize her. She had the mentality of a child: naïve, passive, and trusting—not so different from Baby Girl, before she was wrecked by marriage.

The twins finished high school near the top of their class, cooking and cleaning for their old dad, who, at fifty, looked closer to ninety. Their mother lived to a ripe old age, still up at Howard, where she was at home visiting with old neighbor and school chums. All three Flynn girls went up every Sunday, bringing candy or a coffee cabinet, and sitting for an hour in the parlor. It was all female, so not unlike a convent.

Doreen Flynn eventually went to med school and now keeps a practice in the old neighborhood, seeing old friends and their kids, some new families, and the few remaining FFJs. There are still a handful there, knocking around in the convent, too old to teach and too proud to lend a hand at the rectory. Doreen lives with her twin and Ann Mary Flynn on the second floor of the old Lynch house. She keeps her office on the first floor. And, if the monsignor or any of the clerics at St. Ann's should ever need anything done, however big or small, like, say, getting up a clothing drive, teaching CCD, or running a raffle for the Little Sisters of the Poor—he thinks nothing of calling on the Flynn girls, true pillars of the church.

II

The Cones

I

THE CONES WERE sitting in their office, Mr. and Mrs., waiting for the mail, the highlight of the day. They had six employees, and one office boy, Terry. There were two businesses, and Terry ran one of them. The rest of the employees were girls and women: Dorothee, Angela, Maricruz, Tristana, Irene, and Sidney, and they were all beauties, each from an immigrant family. The Cones carved out of their loft six stations. The office boy had his own airy space, where he cut up newspaper with a straight edge, and stuffed the fragments into envelopes for firms, outfits, and clubs that wanted to test the waters for the spread of their word. Terry received papers from everywhere, and he loved the job of reading and sorting.

The Cones sat facing each other at antique desks that kissed on their front end. Pencils went one way, and pencils went another, her coffee cup, his. Scissors and glue passed down the middle.

Their son was on the payroll, as was Mrs. Cone's ancient mother, bankrupt now, but whose husband's legacy had launched and fueled both businesses. The old lady was tucked away with an immigrant minder, Astrud, who was on the payroll.

In the post that day was a letter blackmailing Mr. Cone, and it was in the hands of Mrs. Cone, who had a gold slicer and was working it along the fold, bit by bit. She knew who it was from. It was the third letter in three months, but nothing had been said, no word spoken. She had answered the first two, the first unsigned, the second signed, and this third from a law firm.

Mr. Cone was the object of a suit for alienation of affection, a crime in their state, run by immigrant Catholics with a stake in the sanctity of marriage, and not just for themselves. Mrs. Cone read the letter, and set it aside. She looked up to see her husband's meek eyes gleaming and glowing. "Dream on," she said, under her breath.

"Come again?" he said, hearing something.

"Just a bill," she said.

"It doesn't look like a bill," he offered, spreading out his hands, shrugging his shoulders, and making his eyes tender and moist.

"No, it doesn't," she said.

The six employees tuned in. Their lives rang and thrummed with the conjugating energy of their bosses, and today's weather was "extreme clear," the worst kind. There was a snap in the air, and only one place to hide, the single-stalled bathroom, dressed with Mrs. Cone's thick towels and fruit soaps, but even to rise, to adjust a gored skirt under a smooth thigh, to light a cigarette, or pound the typewriter, to sip water or suck a lifesaver could trip the wire of contentment, Mrs. Cone's element, the tent she created for them to crawl under each morning, leaving at five.

So, they sat there, tingling.

Taking a sheet of letterhead, rolling it into her typewriter, feeling the weight of all eyes, Mrs. Cone scanned the perimeter like a searchlight, watching each head drop down, except one. Maricruz was the oldest of the immigrant daughters, married to the contractor who had transformed the old print shop into an office, and still sending out bills for materials and labor. With the first one, he got back only a copy of a page from the contract, and a sheet of cancelled checks. After that, nothing. Both Cones had taken Maricruz aside—Mrs., to deliver a warning, Mr., to make a date.

The date was not the first. The first had been an accident. Mr. was running into the city to pick up a turkey dinner and fixings for the extended family. It was late on a Wednesday night, and Mrs. was in bed with a migraine; the maid-cook had a day off, or was fired, as the previous dozen had been in the course of the five years the Cones had resided in the old mother's house, sending her to a city flat with the immigrant. Before moving, as city people, the Cones preferred to dine out, or order in, with shopping delivered to the door and unpacked. Once they had the room, and the parking, to entertain, they did. The tiny town on the main line had a shop for everything, but no caterer, so Mr. drove into the city for the roasted bird. He found Maricruz behind the counter, boxing, wrapping (she'd been hired for the holidays), and stuffing picnic baskets and Styrofoam coolers, for pickup and delivery. The floor was lined with sacks and baskets. Maricruz, all in white, smiled at her boss, but told him to step outside, and his order would be rolled out to the car, but Mr. Cone lingered. Mrs. Cone had taken, by his hand, a double dose of her headache drug, and would be out for hours, probably overnight, so Mr. Cone lit a cigarette, leaning against the wall, knee-deep in the contents, sweet and savory, of the scores of festive dinners.

"Put it out," she said, and he said, "Okay, but where?"

"Out," she said, pointing to the door.

Stepping over the pure white sacks (specially made for the caterer), baskets and coolers, and over the jugs of cider and applejack, he tossed the butt into the street, where the waiting cars were queued, motors running, some chauffeured. It was a rainy night, and the streetlights and headlights made the streaming water glisten and sparkle. Mr. Cone hadn't felt this happy since the day his old mother died, and left him an unexpected nest egg, which Mrs. Cone, to this day, knew nothing about.

He waited an hour, walked across the street for a scotch and no ice, and returned to escort Maricruz to a wine bar and jazz club a crony from a different day, different job, was forever hawking. Mr. Cone had friends; Mrs. Cone didn't, so Mr. Cone saw his infrequently and on the fly—like this, on an errand with time to spare.

Why was Maricruz, thirty-two, willing to go with Mr. Cone, fifty-nine, to the wine bar, when there were crying babies at home and a surly mother, who begrudged her daughter the time and indulgence, but family was everything to an immigrant, and this one—fresh off the boat? Maricruz didn't give it a second thought. Her Polack husband was in Vegas with his cronies, flying back tomorrow, and she was pregnant again. No one knew—not even Sheila, her mick friend, who envied "Mary" the hunky husband, the twin cuties, the live-in babysitter, and cushy job. So, Maricruz, with or without the apron, was going wherever it was, and wasn't calling home first.

She kept a little dress for just this kind of "accident," luck, and wild card, and this was by no means the first.

Second date was to the nightclub, a ritzy boite, long on the list of to-dos and to-gos. She knew (she kept the books for both businesses) that Art Cone was a big spender—gifts, vacations, dinners out, antiques and jewelry, expensed when possible, and what wasn't? If you had the gift (which she did) for a good story, or "cooking the books," as the competitor across the street called it. They'd only been audited once, and it was a lesson to all of them how easy it was, if you had the brass, which the Cones did, especially Mrs.

He wanted her to get a blood test; but, then, they couldn't wait, so off they drove, that night, to an airport motel—a nice one, as she insisted, and he paid in cash, as past experience had taught him to do. Yes, he'd been to that motel before. How did she guess? Mr. Cone was smooth, clean, and fast, but he didn't think to peel off a couple of hundreds folded into the gold clip, although he did promise a raise at year's end. They didn't discuss the trouble over the contractor, the broken deal, half of which was in cash, under the table. Mr. Cone was curt, and Maricruz, sulky—both determined never to let it happen again.

But, it did. On Good Friday, when the help was let out at noon to flock to their churches, and prepare the big Easter feeds, Mr. Cone left a note on Maricruz's desk, and they met an hour later at the motel. Still, no crisp bills, but a basket of fruit and a drum full of caramel corn for the kiddies. Maricruz was touched because, although Mr. Cone had never mentioned the twins, little Bobby (Adalbert) and Louie (Luiz) were named on a card, taped on the drum, with a packet of chocolate drumsticks. Mr. Cone was a peach, did he know that? He was a peach. Yeah, he said, I'm a peach. And she kissed him again, and fogged up his glasses, which he ran under the faucet one more time, and wiped with his handkerchief (ABC stitched in a corner), the one she kept in her purse, flaunting it at times in the office. Arthur Cone had nice things, and he kept them nice, where Mrs. Cone—although she spent a fortune on earthy, homespun clothes and chunky jewels—looked like a bag lady. But, they never mentioned Mrs. Cone. If her name came to mind, they smiled, winced, or put a finger to lips, savoring a moment of telepathy.

***

Mrs. Cone was on the phone—using the letter to fan her face—with her son, a lawyer still trying to pass the bar, when he never wanted to practice law in the first place. He was a born critic, enrolled in a nighttime doctoral program in media studies. The weekly town newspaper ran his column on new movies, TV shows, and what they signified for the culture at large. She mouthed the word, Jaimy, when her husband drew a question mark in the air. She was in menopause, but Mr. Cone was feeling the sudden engulfing fire. He let his eyes dart left to meet Maricruz's, behind their cute horn-rimmed glasses. She needed to be phased out, but that was exactly what he couldn't do, unless he fired them all—not a bad idea—and fold this absurd, money pit of a business.

Mrs. Cone made a lunch date with Jaimy, and when Mr. Cone heard about it, he ordered the car and checked his money clip, but his wife told him she was going alone. They were two days from a deadline, and someone needed to stay in the shop and make sure the galleys were corrected and returned. Mr. Cone knew something was up.

His wife never went anywhere without him. He prepared her morning toast and tea, brought in the papers, drove her to the office, arranged for lunch and dinner, and ferried her home, helping her off with coat and hat, and settling her with a weak drink under her reading lamp, with her feet up and covered with a soft throw. And a dish of something to nibble on. The son, up to now, had never been enough of a guardian.

He went for her coat and hat, and called her a cab, helping her negotiate the slippery plank floor, and double-bolted door. He rang for the service elevator and ushered her in, waiting with her at the curb, and handing her a fifty and a twenty. For a woman who loved (and even lived) to talk, she said nothing, but he heard a sniffle and offered her a fresh hankie, which she kept.

"Arlene?" he said a few times, testing her nerves, but she didn't answer. He sensed more bewilderment than rage, a novelty.

They'd been married thirty years, their marriage firmly rooted in mutually satisfying routines. She'd organized him in the first decade, and he was ready to be organized. The second decade was marked by flashes of malaise and rebellion, but the growing boy—with his own set of problems—fitted like a puzzle piece to their marital grid. The third decade was given over to settling the parents' estate, and to the founding of the businesses, one nesting inside the other.

Mrs. Cone settled her small but plump frame into what was not clean upholstery—far from it, but she wasn't prepared to squat, or call the greasy-haired driver to halt. She scribbled his license number with a silver pencil, and held her breath. Her mind was arrowed with thought—fiery scenarios, and killing endgames—against a background thrum of hurt. There was a place in Mrs. Cone that had been beaten, burned, and cut. The hurt grew every minute, from the time she was old enough to locate, in a separate place, the corrupt and vicious mother. Unequal to the role of protecting his only child, his darling, was the father, who lived to work, to work and make money, to read the newspaper and play the stock market. The sore spot grew, until every inch of skin was stretched over poison pools of grief and resentment. She was a star student, with her doctorate; she had a coming-out party; and, finally, she was a war bride, because Arthur, then on her father's payroll, popped the question, and was inducted, in spite of myopia, flat feet, and a heart murmur. He sold advertising for *Stars and Stripes*, and never left the base. But, still, a soldier, and not free to marry until after the armistice; and, then, spent a couple of years on the west coast, floating a movie career, foolish as he always was, until dragged back and re-appointed treasurer in the office of Furnace and Furnace Realty. Their wedding was small and stylish, but better forgotten because, even then, the bride was far from photogenic, and the little, bell-shaped virgin with her cat glasses and wispy pageboy did not engage the eye—not even her own eye, then or now. Arthur, as she called him, was a radiant bridegroom, but tiny like her, and their attendants overtopped and outshone them. Her mother was quick to point that out, but insisted it was a joke, no harm done.

Then, the work of marriage and the agony of childbirth— so difficult, such an insult to body and mind that Little Jaimy was consigned to the grandmother's care, while she recovered— first, in the hospital; then, in a month-long stay in a cottage by the lake, opened and staffed just for her. Motherhood and housekeeping were not congenial, although she found a friend and confessor in her only child, as soon as he was old enough to sit still, and not blab or cry, just to play quietly with his soldiers or elaborate puzzles, while she made them snacks and drank countless cups of tea. Jaimy was a good listener. He remembered what you told him; sensitive, too: he cried, even bawled at some of the stories of her life, the first part, second, and now, this. True, he had his own problems: hated school, hated his schoolmates, and beat on any child smaller or weaker; then, ran home crying. He told lies, and they'd spent a fortune on a child analyst, to no avail. He was who he was; and, in her eyes, he was good enough. Theirs was still the closest family tie, when they weren't at war, because of the present wife, and the first, ill-chosen and despicable.

By the time Jaimy was ten, he had the whole history of his father's failures and weaknesses: when, and where, and with whom he'd cheated, as well as how he was forced back. Jaimy himself, to his infinite credit, had done some of the forcing, passing on tidbits, hints, and secrets to the grandfather with the payroll.

But, this was different. This, she thought, was war, and Jaimy had long since been committed to the cause. His present wife had changed him, and not for the better. In the family circle, Jilla seemed deaf, dumb, and blind—impervious to the web of feeling, the fast talk and sarcasm, the patronizing and condescension that went with it. They gave her everything they had, because they were a family of quick wit and artful improvisation, and could dish it out at every level, but Jilla proved a dull, almost insensible blob, enclosed in what even she could see was an attractive package. Was she the real enemy?

They were there. And here was Jaimy, waiting on the sidewalk, but too self-absorbed to open his mother's door and envelop her in his wiry arms. He didn't, in truth, like to touch Arlene, as he called her in his mind, and even to her face. She didn't like it. And she didn't really like to touch him, even as a little baby, a tiny boy, who needed touching and soothing and holding. There was always a barrier of air, of resistance between mother and child. Even now, it was his dad who kissed him, who tended him and his baby child, when Jaimy could get Jilla to visit the homestead, and to stay longer than an hour. It was embarrassing, shameful the number of times she found something else to do, or some place to hide in the sprawling house, when she was there. "Don't be allergic," he'd say, and it was a joke, but only partly. A flash of rage had colored his temples and forehead, sorrowing for himself in the center of these frigid and sadistic women; and yet, they were all he had.

And now, Arlene had insinuated herself into the crook of his arm, burying her face in his coat, but here the driver was waiting for his pay, and didn't she know first things first!

She was pushing a ball into his hand, a fifty—that was no good! He nudged her away, glaring at her small, crumpled face. "Do you have anything smaller?" practically screaming.

It all took too long, and the driver, pulling out, honked his horn and honked it again, giving them (Arlene didn't see) the bird.

"Mother," he said, "take it easy," for she was sobbing.

Jaimy despised his father, but also adored him. Settled in the snug café with a balloon of beer, he wasn't surprised at what streamed from Arlene's little mouth, twisted into mesmerizing shapes and wet with tears, and yet he *was* surprised. His dad was fifty-nine, and no Adonis, even at twenty-nine, and yet he'd had dozens of women at his beck and call, by his and his mom's estimate. He was incorrigible, and Jaimy had even seen his hairy hand pinching and fondling Jilla's trim waist, and looked the other way. Jilla could take care of herself. She was capable of sealing up all openings—even, it seemed, the pores of her skin.

"Take it easy," he said again, as he ordered a second balloon, his belly already twisted with whatever twisted it when he was looking at this face, and trying to eat or drink. When the food came (lobster salad sandwich and fries), he squeezed his eyes shut, and bolted it.

"I can see it hasn't hurt your appetite," he heard, and kept chewing.

But, they had to make some plan, because the business (its sale) was Jaimy's future, and his baby son's.

His mother handed over the letter, delivering her theory. She

was paranoid, but it added up. The contractor was behind it,
which meant Maricruz *and* the Polack husband. What to do,
what to do? He drummed his fingers, first on the table, then
on his forehead. "Eat your lunch," he said, at the familiar and
galling sight of his mother playing with her food like the infant
she was, first taking it apart (bun, tomato, bacon, burger), and
making of it a ring on her plate; then, knifing the overcooked
meat into rubble, and spooning up the center with a lapping
of ketchup, and quick sip of ginger ale; then, pushing the plate
away.

"Eat more," he said, pushing the plate back.

"I can't," she said. "You have it."

And, of course, he was ravenous and restacked the burger,
without the tomato, and consumed it in three bites; and now,
he really was sick, so pulled the packet of Tums from his pocket,
and ordered a seltzer.

His mother would take a bowl of ice cream—strawberry, her
favorite—but no solution was in sight, and they eyed each other
over the empty plates, cups, glasses, and bowl.

"He should be behind bars," Jaimy said.

"Don't say that," she whispered.

"Well, he should, if the IRS had any brains."

"This is not helping."

"It's helping me."

When Jaimy returned from the men's room, his mother
was scolding the waiter for something, but she had a plan:
fire Maricruz, and countersue the contractor for breach, code
failures, and kickbacks, and she knew just the man for the job.

Jaimy knew this man, too, the eagle who delivered the
grandfather's estate, lien-free and nearly tax-free, into the hands
of the profligate parents—really the mother, although Dad was
the banker and investor.

"What about Dad?" he said.

Arlene had a plan for him, too. A second wedding to renew
their vows on their anniversary, which was coming up.

"It'll be a surprise for Arthur," she said, "but we'll let the girls know right away. That'll fix her! They'll all help with the planning. We'll have the reception in the office. It's the perfect place for a party—isn't that what you always said?"

"Or, on the roof," Jaimy found himself saying; then, "you'll tell them today, say?"

His mother grinned. It was his favorite face, and he remembered it from forever. It was her signal, and he returned it in kind.

But, when Arlene was dropped off in their shared cab (who'd trust her to get back alone, and in one piece?), and walked herself up the steps and into the loft, Arthur was gone. All eyes followed Arlene's, as her head snapped from the kissing desks to Maricruz's vacant nook. It only took a few seconds, but the boss went down, and stayed there in a heap of fabric and paper-white flesh. Her glasses had flown off, and skated sideways. Maricruz was first to spot them, and pick them up, as she exited the scented bathroom.

II

MRS. CONE, SEDATED, was in the emergency bay on a saline drip, as the resident entered with Arthur and Jaimy, still barking and hissing, as each assigned blame to the other. "Pipe down," the resident said, "or scram." But, when Jaimy turned his heel, his father grabbed his wrist. "Stay put!"

"Get your mitts off me!"

The resident backed them out of the bay, closing the curtain behind him. He'd signaled to the officer, never far away and ready for anything, but by the time the cop hustled over, clinking with keys and cuffs, the Cones had separated, with Arthur reentering the bay through the drawn curtains.

Mrs. Cone's eyes were open, but so was her mouth, and no sign of intelligent life. Mr. Cone had never seen his wife so prostrate and so quiet—not peaceful, exactly, for a flicker around the eyes and a slight paddling of the feet, reminding him of a dog dreaming. (Sleeping in their bed, she covered her head with a pillow, curled up tight as a worm.) She had an unlined face and a spiny nose like a scimitar, with hands and feet, fine and supple as a fly's. All of her flesh was massed in the trunk, a part he hadn't touched (huddled as it was in woolly bags and homespun tents) in a decade—longer, maybe, for their bed, handmade, and capable of holding five, filled the low-slung, forever shadowy bedroom. They slept on either edge; or, rather, he slept, and she read—all night sometimes, and well into the day.

The doctor listened to her heart, holding the tiny, pallid wrist; shook his head, spoke into the mike strung around his neck, and left, glaring at Mr. Cone, who pretended not to see. And then, the mates were alone.

He kept his distance. When a chair was slipped in by a pair of hands, he sat, dragging it a few inches closer, so he could watch her face and the rise and fall of her breathing.

She was old, but looked like a crumpled child, with a wispy cap of hair—a child with leukemia or polio, alive, but barely. Who was she? In Mr. Cone's mind, she was layered like an onion, with so many skins; some papery, some slick, all giving off a spicy and penetrating scent. He couldn't see her without seeing her father, and horror of a mother, his own mother (whom she resembled, being too thin here, and too fat there, and all painfully soft and dangerously brittle). Jaimy was there, too, and the million layers of all the books she'd read, absorbed, and could rattle off in loops of speech; the dressmakers, the jewelry dealers, the aunts and uncles, and even the office girls and Terry were there. She was a dead queen of millennial extraction, refining now, attenuating, which is why he'd picked her: brilliant, high-strung, possessive, willful, majestic.

III

WHEN JAIMY RETURNED, the bed was empty, the nurses stripping the sheets and rubbery bed pad. Under the thin mattress was a folding contraption, with springs and pulleys, handles, cranks, and wheels. The chair was gone, and so was Mr. Cone, who had not passed through the waiting room. Both Cones were sucked into the inner core, and so he knew his mother had been admitted, maybe never to return, and his eyes stung with tears.

Abandoned, as he'd been as a tiny baby, Jaimy panicked, raged; then, concerned that he was driving his blood pressure to an unsafe high, he sat and intoned the self-soothing formula: Jaimy Arthur Lorenzo Cone, Jaimy Arthur Lorenzo Cone, and left.

And went straight to the loft where, after glaring at the ring of girls—even the puny Terry's face crowned at his doorway— he sat at his father's desk, facing his mother's. The phone was ringing, but it soon stopped as the globe continued to whirl, the four clocks to tick, not knowing or caring whether Arlene Cone was alive or dead. It was a new world, and Jaimy rolled a fresh page into his father's machine, hearing around him the others' response to advancing time.

His first act as heir to the firm was to call Jilla, and send her to the hospital for an update. Yes, it was the city general, and yes, she was admitted. "Where are you now?"

"Just go," he said, the new tone connecting to its severest critic.

A gofer appeared beside him, and without his having to ask, told him what was to be done that day at the printer's. Another appeared with the galleys for his signature. Off they went; the afternoon ripened with fiats, a steady thrum of activity. It wasn't until day's close that the phone rang again. His wife with her report: overnight supervision, possible heart attack and stroke. He steadied himself, and locked the vacant office behind him.

A bubble of laughter was in his throat, but he swallowed

it, reserving for his face the mask of a commander, flexing it, reserving it again, unleashing it on the stranger, who looked the other way, unnerving him, the man behind the mask. So, he ducked into a coffee shop; and, in its stinky restroom behind the kitchen, looked. In the rusty glass, a vengeful god, handsome, plump and courtly. It was perfect, so he swept to the garage to order the car, no questions asked.

***

At the hospital, on the third floor, in a ward designated for cardiac observation, lay Mrs. Cone with her thin fingers resting in Mr. Cone's. She was still out, but it wasn't a coma, they said, although coma-like. It was peaceful, and Mr. Cone soon fell asleep, sitting up. He could sleep anywhere. In his dream, he was on a white ship, and Arlene was the figurehead, hammered in silver. He was in white, and shucking an ear of corn, when he came to see the necklace of fine silver and onyx lozenges dripping over his hand. "Take it," he heard. He leaned over to kiss her papery cheek, and saw her lids lower and squeeze shut. She grabbed his hand in one that felt like a bird's claw, fashioned in ivory. He lay his head on her pillow (ignoring the cruel twist in his back), and lowered his gaze onto hers; for his gaze felt to her, and to him, like a caress.

Into that precious moment burst their son, for Jilla had caught them both asleep, retreated, and received her husband's wrathful gaze in the waiting room, as he swept through.

And, they turned on him, sealed up as they were in that fearful unity.

"Come back," his father said, but when the son returned, it was with his guardian, so quick she was to normalize what was legendary.

The young Cone wanted to climb into bed with his mother. Either that, or bring back the mask and strike his wife, the harpy, or turn into something—a bull or an eagle.

And, she was patting the bed, his mother was, patting it for him in his full-growth manhood.

The sky darkened, the lights flickered, a tray was brought, and the normal one returned to her own cave, there where the baby boy, all theirs, all Cone, was waiting for whom he loved.

IV

Mrs. Cone was once again asleep, and the buzzing, beeping white cube held her tight, as its own. She stayed put a long time, as one thing led to another, and parts were removed and replaced, refurbished, scoured, and polished. One day, Maricruz arrived, the first guest of the day. She, and her babies with the grandmother, were moving back to Havana, she said. The Polack contractor would remain behind, but just to finish what was unfinished. And what would that be? Mrs. Cone asked with her eyes starting from her head.

The head, recently mined, was wrapped in a cloth turban that was very becoming to her own severe eye. She was all points and sharp angles, dramatic curves and bright metal.

But, an alarm went off, and the guest was brushed aside, as a cart careered through the doorway, and the team deployed all its powers to brazen death's sultry wing, closing now over Mrs. Cone. And opening again, but now closing, as the royal sacrifice envisioned, the king's treasury, or war chest, delivered on the back of the lecherous Cone, her consort. And, into the hands of this barbaric slave. Heaving now, as the thunderclap and bolt of flame raised her an inch above the white and salty plain.

The Meat Eater

HE CAME IN a strong size, making his parents look like pygmies, and his parents were tall to start with, not that he cut them down, more wore them down, looking up to see his head large and bright as a sun. His father was fifty when he was born, joining a ten-year-old sister, as plain as he was fancy, not fancy but choice. She was average: height, health, and intelligence. She even had an average name: Fran. His was Karl, but the name grew with him so that the r purred like an outboard motor. The K hardened the opened mouth, where the C had just the round shoulders. Karl came into the world a strong syllable, butting the doctor with his head, making his mother (always his champion) laugh, craning her head to see him in his full length, stretched in the nurse's bloody hands, with his screech filling the swampy room.

Cleaned up, measured and weighed, he took up his life as a baby, but no one really thought of him that way, not with that head and those mitts. He was in command upon arrival home in his whites, and no matter how tightly they locked his cabinet door, and turned up the Victrola, they could still hear him. Their ears and nerves were all his. The first word he had to say was Karl. Everything else was mush in his mouth, even when Fran pinched his lips and stuck a finger down his throat. He had just enough dental ridge to bite the finger, masticating it. He always called her Frances, when he called her anything, and she became a Frances. Everything he told her to do, she did, but that was later. In the beginning, her hateful face mooned over his cradle, and sometimes under it, butting it, or stuck a pencil through the webbing so he could feel it. Or bouncing the cradle till he spilled a bellyful of milk over his face and garments.

All of this he stored up in his infant memory, delivering his reply over a decade's span, from the time he reached half his height at seven, and the remainder at twelve. By then, they were all shattered, not so much shattered as depleted, their lives a bad taste in their mouths. She became a nurse to transfer some of the aftertaste to others.

But, go back. He came into the world full of ideas, but how could he capitalize on them, wrapped like a mummy, impotent, and full of cravings. His mother told Fran that he'd come in the beak of a large seabird, but not wrapped in a diaper, the way she'd seen it. No, it wasn't that simple a story, and his mother didn't want the plain-faced one anticipating the flight of the beauty. Fran was her mother's helper, and then a nurse. She'd cleaned the house he lived in for nine months. So, even at ten, Fran had in her mind's eye, put there by her mother, a boy-bird. Don't simplify. Not a boy with wings, or a bird with a boy's face: a boy-bird, both and all, no overlap. He'd been flown in by a bird, and was a bird, although he looked like a baby.

She'd been discouraged from encapsulating him in any of her categories. He was an energy field. Try that one. But, that scared her, hearing his breathing in the night, in the room she insisted on sharing. If they loved him so much, she wanted a piece of the action. But, was it love when birds are so fierce and love so feeble?

At first, they barred the door. Let her keep her bed where it was, in the pink room against the wall. One day, she rolled it through the doorway, down the hall, and next to his basket and nest, then locked the door against them.

Please and pretty please was to no avail, but the sound of the strap smacking the door to alert her, then the unscrewing of hinges made her say: "I'll kill him right now with my hands," and a plea bargain was accepted. For the moment.

When it was clear there'd always be a moment in the long days and years, before he reached half his height, for her to fulfill her promise, they stretched the bargain, gnashing their teeth at how they'd been gulled by a kid.

And, he cried until they rolled her back, so back she went, although the room was small and they had to crawl around to reach him when he called. The dad was not so available. The second child was another kind of plea bargain. He'd been cornered by the mom with receipts for a hotel room and dinners at a place to which she'd never been invited. The dad had had a score of mistresses, and evidence there in front of her eyes, but she chose—as a younger woman with her own prospects—to ignore the way he flaunted his outings and escapades: lipstick stains and stale perfume and odors less definable but more telling. He was always amorous during these episodes, but it wasn't until Fran was nine and she, forty-one, that she failed one night to poke in the protection. A sick pregnancy and surplus weight transformed a striking, horsy woman into just the horse, and altered a temperament that had been sunny and hard-plated to volatility with storms of weeping and rage, sometimes at once. She was strong, even while sick, and he feared for his life, for she was a skilled gunwoman, and had once broken his collarbone by a shove into the fireplace. He was off balance and didn't see her coming. He could defend himself, but beating or braining a pregnant woman was something not in his character. He'd come close.

When his career took a rough turn and the traveling was restricted to their county, and without the means to support two households, even if the second was just a room at the Y, the receipts turned up. She was looking for money to pay the grocery boy, or so she said.

Truth was, she planned to abort this baby, but for the offer that saved its skin and their home from turning into a bullring. He said: "Have the child and we'll move." They were Canadians, but they moved to the states, where Karl was born on December 24. The child was so different from their first. He was a champion and no person, nothing had made him so proud. They gave the baby four names: Karl for his father's father, Pierre for his mother's, Delavigne, her family name, and, of course, he would carry theirs, Foxman. It gave him many combinations, not including F. Fox, which you'll see on his work, which is everywhere.

For a long time, he let his father keep the stage, but when he was ten, and his father, sixty, the struggles began. Not much of one, at first, because Dad spent a year in prison for transporting contraband—explosives, not drugs, although he'd been trained for both when the company that hired him out of Canada diversified, and his career picked up enough to buy a penthouse and a house in Florida. Mom had gone from horse to dragon, but harbored a talent for portrait busts in bronze, stone, and glass. When her husband was remanded, her gallery hired her, and a fat policy was cashed out to keep the penthouse and pay for private school. Frances Foxman was long gone—no one had heard from her since she'd run away from home, after she and the dad nearly killed each other the night of the blackout. Frances had raced down the twenty-five flights of stairs with the crazed man behind her, cursing and swinging till someone called the police. When they arrived—the only lights there on the street—Frances was gone. There were no charges, just the filing for a missing person.

Karl Pierre was a day student at St. David's, not quite ten, beautiful as a god, and as tall as his mother. They had the same color eyes, brownish orange. Mother taught him to cook and make a decent drink. She'd grown up with a houseful of servants, but her father, like the husband, had suffered reverses, which he corrected through crime. She had a way of telling the story in two parts that made Karl Pierre laugh. First time she heard it on the cynical, ten-year-old face, she slapped him. Then, she saw the funny side—the stupidity of it—when he pointed it out. She saw it, and after that they called each other Gertrude and Hamlet, for laughs. Her name was Gertrude.

The year without Dad and Frances was a wonder year. They

golfed in good weather, they played bridge with the gallery owner and his boyfriend; they redecorated with a windfall from a sale of Karl Pierre's bust, with wings lightly incised, to the archbishop, gift of the diocese when the arch was anointed cardinal. They visited the chancellery where the cardinal had his apartments. The boy-angel (really a bird) was set in a niche in the chapel.

Karl Pierre liked to sit on a wrought-iron chair in the churchyard with every kind of biblical flower, and herb, watching the peacock parade. His mother decided to take "instructions," and the boy went along. He'd been reared in no faith, but guided by a stubborn and well-hidden streak of Marxism, for both parents had been party members, luxuries and avidity notwithstanding. Karl Pierre thought nothing of Jesus until his crowning hour—that gory finale and reversal of fortune. He was a boy-bird, too, but more of a turkey. Karl Pierre was between "stages," as child authorities were saying: between play and puberty, but he never played in earnest, and puberty was just a simple return on plenipotential.

Before the father was returned to civilian life, Frances Foxman made an appearance. Their mother was received into the church with baptism and first communion as a pendant to a high mass. Karl Pierre escorted her, in black with a shot of white in her hat, to the baptismal font, where the cardinal awaited with a bowl of hosts and a salver of holy chrism. An announcement in diocesan churches named the adult catechumens to be received into holy church, which is how Frances knew where they'd be on the fourth Sunday of Lent. Frances heard mass that day, and lingered in the nave, appearing in the churchyard as the Foxmans were sipping champagne with His Eminence. Karl Pierre spotted her first, hatless and in a maroon dress. She looked older than the dragon.

"Let there be peace on earth," she said, "and let it begin with me." He saw his mother's lipsticked mouth drop open. It was the beginning of something different, not to be despised.

They cozied to Frances, as Frances took over the chores, adding her mite to the family budget. She was a trainee nurse, working with children facing death in a locked ward. It was work she'd been cut out to do, cut out from them to paste herself onto St. Jude's. She was good with kids, especially those whose parents found the scene unbearable, and who wouldn't? She cuddled (Karl Pierre laughed to hear it), spoon-fed, changed, washed, and drove in the needles. She was good at it: her hands were steady and she could talk them through it. How long, though, had she been in their city, hovering five blocks away from the penthouse? They didn't ask. Suffice to say, she stayed under her own roof, although fell in love once more with baby-bird, no longer a baby, and a bird only to trained eyes. He was eleven, but looked twenty, and had long been man of the house. "Come over whenever you want to," was what their mother told Frances, but it was Karl Pierre who filled her in on Dad's location. All was forgiven from her end, and Frances was the one to visit Dad in medium security and bring him what he needed. He'd taken up the Russian language, and was lining up work in import-export.

***

Karl Foxman was a senior in high school when he took inventory. Dad was in the money once more, Mother on the cancer ward where Nurse Foxman had transferred her posting. The cardinal himself visited once a week with the viaticum and latest chancellery news. With Dad working the Iron-Curtain countries with fossil fuels, Mom gone forever, and Frances still in her own digs, Karl had the penthouse to himself. He cooked his own grub and limited himself to two drinks a night.

Colleges were banging down the door to recruit the scholar-athlete (his games were golf and tennis, but the track coach showed up, too). He was good at everything: math, painting, reading, writing, and "leadership"—although it wasn't yet called that. His father wanted a business partner, his mother a saint, and Frances, as always, an idol.

None of this desiring did Karl feel. He could hear their peeps and see their famished faces, but the world with its human fragment was behind glass. He could tap its smooth, cool surface and watch the flies buzz. Fun to do when you're five, or younger. He felt another kind of desiring finger tapping his breast and just at the temple. Something a bit more insistent.

"I'll go when I'm ready." He was a master at self-communing. He could divide himself into a multitude, a roomful, or just a pair. He had audiographic recall of his thoughts and speeches, and everything he'd read, but what he'd read was what he could think, had he tried.

He was nearly fledged, and there'd never been so much they could show or offer that he couldn't produce himself. His mother had supplied him with flesh and food, and the example of terrestrial grace. She'd also given him the maquette of the cardinal's "Bird-Boy," and he'd painted it. It had no eyes, so he filled the holes with whatever seemed right: gluing in and scraping out rhinestones, seed pearls from his mother's baby necklace, salt, blood, turning an artwork into something visionary.

One day, as he was packing his father's yellow leather case to fly off to college (he picked a lusterless place that showered him with everything it had), the bird toppled off the dresser, crushing his elbow and ricocheting on the floor. Dazed with pain, he buckled, his mouth open in resonant howl.

Later that day, with his good hand, he wrote a history of what happened in terza rima, as his right arm was throbbing in beats of three. Leaving out the event itself, its qualities and agents, the words remaining in the poem were sharp as mica: they cast no shadow, hooked no comparables, caused no echoes. They were a grammatic fossil, resistant to alteration.

This poem was no fruit pie or feathery crown, but still he hid it away and went about the business of traveling. Frances drove him to the airport, for he was repatriating to their native Canada for this interval. Sister and brother looked like mother and son, if such a one could produce such another.

From the round window of the plane, he saw the world's hurly-burly snap into place as a map, then a stamp, and that taught him something that staying at home never could. This became his new material when the old stuff wore out. His mother had converted, going from nothing to Catholic, his father was a trader and his older sister, Frances, nursed the sick. He was from them, but not of them, and bore lightly the burden of their names. His papers, including the important ones to come, would be scratched with their mark, even when they were gone. On the plane, he tried out the initials, squeezing them tight as he could, but then surprised himself by announcing, on the ground, that he went by Francis, then laughed to hear it, and became known, in fact, as a funny man, whose interior forever bubbled with cheer. He was the one who could always think of a good one, but he insisted it was Francis he was called, not Fran, or Frankie. Someone spotted Karl Pierre on an envelope, and another quality emerged: murderous rage.

He had no self—this he'd always known. His mother was selfish, his father was sub-par, and Frances borrowed from her profession once she was finished with family strife. But Karl Pierre (renommé Francis) was, like his pottery bird, hollow. In him was the cool of a sealed cave. Had they made him like this? Did they know? Was there something else he *did* have? He took his pencil and filled in the oval: none of the above.

Testing was something he liked: to test and be tested.

He tested out. He was forever testing out, but what was left over? "Karl Pierre," his sister wrote, "every week I'll send you something from home." He kept the letters from Frances to Francis, although addressed simply to Foxman with a box number. School bored him sick, so he started playing cards, then chess, anything to fill the tedious days since he'd stopped going to classes. All they did, when you look at it from his angle, was recite the alphabet, count to a hundred, name the fruits and animals, and tell time. (He won cash and other boys' treasures: a violin, fishing tackle, cufflinks, and a signet ring.) "Take me home," he wrote to Frances, but Frances was wary. He transferred out and landed back in the States, finishing a master's degree with nothing underneath it. By then, Mother was gone, and so was Dad, whose heart stopped in Novosibirsk seventy years after starting up in Nova Scotia.

Frances wanted to make him a home, but what kind, and where would he drop from the sky?

But, he wasn't coming down or even over. He didn't want to give what he had or take what was offered. He preferred flight, or even rotation on a spit with eyes wide open. I am what I am, he said, when anyone insisted.

But around him was deflation. As a void, he produced a vacuum, annulling what filled the space around him: the heads of humans and dogs, streets and tidy rooms once replete. He had a kind of nulling touch. He painted and wrote in his special style, creating things on the flat. But, look close, and nothing. Time, though, had come to favor nothing, the world was so stuffed. Even the discard pile was growing and crowding out the new. *Nothing* seemed fresh because it was so poor and so rare. His paintings were one thing: an island like a lily pad on the straight line of the sea. His poems limned the borderland between void and vacuum. There was a magical value to both: a sucking action that depleted viewer and reader. This was catharsis as never felt before.

But, even that grew stale. There was none of that crisp joy in filling a bubble, that tender bluish cancre, with his breath.

The world took his products and supplied his needs. He was adored for his looks alone, which gratified, like the art and poetry, sucking out the homeliness and filling the emptiness with air. It was nice work, and it paid.

Frances watched from her angle, still a nurse and pegged to the bedside, while Karl Pierre flew and buzzed around her.

Frances was home base, ever watching and hoarding, although she was no reader or gallery bum. Nothing he did ever cleaned out Frances. Did he even try?

She was a merciless recorder of his flights and touchdowns. Her clock told the right time all the time. And boy-bird would come home when called, although she'd never called before.

One day, making this call, he answered. "Karl Pierre," she said, in her bristly voice, shrill and clear, "where are you going?"

Where was he going? And where was there for him to go? He was the god of art. He would never exhaust what they gave him, the dragon sculptor and the felonious father, a smith who turned coal and oil to gold. Even dead, they stoked and they fueled. And he also had his groundling, who kept track.

In this long life, Brother Sun and Sister Moon had found no mates, and as afternoon drove down and pushed up its cycling orbs, the sky looked shaved, skinned of its airy veils. It was time.

"My lips are sealed," Francis said to Frances.

"Just where are you going?" the sister asked again.

"My eyes are closing," he replied.

It wasn't for lack of fuel or will. His broken parts that stayed broken, the big things shrinking, and the magical voiding finger were all his, but it was no longer the same once she'd hinted at more. Where was he going? His perfection was granite. He was no bird.

That afternoon, Karl Pierre was in the hospital. He was asleep but had no dreams, as his sister swarmed above him in her white hat. He was a beautiful corpse, even with some life left to him. "I love you, baby bird," she said, smoothing his eyelids, then kissing them.

She had a last question. "Where are you going now?"

She ordered an autopsy and they found him stuffed with things they'd never seen before. His life had unfolded inside his skin, in the arch of his ribs and around the long bones. There was inside him another man: had he been a twin?

Nurse Foxman kept his secret with his archive. Come and

look. Birds and islands, yes, but with a round earth, there was no place to go but in circles. So, he had worked the inside and struck this new model in his own flesh. She called it, "The Meat Eater."

His Louise

"IF I HAD wanted a dog this size," she said to husband number five, who built flat-roof houses on coastal flood plains, "I would have stayed with the ballplayer, whose sideline was dogs."

"But to him, I said," she told the builder, "'no home dogs, no garage dogs, no dogs lying on the stoop in the noonday sun, or with moonshine on their backs.'"

One thing the builder didn't like to hear was how she talked to number four who, deaf in one ear, and with broken English, had published a book of poems on the sport and liked a word, translated or not. His face (number five) was saying: so what have you got against dogs? But it was saying other things too. The five husbands each had a beautiful face that talked a blue streak. Talk was unnecessary with the visions these faces gave, but she was living in a cage, and that big, brown-eyed dog was a free man. That was her point, but to make this point to the flat-roof builder was to give him the wherewithal for a national gallery of faces, each one communicating a volume, meant for one reader.

The dog was reading faces, too. She didn't have the heart to admit that the hairy bag of bones had committed itself; she was already part of his library. "Get your eyes," he heard (number five), coming home one night, "off my face, *cane grande é biondo*," and through the window he saw the dog's killing sweetness adulterating the dry ice of his wedded home, the only house he hadn't built flat, because flat roofs—or rooves as she insisted, a stickler for form—she could not stand.

It was his dog. The dog had arrived. It was more part of them than they were part of each other, or of some third thing. It was the third thing, but already in second place. The ballplayer had bred Latin dogs: shorthaired pups, yakety-yak all the livelong day, and everything in the same extreme tone. They were stupid dogs and he, Alfie, was in some ways a stupid man.

Stupid, grandiose, a crybaby, but everybody's favorite short-stop. "How I love an athlete," Louise's sister, Janice the fish, said to the hearing ear, but Alfie was picking no more wives in the same family. "What a family!" he told number five, when the latter built number four's house on Pinecone Island. One was all brain, one all tooth, one a drinking fish and one a stripper. The builder was puzzled by the warning because the ballplayer'd had only one wife, Louise, but what he meant, as Louise filled in when number four went back to Cuba to live with his mother, was the tooth had gone after him, and the fish, too. The stripper never came home. There were enough men on the west coast for a lifetime, or so she said.

Louise kept a picture of all five on her dresser. Horace, number five, put up a photo of the dog next to the only other wife he'd had, Laela, a modern dancer now gone to seed, but not yet seedy in the photo. It was a cozy scene: five men, one woman, and one dog. Louise refused to have her picture taken. One face she was never going to have to look at was her own.

The dog kept knocking over his own picture to chew the wooden frame. Louise moved the picture to her side ("Why did you think of that?" the builder asked), and only then, did Peaches desist. After a while, Horace removed the dog's picture. He kept it on his desk at work.

Was the problem that it was a dog, or so big? Or both? Or that Horace, number five, had bought it from the breeder? Or that Horace was number five and the first to introduce such a novelty with no discussion or allowance? This Louise thought while Horace was off building his houses.

The demand for these houses was fierce. People loved the way you could use the roof for a picnic table, observation deck, or high-risk field of games. Everyone wanted to be on the roof and family life revolved around a strictly policed schedule. Some people ruined it by roping off or fencing sections, trellising or building a sunroof. That made the roof into just another story, but some people had that instinct for going too far, where "too far," as Louise the brain knew, always turned you back to the original, to the time before the flat roof was devised.

Men loved a flat roof and they mostly occupied it, doing nothing to doll it up or partition it, or save the mammals from tumbling off the side. Men—and this Horace knew, and was the reason he'd become a builder—loved a roof with nothing on it but openness. They liked marriage, too. Marriage was what was underneath the flat roof, and perfect as a flush toilet, tailored to the one use.

The dog was big, but it was handsome, too, and betrayed no signs of vanity. It ran, jumped, ate, slept, and looked. It only barked when Girl Scout cookies came to the door. It hated kids, but that was its only sour note. Big simply meant that it must be allowed volume and air in the A-frame, not to mention its unerring ability to sight line itself at the center of your field of vision. That hurt, because it was a constant to a stay-at-home person like Louise, who worked for a living, but at her kitchen table.

Louise assembled first-aid kits, a wonderful job it had taken her a lifetime to think up and to land. And the moment was right, too, for hand labor was as often farmed out to housewives as out-sourced to China. Housewives proved faster than Chinamen, who still possessed artisanal yearnings, and made things too nice for the price Americans had been to the manner born to pay. Louise was no housewife; she was taking a turn away from the world and living in her A-frame. The fifth husband was in and out, but the dog stayed home.

Horace was the best husband, so far, or up until the introduction four months ago of Peaches. He had his work, and the gratifying way that couples and young families and even old people loved his houses. He couldn't at the moment live under a flat roof, true, but he enjoyed the satisfaction of slotting new homeowners under one. The new contracts were for manufactured homes, homes on wheels, and homes on pontoons and stilts. Horace was at the beginning of three lifetimes' worth of inventions. The energy was within him, and the new marriage, so far, was drawing off none of it. Louise, to the average eye, was a simple, plain girl—not plain to look at, because her face was so mobile—but plainspoken and plain living, and asked for nothing but the air to breathe and no flat roof lowering over her pale-blonde head. She didn't care for the dog, true, but its presence was allowing her to talk about her favorite subject: the first four, and especially Alfie. Horace, although he'd liked Alfie, didn't care to hear about the men who'd shared Louise's bed, but the few blurts Louise allowed herself in venting about Peaches, cleared the air and evened the score.

What Horace didn't know, as the happy fruitful builder, was how this talk was burning a hole in the back of his head, where he couldn't see it, but could smell the scorched hair. In short, it was hurting him, and now—thanks to Peaches—Alfie the ballplayer and part-time chow-raiser was alive in their house.

Before Alfie, there had been Fredo, number one, who came from a fortune-telling family, a line of matriarchs and carny fathers, with the accumulated bucks and brains to send one offspring to junior college, where Fredo learned the electrician trade, and, only then, joined the circus. He was freelancing at a county fair when Louise Pilkington waltzed by with a paper cone of frozen lemonade, dragging behind a rolling suitcase full of scarves knitted with organic mohair and fiberglass, a first in knitting history. Fredo had followed Louise with his eyes, then walked a cable, hand over hand, to where she was coiling her wares like snakes to fit in the pockets of milk crates. Louise had the blondest hair Fredo had ever seen. That's what he told her, then and often, until Louise began to feel the compliment taking on a life of its own, and whittling her manifold into the single qualifier. She started working in white, pale yellow, and shell pink, and the yarns got finer and finer, until they were as translucent as silk stockings. "Get me out of here," she mentioned to the fish, a capable girl, who bundled Fredo off to Anchorage, where craft electricians were rare as hen's teeth, and recommended a destructive perm to her older sister. The perm solvents turned the flaxen hair a coppery blue-green, and addled it into a large sea-sponge. Louise was so new and so different, she was forced to turn in her license and passport, and start over. Fredo's admiring attention had been so acute that it kept her from knowing the least thing about him. His face had the one expression, but Louise had never been loved before, and the three-year diet (Fredo was no talker) made Louise curious about circulating humans, above and beyond the immediate family.

Every husband had had a particular genius; some worked with their hands and some with their heads, and some, like Alfie, with head, feet, hands, hips, elbows, spit, and fingernails. With each one, Louise's own craft had changed. After Fredo, and with the hair still tortured into a rough and almost-living plant, Louise had taken dance lessons, then speech therapy, glassblowing, and fancy cooking. She was good at each, and had short, successful careers starting at zero and rising to just under management, which dissolved the crafts into one dull science, at which point, Louise quit or got married, or both. Horace, the latest and best, was self-employed and also employed others. Every part of his business was personal and he involved himself, tastes and instincts, in the smallest details, not exclusive of counseling and arbitration for his homebuyers, because a new house, as Horace knew by now, always busted up an old way of living to make way for a new. Building the house to specs was only half the practice; the other half was building the characters and personalities and relationships to fit under the new flat roof.

So, why oh why had this wise man introduced the dog? Let's start with the A-frame, Louise was thinking, now that she had time to think, as she'd curtailed the number of kits she assembled to rest her sore and achy hands. The dog's back was useful in hand therapy. The thick blond hair and rubbery flesh and natural oils were a nifty hand spa. The feel of the dog's muscle-rippling back inspired thinking of a closely meshed nature.

The A-frame—she talked out loud to the dog, who seemed interested and even barked from time to time—had come from a Maine commune, wood-house and wood-boat. Its parts were shipped by truck and snapped together in no time. There was just one large room with its slant roof and a sleeping loft. The outside was barn red and the inside pale yellow. Two walls were glass. Louise loved the house, and so did Peaches. Horace accepted it as a compromise; he understood how delicate the matter of housing was, but a flat roof and a dog were things he had always wanted from life and—up to Louise—he'd been too busy building a business and taking care of Laela, whose fall from health, mental and physical, was precipitous, commencing with marriage, to build his own perfectly realized design. He had long since been living vicariously under his clients' flat rooves, and with their wives, children, dogs and cats—that's how well he knew them, and how gifted in the art of psychic transport. He'd never met the carny family, but knew in his heart that arts and crafts (and building) were closer than people thought to magic.

The A-frame was the antithesis to flat, especially as the wood-house commune had designed the kit with "legs" that spanned from the peak to the ground, and even under the ground a little. The pitch was steep and the house legs were unbroken by windows. Snow and rain slipped off so fast that a moat of concrete was built to collect the run-off and feed it onto the flood plain, where nothing grew but ferns. If Louise had to be encased in anything with a straight edge, it had to be without the box or cage shape. The A-frame felt light and even portable, in spite of the fact that the legs were rooted into the ground.

Sometimes Louise felt the house divided in two just along

the roofline, and other times perpendicular to it, but she could not instruct the dog in the offices of the binary. If she moved her table of health kits so many inches toward the south pitch, the dog waited for the table to settle, then he moved. If she moved her chair to face the opposite glass wall, the dog waited for a final settlement, including the righting of stacks that had tumbled in the jostle, then re-oriented. If Louise faced the east windows, the dog faced west, as if they were enjoying a dinner out together at a special restaurant.

Horace worked long hours, especially in summer, the builder's season, and more than once Louise considered Peaches to be a spy or warden.

Alfie had worked long hours, and spent weeks away from home. They had lived in a flat in downtown Foxborough, where Louise kept a shop for the ceramic tea and coffee sets she "threw," and then painted. It was absorbing and fruitful work, and even the White House had a set of both. The Foxborough flat was a junky jumble of sports and exercise equipment, Spanish-language magazines, papers and videos. There was barely space for a bed, and the dog-breeding apparatus, bought when Alfie was benched with a heel injury, was the last straw. Louise filled a suitcase with dresses and underwear, and another with correspondence, and moved back home to Watertown. Alfie cried and begged; he promised and threatened and tattooed one side of his face with a kitchen knife, but Louise wasn't going back. Alfie was a dear, but he had too much stuff and was getting worse, and he still didn't speak English.

Every single time, four times out of five, the husband had trespassed the line, and each time the line was different, because the substance of life was different: a baseball player's line could not coincide with a flat-roof builder's, or a carnival electrician's, a cartographer's or a musician's. The line had to be redrawn, and Louise had each time retraced it. Had she told any of them just where it was? was the question the fish liked to ask, especially when she'd had a few. Needless to say, the "line" was the fish's theory, cold and arbitrary like the fish.

"I have an A-frame house," said Louise (and Peaches barked, but a low bark because it was early in the morning and Louise was staggering in the kitchen zone to find ingredients for her hot coffee), "with room inside it for this table and chair, but the house comes with him," she said, eyeing the dog, a healthy dog with fifteen good years ahead of him.

Alfie was in Cuba, Fredo in Anchorage, Dicke (number three) in Key West, and Gary farming onions in Georgia. Would each of them need a place, mental or otherwise, in this new life with Horace and Peaches? Peaches barked to hear his name. If lines were drawn—arcs and tangents to quarter each husband, then Horace would be playing hopscotch in his sleep, which wasn't good for a brand new marriage. Even if they were layered like mummies and slung from the "A," they'd collect dust, and swing, and otherwise trouble the space. The old husbands, ergo, had to be eradicated.

Louise folded up shop for the day, just as the day was beginning. The hard items were crated and the soft items rammed into a paper sack.

Louise folded her hands on the kitchen table and did nothing but wait for Horace to come home. He wouldn't be home for eight to ten hours, and when he got home, he'd be tired and sweaty, and good for nothing but a drink and dinner and flop of the couch with a magazine over his face.

The A-frame buzzed and ticked in the heat of the summer day. The planks of the A swelled, as the barometer rose. The glass was indifferent to heat and humidity, but as the putty softened, the sheets ground deeper in their grooves. Louise felt the first sticky thread bind her from the temple to the knob of the sugar bowl. She had never sat still long enough to become a spindle for a spider's cloth. The line was just a tickle, but soon there was a second from the corner of the mouth. Stillness was a weapon, but not a good one for men that were already gone. She must do more than wait.

It had to be a big dog, Horace had said, because otherwise it would get lost on their lot of twenty-five acres. But, then, he had said that it had to be big to scare off the crows and the foxes, the deer, coons, groundhogs, mice and voles. To scare them from what? The crops, he said, the ferns, flowers, topiary and grapevines. All these beautiful things could be seen from the wall-windows facing east and west. The world outside was sculpted, wetted, and trimmed by Horace's able hand, but wild animals found their way in the dead of night. Did Peaches ever scare any of these night stalkers? How could Peaches scare them, if he slept eight hours under their bed? Just the idea of Peaches, Horace had said, his smell and the sight of his eyes through the glass would do it. But, then, he said, it was because of the isolation of their house, and Louise's need for living protection. From what? she asked, but the answer he gave (vagrants, hooligans, Jehovah's witnesses) was not the real one, and Louise didn't press him further.

There was no basement, so the four couldn't be packed under the plank floor, and they weren't, to her knowledge, dead, so why did she think she possessed them like junk too junky for a yard sale, but too personal to leave out for the garbageman? The question was academic: she did. Where she went, they went, just as Peaches the dog revolved with her like two planets around the medical kits. Number two had overlooked number one; number five didn't see number four, but in time these earlier ones, long gone but not forgotten, had made themselves felt. They had thickened out Louise, and slowed her down. No, they haven't, the fish had told her. If anything they've speeded you up, but Louise felt slow. Big chunks of time had been spirited away like the best of Horace's vegetables and flowers by the night crawlers. The time taken by the first four was like a set of bulky cubes wrapped in plastic and string. Inside were layers of glassine, soft shelves of a beguiling translucence, a wonderful way to trap nothing useful. The first four had their own lives—that's what people would say—but did they? When Louise happened to see them, or hear about them, they seemed the way she imagined them: lost in space, boxed somewhere loosely with a lot of air. Some were busy and some were idle, but the clocks all round had stopped.

"I know why it is," she said to the fish. "You don't," of course, the fish replied.

"It's because," Louise was talking out loud again, with Peaches awake and listening, "marriage is something you can't repeat. The repetition of even one drives the nail of non-being into the original."

This had the ring of something, so Louise locked up the house and took Peaches for a walk. As they walked, the A-frame got smaller and smaller behind them. Such pleasure did it give the dog to be accompanied on his walk, that some exceeded what the dog himself could contain and spilled over onto the mistress. The dog trotted and trekked; he dashed onto the fields of nodding grass; he leaped and frolicked. He nosed out a groundhog and baby rabbit. The birds seemed to know him and his ways, and they silenced their pecking and cheeping as Louise and Peaches passed under their boughs. The farm was full of creatures, Peaches just one of them and Louise, just another. The A-frame was now just a matchbook, but raised at the horizon was a limpid plate of blue Jell-O. Dog and friend walked in one direction, then turned straight back.

Fish was not anti-marriage so much as anti-anything that stood even idly in the way of the union of brain, fish, tooth, and stripper. These four were a legendary union and under the auspices of their Mam and Pap, a married pair who drove that car to its death. The brain had had too many marriages, while fish, tooth, and stripper had a sum total of none. It wasn't just the unfairness, though, that griped Janice (number two); it was the imbalance. Louise, Janice, Alice, and Diane were north, south, east, and west; and north had gone and wrecked it, and not just once, but five times! And she carried them all on her back, so where were Janice, Alice, and Diane supposed to go? Di had blown off on a beeline west, as soon as Louise had paired up with Fredo, and was never coming back, but Janice and Alice were lonely as clouds, drinking and eating, but with never enough to fill in the gaps. Janice nagged and Alice sighed.

"I'll find my own way," Louise had said to fish, when the grumblings and pot shots were too much, even for someone like Louise, tolerant to a fault. "You won't," were Janice's famous last words and then, not a whisper.

I've got this unusual house, she thought, after the happy walk was ended, and a new husband with a useful and high-paying job. But she was dragging around these other bodies, taking up more and more room the more lifeless they became.

Before long, Horace's round car drove up to the car park, a concrete slab outside the moat. He parked his white car next to Louise's identical red one, making sure the front and back tires were as exact as bars of beads on an abacus. He received the dog's complicated and all-engrossing welcome: paws, drool, bites, rearings, yelps, and rolling eyes. The dog galloped around him, leaped over the moat and back, spun, jumped, and laid his front paws on Horace's shoulders to look into his face. "Down," Horace said, showing the dog his fist.

Over the moat they came, and the hug offered to Louise was shared by Peaches.

Something was different in the home, and Horace could sense it. There was a torpor, as if no life had transpired in his absence, as if he'd left an empty house. He glanced at his Louise. A shadow covered her face, so that he couldn't gather the skin, colors, and features into a whole. "Who are you?" he felt like saying. For the first time since their marriage one and a half years ago, he felt grateful for the health and communal bulk of the exes, all men after all, and each with his own story, hobbies, failings, and a grid of natural relatives, who filled out whatever part of the picture was vague. Take Alfie. Eight to twenty percent of his life was Cuba, fifty to sixty percent was baseball, ten percent—but an important, forceful ten—was Castro. Castro—just the mention of his name—wound the shortstop to a high pitch: hysteria is what it looked like to a North American—especially one as far north as Horace. Still, when you named and accounted for your percentages, there was nothing left over. Alfie was squared. Same with Dicke, Gary, and Fredo, although Horace hadn't met them. Fredo was still in the Alaskan wilds. He always sent them a case of smoked fish for Christmas, signed Uncle Fredo, as if Horace were a subordinate and not an equal. To Alfie, Horace was more than equal; Alfie looked up to him, but that was all latitudinarianism. Alfie was pure Cuban that way, with a built-in inferiority complex. Gary and Dicke were middle Americans—Colorado and Alabama. Their vitas disappeared in the air, so similar were they to Horace's; easy living in college, busted career in a white collar, a cool hobby become a profession. Louise fitted in somewhere. Oddly—and was Horace realizing this for the first time, as he looked into Louise's unintegrated features?—Louise belonged to each of them, and matched them to a T; or, at least, did whatever a partner should do to fit or complement, to oppose and reformulate, to combust and recompose. In each couple, she was a perfect fit, although in a different way. This thought (so treacherous and corrosive) brought things to a standstill in the A-frame house on that night.

Louise was sitting with Peaches's head on her lap. "He likes you," was the first thing Horace said that night. It humanized them a little. They could retreat from their lonely perches, climb out of the clouds, the self-satisfying cones of thought; breathe and let the A-frame do the rest.

There wasn't enough time on their clocks for the full unravelling and evaporation of what separated them. But the cooperation that had gone into the A-frame, and the big dog, had its own sturdy half-life. Many numbers had been played, cities of dreams built and crumbled, and storage was

NO HARM DONE   105

fast running out. Horace, still starchy, and with the burn hole irritating the back of his head, looked across the kitchen table at his Louise, and said it that way to himself, and then out loud—my Louise—and felt from that moment how hard she would try to become it.

III

Someone Is There

HE LOOKED LIKE nothing, which depressed them as they entered and took their place. There were three places: a couch like an altar, and two matching chairs, separated by a table with a box of extra-large tissues. It was the most inviting thing in a room without so much as a poster, a plant, or ashtray. He had his own lounge chair, into which (once they began) he disappeared, to become a voice that each strained to hear. His name was Doctor Kowal. Someone not too distant in time had sheared off the terminal syllables to what was once a real name, the kind you could trace on a map of Eastern Europe.

He rose early, while his wife was still a lump in the bed, to his full days. He ate cereal with a sprinkling of fresh coconut and dried fruits, and drank a protein shake, for he worked through lunch hour. He had an antique car, a Benz, with cream-colored leather seats and chrome fenders. Every night, secure in a locked garage, the Benz was shrouded in a chamois cloth. First to arrive in the lot, the car claimed space number one, close to the entrance. Hildegard was its name; its original owner was a trainer-breeder, and had had the car shipped from the factory. Hildegard was a family name, according to the dealer, who had filed the paperwork, including the car's maintenance diary. Dr. Kowal kept the diary in the glove box, required reading for the mechanic who'd lay a hand on the hood.

The drive to work was made over to the Benz, listening to its six cylinders, to the smooth interlock of the gears, and the way its tires, capped in chrome, took the speed bumps in the corporate park. The trunk, a velvet case, was empty. He kept a folding umbrella under the passenger seat.

Few patients had spotted him in his black 300SL, but those who had, brought it up as a key piece of evidence, which he skillfully turned back on them. His clientele were mostly men of a certain age, with the money to see him four or five times a week—very early, at lunch, or late in the day. In the interstices, he saw (at a low fee) students, women, and children, and the rare retiree, driven in by an exasperated spouse.

Dr. Kowal was the best-known shrink in town, reached solely through referral. He shied from publicity, and did any forensic work anonymously.

Marie, his wife, and Hildegard, were his life, when he wasn't at work, or writing up cases in his home study, where he had a chair to match the one in his office.

Marie had been his first inpatient, when he was a green intern. She had become a nun at sixteen, whose failed vocation (as they put it), and return to a family of priests (she was the youngest and only girl), had triggered a major depression. She had already cut her throat with her father's razor, ingested rat poison, and thrown herself from a second-floor window onto her mother's rose trees. She was in four-point restraints in a locked ward when he first met her. A comely girl whose thick black hair was just beginning to grow out, her emaciated face made her pale eyes large and shiny as a cat's. Just over five feet, she looked like a child.

That first day, he pulled up a metal chair to her bed, and sat there. Even then, he was plain to look at, and slight of build, but before long, she was willing to stretch out a finger, once he'd released her hands, to touch his sleeve. She told him (when she could get the words out) that he looked like St. Francis, without the tonsure. She'd been (she told him later) a Poor Clare, and then explained what that was. He'd heard of the saint with a bird on his shoulder, but not of the sister Clare. They had no children.

In time, Marie seemed just like other doctors' wives, if a little quiet, and always dressed in white. She had shaped her peculiarities into styles and choices. She did her housework at night, and spent the days reading. She had become an expert in her own disease, and in church history, especially the violent schisms and healing councils. She studied Jewish history, too, when first married, and considered (with no pressure or encouragement) converting. Raised in doctrinal Catholicism, the Old Testament was fresh ground, a marvel of strangeness and funny bits, and the way the different authors tackled the job of storytelling. Her religious name was Sister Mary Divine. She had made her first and second vows in a black habit with white veil. It was before the final vows, with the advance to full black, that she suffered the breakdown.

Arriving at his office when the sun was breaking upon the horizon like an egg, he sat down at his desk and opened his ledger. All his patients had their page, some with a slash drawn corner to corner. He blacked in squares on several pages. Sister Divine was in there—not on page one, which was blank, but the next page, for he'd ordered the ledger the day after commencement. First in his class, he was offered the single spot in the teaching hospital's psych ward. He had no office then, so he kept the ledger under his bed, the only place it would fit, and made his entries sitting on his Kilim, gift from his family.

Marie Divine still had a scar like a fine chain around her throat. She wore scarves and chokers until the white flesh loosened, and all but swallowed the scar. The early psychotropics were crude, and his first conception of Marie Divine was of a record revolving at the wrong speed. She seemed miles away, but the nurses reported late-night pacing, when they took off the leg restraints to give the sores a chance to heal.

She was still a marathon walker. Setting out in the early afternoon, she tracked the length of their town along the north and south arteries, and knew every cat and dog along the way. She was shy with people, but housewives and shut-ins, perched by their front windows, waited for the sight of the tiny woman in the hat and heels. "Religious," as she termed her colleagues, were, by vow, poor and homeless, and performed their corporal and spiritual works of mercy on foot, and in silence. She had broken away from the articles of faith, but was faithful to the practice. He had his time carved into fifty-minute chunks; hers were the canonical hours, beginning at midnight. At the end of the parkway was the bay, where she stopped for coffee and to read the paper, starting home in time to fix their supper.

His pen hand was on one of yesterday's patients, but he flipped back to the beginning, looking at the marks he'd made with a fountain pen for the hours spent with Sister Marie. She'd been two months on the ward and, in that time, he'd met the family, and even paid a visit to the convent where he was received by the reverend mother. You weren't supposed to fall in love with your patients: that was a cardinal rule of his craft, but people forgave the Kowals.

He'd grown up across the street from a Catholic church, and played on the parish basketball team, but he'd never seen a family like hers, or an order so backward. He kept his notes and had used them for a paper on difficult-to-treat cases. He was surprised to see a strain of dogmatism in his views. He was himself, as he now saw it, a convert, but his sect was on the rise and hers in decline.

He smoothed her page, and turned it.

His first session was with a chemist, a man who'd lost two wives to the same cancer. He had grown children, who'd forced him to seek help when they'd seen what their childhood home looked like. He was burning the furniture, piece by piece, in campfires on their fifteen-acre lot. He also fed the fireplace. When the oldest girl visited, she found the first floor stripped. She'd moved her father into a hotel, when he refused to go to the hospital. Dr. Kowal knew the man from an advisory board, and the daughter was able to bring him in for a consultation. The patient stayed in treatment, but came only once a week. He brought coffee for himself and Dr. Kowal, and they shared a bagel. They talked about organic molecules, and sometimes they drew them. Dr. Kowal always left him with a problem to solve.

Michael was the man's name, and he insisted on first names. The doctor's name was also Michael. Michael the patient sat in a chair, with the doctor at his desk. They passed a quad-ruled pad between them, with the organic compounds (balls and lines) spread like maps. If this is this, the patient would say, pointing to the formula under the map, and I add this colony (he was quick with a pen), what is it now?

Dr. Kowal would take the pad to study the enlargement. I don't know, was usually his answer, but I know you do. The patient would reclaim the pad, erase the old compound's name and write in the new one. He had a photographic memory for molecules. They meant more to him than stories and people. "But not as much as combustion," the doctor had said, adding, "the force that combines them."

Dr. Cormley was still working at the plant, which made eye solutions and lenses, the only other thing he did besides "visiting" Michael on Mondays. The daughter had said he had a bed, table, his kitchen stuff, and a few lamps in the eight-room house. He wore two wedding rings.

Dr. Kowal closed his ledger, and opened the blinds to meet the sun head on.

Michael walked in on the minute. He refused to honor the ritual opening of doors. He didn't want to dawdle in the doctor's waiting room. If the doctor's door was still locked, he waited right outside.

When the doctor turned around, the patient was already sitting in his chair. His right hand was bandaged, with the fingers bound into a club.

"What happened?" Dr. Kowal said, and Dr. Cormley started to cry. They sat like that until Dr. Kowal said it was time. He had an hour free on Tuesday, tomorrow, and when he wrote the time on appointment card, the man took it.

He had anticipated a break, but nothing so drastic. His way with patients was a gentle but steady forcing. There was no word in the psychiatric lexicon for this, but the best practitioners knew it by instinct. You either had a taste and a talent for it, or you didn't. The poets—as his wife, a reader, had told him—called it negative capability, but that seemed the least of it.

He had wanted to be a surgeon, and he had the hands and the patience to resect the finest blood vessels, but he'd been struck by what he saw on his first visit to the back ward: the faces, the mannerisms, the barnyard noises, sparks firing in the skunky air. Compared to handling these deviations, cutting out tumors and transplanting organs was mechanic's work. And it was there—in the state hospital—where he found his calling. He found he could call *them*, and they would answer. Something in him was visible and palpable, and pulled them out of the netherworlds they found so congenial. The mute ones opened their jaws to bleat; the chatterers closed theirs to listen; the screamers piped down, if only for a minute; the head-bangers, shakers, and spinners slowed their sickening beats and revolutions to take a look, when they'd seldom shown an interest even in each other, much less the uniformed staff. The ward officer noticed, and the new med student was sent to the hospital director, a graduate of the same school. Upon a good word, the student's progress through the ranks was foreshortened and accelerated. He received an M.D.-Ph.D. in three years, and then turned to analytic training. He tried to find the words for this skill or talent, something to bind it to what was already known, make it less epiphenomenal. Transference, though, was the patient's own forcing, of fears and fantasy, and frustrated desire. What he did (and he was forever refining it) was faster and targeted; something closer, his wife said, to exorcism.

As far as his arsonist was concerned, the devil was now out. The rest of the work was finding something to stuff into the hole, dug in childhood, and still sucking air.

How can you be so sure? Marie had asked, as he shared some

NO HARM DONE   113

clinical details with her. Look at you, he felt like saying, but he
knew that each patient felt like a singularity: the alpha and the
omega.

He was, in this case, the prime mover. Was healing, though,
such a one-way street? It was, he knew, in her New Testament,
where Jesus walked about with his disciples among the
unbelievers. In this case, though, better not to put a name on
it. He was a molder: he shaped the cloud-like force around each
patient, until they lost the urge to hurt themselves. It didn't feel,
Marie had said, like invisible restraints, but it worked that way.

She still kept the habit of the Poor Clares, in the back of
their closet, covered with a sheet. He'd suggested professional
storage: isn't that what women do with their wedding gowns?
The convent had retained three wedding gowns for the day a
novice made her final vows, but you didn't get to pick your
own, Marie told him, because vanity was like a skirt you stepped
out of, before drawing the veil over your head. Picturing her
walking down the aisle in a dowdy, ill-fitting dress was too
painful—not for her; she seemed to cherish these moments
and stages in a life wholly elected and reluctantly abandoned—
but for him. He thought of himself as raising her, like Lazarus,
from the dead, but raising her in a way that improved upon
her life as Baby Sister to three priests, and daughter of a candy-
store owner. For their wedding, she'd worn a white suit with
polka-dot blouse. The suit was in the closet, too, but the blouse,
worn for ten anniversary celebrations, was in the bag kept for
dusters. She'd washed it and it'd shrunk to doll-size, the ink of
the dots scribbling into the white organdy. She kept everything,
reassigning cast-offs as they degraded.

I don't plan to continue to treat you, he'd said, the day he
proposed, but that was a vow hard—and maybe impossible—to
keep.

When Marie was released from the ward, but still living in
the convent, she came to his office with an older nun, a silent
witness in the consulting room. Sister Veronica was a tall, thin

Irishwoman, with dark eyes and pale skin. She kept her eyes down, but she was listening: she blushed when he addressed his patient by her first name. "Is it Marie," he asked, "or Mary?" He'd heard both.

The two nuns answered in unison. They laughed, and Marie explained that her given name, Marie, was altered when she'd made her first vows. No sister kept her given name "intact," was how Veronica put it, blushing again, because it wasn't her part—and she understood this—to speak for her subordinate, even though in any other "street" context, she must speak.

Dr. Kowal had studied the patient's face, noosed in stiff, white ruffles, with a tight band across the forehead. Somehow, the face looked older.

It had been on his advice that she return to see if, together, in their biweekly meetings, they could resect the broken thread of thought and events that sent her to the hospital. "Our lives are not our own," she'd said as an inpatient. He asked if she were hearing the voices of Jesus or of God. "I meant corporate life," she said. "We're not individuals." They'd talked about her childhood as the "mascot" of three priests (one, a Jesuit; the others, parish priests). She'd gone to all the ordinations, first masses, and installations in remote parishes. She'd gone shopping for chalices and vestments, suits, and black shoes. The parents had had Marie in their early fifties, and the father died when she was five. The priests had to read books on the Index, to know what was there to test their chastity. In junior high, she'd found these books in a trunk, and absorbed what she could of the "facts of life" from *Fanny Hill,* Casanova's memoirs, *Lady Chatterley's Lover,* and assorted detective novels with the black-cat label. There were other books harboring heresy, or spin-off cults of Mariolatry and devil worship. The Jesuit was a theologian in a Canadian university. Dr. Kowal had seen photos on Marie's bedside table of Mike, Ed, and Neil, in their Roman collars, but had only met the mother, who was the most devout—a daily communicant, with a crucifix and holy water

NO HARM DONE   115

font in each room of the house; a Mary altar with a vigil lamp, dried palms, the papal blessing. The philodendrons and rubber plants were housed in sacred effigies. On the walls were copies of Italian religious art, "Madonna of the Chair," "Light of the World." The house smelled of scorch, smoke, and candle wax.

Father Mike Divine, the theologian, had married the Kowals, assisted by Fathers Ed and Neil. A rabbi—present for the sake of old Mrs. Kowal—inserted a Hebrew blessing, as the Catholic vows were exchanged. Marie wanted a plain band, like the one she'd worn as a Clare, but Dr. Kowal enriched the band she chose with pavé diamonds from his grandmother's wedding ring. Marie had bought him a silver ring, woven with a pattern taken from the Book of Kells. He liked it better than he thought he would, and liked the brothers, too. The eldest, Mike, was fat and stolid, but the younger two, assigned to neighbor parishes, played basketball and hockey, and seemed like schoolboys. They sent him a few of their troubled parishioners—the hard cases, as they called them, drinkers and philanderers, men who couldn't keep a job, or those for whom rectory advice, or a retreat, wasn't enough. Father Neil had come in himself, when he felt his faith slipping away, but found, in time—and on his own—a second vocation as a missionary, with a posting in the mountains of Peru. Father Ed followed him there, but the oldest brother, the theologian, stayed put. He was newly launched into the chancellery, assistant to the archbishop.

The brothers were glad their baby sister had found someone to look after her. They were confident she'd find her way back to the true fold. "They don't know me very well," she said.

Dr. Kowal knew that Marie's vocation was to be his wife. He'd even said this, when she'd complained that she wasn't doing much with her life, since taking it from God. They were talking one Saturday, a few months after their marriage. On Saturdays, they spent the mornings drinking coffee on a porch he'd winterized. Marie was a birdwatcher, and had hung up different kinds of feeders. The Clares—because they work with the poor—were trained, she said, as social workers and nurses, but she'd entered right after high school, and had gone no farther. Teach yourself a language, he'd said, or paint. She'd worked selling "better" dresses over that first Christmas, and was good at it. She liked the clothes and the customers, and was even sent to a trade show with the boss. She still worked in busy seasons, but selling dresses and suits wasn't a life's work, not the way—before entering—she'd conceived of a life. Be patient, he'd say, and, of course, she had infinite patience. Each day blossomed with something new. He'd come home and hear about it—someone new seen on her walk, or some oddity she'd read in the paper, or spotted through their backyard, when the kids were released from school onto the playground. With such zest for life, why bother with a vocation? was his thought.

She wasn't strong. There was no organ weakness, or disease, but for a youngish woman, she lacked vitality and endurance— except for the long walks. She drank too much coffee, slept poorly, and finished the bottle of wine they opened for dinner. She was too thin, and had a slight stoop. He was ten years older, but looked younger. She didn't like to go to doctors—no one in that family did. The body, and even that part of the mind that wasn't the soul, was an impediment, something to neglect, discipline, and overcome. With no active faith, he wondered, where does that huge subtraction leave a person?

After an hour's lapse, he heard his second patient, a new divorcée, open and close his waiting-room door. Beatrice Lamb had sent her husband, a man just finished his second surgical residency, for treatment, almost a year earlier. The Lambs had been college sweethearts, married for fourteen years when Bruce, a science teacher, decided on a medical career, spending the next ten years in round-the-clock training, while Beatrice, also a teacher, supported them. Suddenly finished with the second residency, and rehired as a hospitalist, the man felt pushed off a cliff. He was lifeless one minute, and raging, the next. He wasn't sleeping, and had put himself on anti-depressants, with no relief. He was afraid he had cancer—the kind he'd treated in much older men—and was losing his memory. He could just manage to show up for work. Miraculously, once scrubbed and gowned, his hands were steady for as long as it took to cut and sew, but no sooner had he finished the day's last work, when it started up again. By the time he got home, he was a mess—sometimes, he cried in his car.

Beatrice didn't know the half of it. He was so angry at *her*, he could hardly speak, and closeted himself with his reading, and whatever game happened to be on TV. He hadn't spoken a civil word to her in a month. She was puzzled and even frightened. It took another month to browbeat him (as he put it) into the psychiatrist's office.

Dr. Lamb was the youngest of four, a doctor's son. His brothers were much older, nearing retirement, when he entered medical school. The parents were dead—the mother just a year ago. He was estranged from them all. Beatrice was his only family connection.

In the weekly visit, Dr. Kowal heard about the marriage, a "disaster." Beatrice had drained him dry. She was abusive, a whiner, never satisfied, frigid, indifferent to his needs, uninterested in his career, reckless and negligent, a spender, overweight, and losing whatever looks she had, which weren't much. He had nothing but his work to call his own. He couldn't bear the sight of her, or of their house, on which she'd spent the money they didn't have, decorating.

Slowing him down and asking him to focus on a single subject only succeeded in speeding him up. There was nothing worth examining in his upbringing, or his childhood. He had very little to do, he said—then or now—with his family. He'd been involved in sports as a kid, and was home only to eat and sleep. When Dr. Kowal asked what had sparked the crisis, the patient glared, his face flushing. "Haven't I *said* this already!"

He wouldn't say his wife's name, referring to Beatrice as "she." She was the cause, but it was more the build-up than a single outrage. When Dr. Kowal pointed out that the crisis coincided with completion of a long, arduous training, the surgeon said he wasn't paying another doctor's fee to hear something so stupid. Yes, he knew the dates coincided, or nearly did, but his problem had nothing to do with medicine. He loved his work; and, if anything, there was more of it now than in the busiest days of residency. He was gone from dawn to dusk, on call through the weekend. He loved teaching; and, having his own lab—a lifelong wish—was now a reality. He had applied for a large grant, and word was that he was a shoo-in. In this part of life, there was absolutely no problem—just the opposite. The problem was entirely, as he put it, "in the home."

Following the fifth or sixth session, the Lambs separated. The patient moved into an apartment near the hospital, but things still weren't right. Dr. Kowal had helped him with step one, though, and he could do the rest himself. (The patient still owed him money, money he was sure he'd never see.)

A week after Dr. Lamb's last appointment, Mrs. Lamb called. That was a year and a half ago. "You don't look at *all* like what I expected," was the first thing out of her mouth. And Dr. Kowal could have said the same.

She laughed, and said she'd received a full report on the office, too: cramped, with junk for furniture, and his presence in it, "like a big spider." And he said, she added, that your voice was the most irritating he'd ever heard: grating and singsong.

Mrs. Lamb was a beauty.

"Tell me why you're here," he said, because she fell silent, after thanking him for the appointment. "You're my husband's doctor," she said, "and you helped him. But you didn't help me. I sent him in the hopes of keeping him." Her eyes filled with tears. "He was hurting so much."

Mrs. Lamb was willing to work, since compliance was, for her, a major defense, but even when the terms changed, and she became, almost overnight, the woman the surgeon had described—she even looked heavier and older—she came regularly, and paid on time. She was trying to discover what part of the marital unit, that had been her total identity, was still hers. "I never thought of myself as a doctor's wife, so much as a doctor's mule. You know how horses need a mule around to steady them?" She paused, then said: "Stop blinking at me."

"Was I blinking?"

"I don't know. Your face doesn't look normal today."

"What does it look like?"

"I don't think you like me. Most men like me too much, but that doesn't last—as you know."

He waited, looking at the now-wan face, until his patient looked away. "I'm sorry," she said. "That was too personal."

He waited. There was so much she had to say, and simple support or empathy was rebuffed. She explained that kindness was an insult, given what he now knew about her failure and inadequacy.

That was the beginning, and the beginning went on for months. Much had changed. The surgeon was remarried, and had moved to California. "He can walk away, but for me," she said, "he's still a noose around my neck, or is it a monkey on my back?"

He was encouraging her to speak out, to claim her own hostile impulses. Her notion was that all the hating was Bruce's. She'd absorbed the hate, and now it was pouring out, but she was just the storage unit. Whatever there was *of her own* was lost. "Don't forget," she liked to say, "how long we were together. I was just a child."

That day, she came in dressed in a short, tight skirt and furry jacket he'd never seen before. "I think I'd like to lie on the couch today. Is that okay with you?"

He waited.

"I guess it isn't," she said. "Well, I'd probably jump right up anyway. I hardly can stand to stay in bed, when I'm at home. I must have slept last night, though," she said, "because when I woke up, I remembered my dream. I haven't had a dream in years."

"What did you dream about?"

"Does it matter? We're not doing dreams here. I'll tell you anyway. You were in it. We were getting married—as soon as I got off the roller coaster—but the car wouldn't stop, and you just stood there with the ring in your hand. I think you were crying, or I was crying, because I woke up crying."

After a pause, she said: "But that was typical. I always wake up crying. And I finally have something to cry about. You know what Bruce used to say? He'd say: 'What do *you* have to cry about?' I thought I knew what I was crying about until he said that, in that tone, and then I wouldn't know. I wouldn't even know what the hell I was crying about! That's how he destroyed me, by taking things away, one by one. I wonder sometimes if you do that, too."

"If I do what?"

"Take things away that I've said. Rob me of my reality. That's why Bruce stopped coming. He, of all people, wasn't going to take that chance.

"I'm sorry," she said. "Where would I be if I couldn't come here and spew this out to you?"

Marie had described a circle of hell reserved for a special brand of sinner, doomed to eat her own flesh, which grew back the instant she'd torn off a chunk. These sinners were ravenous. Catholics considered this a description of the afterlife, but he saw it, for some, as the here and now.

"Did you hear what I said?"

"I think so. Do you want to tell me again?"

"I'm thinking about killing myself. Why shouldn't I? But, I'm too much of a coward. And I'm not good with a gun, or even a knife. You have to have some skill. You can't be a klutz." She laughed at this.

"Do you find me funny?" she said.

Beatrice Lamb didn't need forcing. She had filled a year's worth of hours with a stream of talk: confessions, threats,

NO HARM DONE   121

laments, and rants. She answered her own questions, and asked questions for him. She was the most voluble patient he'd treated outside of the hospital. She'd be talking when the connecting door opened, and until it closed behind her. He'd tried to leave a thirty-minute border, and often had to take an aspirin and close his eyes. Once he'd marched down to the lot to lie down on the back seat of the Benz.

He could see that Dr. and Mrs. Lamb were made for each other. Borderline narcissists in a lifelong dance—until the injury of the end of his stellar performance as a resident dropped the tent onto their heads, a tent like a cobweb, sticky and maddening. He'd broken free, but probably still felt the stretching, tickling fibers. Who starts the weaving in such a match? Does anyone ever stop? There were those (like his Marie) who hadn't the urge or knack for it, or perhaps, their interfering God did all the weaving, leaving them free to dangle or die.

"Why do you ask?" he said, but he'd waited too long. She'd lost the thread, but was remembering more about her dream. Was he interested? Or was that too old school? "Why don't you buy yourself a few prints?" she said. "Where'd you get this god-awful rug?" She was scratching the gray and yellow design with her heel.

Their sessions began like this, until the turn—a thought about the empty, four-bedroom house, or the clothes (the coats and suits he'd left in the closet) she hoarded, or her boyfriend— too old, immature, stupid, clingy, inert, a mama's boy—she was stuck with in her unbearable pain, grief, and isolation. Beatrice Lamb could cry on impulse. Her face (at the turn) would bloom, swell, and transpire like a hothouse rose. But the tears dried as soon as they came.

Toward the end of the session, he talked about the dream, and this consideration felt like the touch of finger upon finger, a charge reversed, something given and received, without a superfluous word.

"It's time," he said, and Mrs. Lamb sailed through the

doorway's narrow port.

He watched her cross the street, sliding herself, in one liquid motion, into her tiny car.

Mr. Browning was late, and Dr. Kowal lingered at the window, until he saw the black Lexus shoot into the spot left by Mrs. Lamb. The man leaped out, and was nearly sideswept by a delivery truck. Two minutes later, Dr. Kowal opened his door to let the man breeze past, throwing himself on the couch, covering his eyes with an arm.

He was in real estate and could sell, as he claimed, any house to anybody, but he had no life. His own house, complete with wife and four children, was as unreal to him as a stage set, but he was so real and oppressive to *them,* that—when not holed up in the den with his TV—they scattered. Except for meals, he never saw them. His wife was a teacher, and they had a daily maid and cook. He felt most at home in his car, or hosting buyers in the echoing shells of new houses. He knew how to decorate the bare, white rooms, and also how to clear and point up the wrecks of old homes, left by the old, sick, and bereaved. In two decades, he'd moved his brood to six houses, the newest and biggest unit in a raw subdivision, and always made money on the deal.

In the minute it took Dr. Kowal to close his doors and sit down, the patient was asleep. Dr. Kowal rang the little bell hooked to his chair.

"I wasn't asleep," the man said, looking at his watch, easing the strap on a meaty wrist. "My oldest," he started, after clearing his throat, "Valerie, wants to go to art school now—not to college. I told her no, but her mother said yes. 'I'm the one paying tuition,' I said, but Val said she'd ask her grandmother for the dough. My wife insists it's her life, her choice. 'You might be a good mother,' I said, 'but you stink as a parent.' And then, they were all crying and picking sides, but I put my foot down, and it stays down."

He paused. "I don't know why every discussion has to end in a battle, but that's the way she wants it, and the kids go along. I'm sick of it. This is not life. I have closer ties with total strangers. Fact is—they hate my guts, and always have. Once Mona went back to work, that was the end of my role and purpose with the bloodsuckers.

"I think I'm going to be sick. Hold on," he said, jumping up, and bolting out the door.

A woman colleague had referred Cody Browning to the analyst, and the man said he was willing to try anything; he was willing to sacrifice himself in any way, but how that was going to affect his family, he didn't know. So far, it had only made things worse, he said, because he was learning how to stand up for himself, to hold his own in that jungle.

Mr. Browning was the only child of a widowed mother, who'd moved in with an old-maid sister after the husband, a lineman, was killed on the job. When the boy was nine, the mother remarried, and the new husband, who owned a body shop and lived over it, moved in with the sisters, but the marriage bombed in a year, because the stepdad was a drinker *and* a gambler, and the aunt said either *he* goes, or you can all find someplace else to live. His mother was beside herself, and turned to God, spending her life at church, or at the rectory, answering phones for the priests. Eventually, the stepdad himself bailed, and good riddance, but by then, nothing was the same. The aunt took it out on them, and rued the day she'd offered to put a roof over their heads. Cody attached himself to a friend's family; and then—when he left home after high school—never came back. It was like having no family at all. And think how he must have felt, he told Dr. Kowal, on meeting Mona's family: they were like a TV show—everyone got along; and, out of four kids: a doctor, lawyer, a social worker, and a teacher. He wormed himself in with Mona's brother, and went to auctions with his sister-in-law.

The patient was in the restroom for ten minutes. The phone

rang until the message cut in. It was only then, hearing the message, that Dr. Kowal recalled that today was his birthday. Was he fifty-three or fifty-four? Funny that Marie hadn't mentioned it; then, he remembered that she hadn't been up. She'd had a restless night and, toward morning, moved to the couch. One of the missionary brothers had called; he was coming back to the States for R&R, and wanted to stay with them. Something was off, Marie said, because the order didn't allow home stays: when stateside, the missionaries had to board with their own, but Father Neil had said what he needed was to come *all* the way home, and he didn't want to disturb their old mother; plus, their mother didn't have room.

"What does it mean?" he'd asked Marie, when she returned to the supper table.

"He didn't say, but it can't be good, can it?"

The priest would arrive in a week, and although Dr. Kowal had encouraged Marie to talk it out, she'd said nothing. Divine family reunions, rare enough, were never less than maddening. For all his twenty years of marriage, Dr. Kowal had not found a place in this family. Sometimes, the priests treated him like their dad, and sometimes, like a stranger. As soon as they arrived, Marie would press to leave. Yet, by the time he needed to be back at the office, she couldn't tear herself away. "Stay for a while," he no longer said, because that made things worse. She went nowhere without him, but the only trips she really enjoyed were times together and alone, unencumbered by family, friends, colleagues, or even a common language. Marie preferred countries where neither of them had even the rudiments of the grammar: she liked to hear people talk, but preferred not to know what they were saying. It brought them closer together as a couple, she said.

The annual retreat of east-coast shrinks to the tip of Cape Cod for rest and rematings was never part of the Kowals' summer. They traveled in January, and went someplace different every year. Marie picked out the spot, and laid out their travel plans.

They had never been to Israel or Ireland. She'd heard quite enough about the latter, and had lived her life in a "replica" of the old country. Dr. Kowal had taken the one high-school trip to Jerusalem, but that hadn't made him any more Jewish than his socialist parents.

Now that Neil and Mike were settled in the mountains of Peru—and since Marie had a smattering of Spanish—that whole continent was off-limits, although the Kowals had been to the islands, and once to Brazil.

Dr. Kowal replayed his message, but just as he heard his wife's voice, his patient was back. "I think I have food poisoning," he said, "so I don't want to lie down."

When Mr. Browning had seated himself across from the doctor, he looked up. The two men were the same age, a few pounds overweight, in brownish tweed jackets. Mr. Browning spotted the run-down heels on the doctor's wingtips. "I can see you don't take good care of yourself," he said.

"So, I come here twice a week," he went on. "I see you. It's like having a friend. I haven't had a friend that wasn't also Mona's friend—or, *mostly* Mona's friend, or *completely* Mona's friend—since I got out of school. But, if I had one, it'd be someone like you, older, stable. I think of myself as stable, compared to guys I know in the business. I've only had one wife, for God's sake! And a big Catholic family—although I'm the only one who cares about that. I sent the kids to parochial school, and I make sure they do their Easter duty. It's the only time they see the inside of a church." He paused. "It means something to me.

"You have to have *some*thing in life. It can't all be about money.

"Say something! I need you to talk back to me today."

"What would you like me to say?"

"I just want to hear a voice not my own. Hey! Guess what? I need to get out of here early today." Smoothing back his hair, he stood, swaying a little, he reached across the gap for the doctor's hand, squeezing it. "Thanks a lot. I appreciate it. You know I do."

Dr. Kowal replayed his message, and heard the message within the message. The priest brother had had a change of heart: he wasn't coming home, after all. "False alarm," he'd said. He was being sent to a facility. It wouldn't be long—a few months. Above all, don't tell Ma, or the other ones. "Your husband will understand." Marie said she was going out for her walk: they could discuss this later.

Dr. Kowal did understand something about *all* the Divines. The particulars he didn't always know—and no one in that family would dream of seeking treatment—although they expected him to intervene in emergencies. "We're all on your case list," Marie liked to say. "We're tied to you like a big, heavy barrel."

"What's wrong with that?" he said.

He wondered if she knew what day it was, and whether he was turning fifty-three or fifty-four. He could do the subtraction, but didn't. Turning fifty had posed no problem to a man who was born old. That's what his mother always said, and she meant it as praise. Mature for his age, thoughtful, responsible, capable—those were her words. She leaned on him, especially after his dad's heart attack. At age eleven, he was the man of the family, although his father lived another year, bent on working himself to death, three weeks out of four on the road. Harvey Kowal was a labor lawyer, and had seen his workload double as union after union folded, and as factory jobs went overseas. Harvey Kowal was the one to rely on, for as long as he could breathe. He'd died on a plane, returning from Cuba. The three Kowals met him at Newark International with the rescue squad and the hearse.

His sister, Sylvia, twelve years older, took over the law practice, supporting mother and brother, because Dad had left almost nothing, and didn't believe in life insurance.

Dr. Kowal was fourteen when he started managing the family

budget, using a checkbook with all their names, and signing his. They sold the house, a wreck, and re-mortgaged and moved into a two-bedroom apartment, with mother and daughter sharing the old double bed. He'd worked his way through school, helping out in the uncle's mortuary. He was the one dispatched in the souped-up beach wagon to collect the stiffs. The uncle worked out of his home, in what had been the grandfather's business. His only child had also married a Catholic, so there was no one to take over, and the Kowalewski Funeral Home was sold, when the uncle was too old to do everything himself. Dr. Kowal played chess with the old man, now a widower and living with his married daughter. What they had in common, the uncle liked to say, was the crucifixes, the dried palms—and the Sunday masses, to which his daughter took the grandson, who was training to be an altar boy, imagine! "Aren't you glad you don't have kids?" he said.

The Kowals wanted a family, and they'd tried, but even after Marie was treated for what was said to be the problem, there were no pregnancies. By then, Sylvia Kowal had taken up with a woman, whom she called a partner (although they lived in different cities), so the Kowal family—under its original and shortened name—would stop with him. And wasn't that also true, he was thinking, for the Divine family?

The afternoon patients included a very sick boy, whose father delivered him to Dr. Kowal's door, and waited outside. The family didn't want to hospitalize Louis again. They'd tried every drug available for what was an untreatable mélange of melancholia and obsession. Nothing was left but ECT, and the hope that age and growth might ease the flood of symptoms, aggravated by hormonal flux.

Wasn't that what had happened in Marie's case? There was a temporal window, when intervention meant most, and development itself an anodyne. Dr. Kowal took the referral with that in mind.

Stumbling in, the boy always glared at the two armchairs, as he calculated. To stop the stream of numbers, even and odd, odd and even, he jerked his head back, and dropped down, his spindly legs and arms like trembling feelers. When he spoke, he kept his eyes closed, opening them to watch Dr. Kowal formulating a reply, then closed them again to repeat; and then, to dissect. He'd say: "What you really mean is this." With that, the doctor's soothing sentence would be twisted into something that cut and burned. "Now, try it again," the boy would say, and Dr. Kowal would enunciate the boy's sadistic recap. They'd go on like this, barb and rebarb, until Louis was satisfied. The rest of the hour was devoted to stories of early life, which must not be broken into. He'd date the story, first by year and season; then, by color, make, and model of that year's car, for his father leased a new one every spring, after the winter auto show, which the whole family attended. It was the best time of year. And there was always a different car: T-bird, Cadillac de Ville, Barracuda, Regal, LeMans, Town Car, Firebird, Bonneville, GTO, Mustang, but American-made, and first issue. Mother sat behind Dad, and Andrea behind Louis. They liked to drive to no place in particular, stopping for lunch or dinner wherever they happened to land: the lower Cape, Foxboro, Newport, Jamestown, upper Connecticut, Western Coventry, rural Scituate. The "mystery" ride was a typical Sunday story, and the brightest number, tunneling into the darkest, for—no matter how long the drive home, or how hard the father worked to shorten Sunday night—at bedtime, Louis would drop into his finished basement and play his records full blast, to ward off Monday, and the forced return to whatever school it happened to be for disturbed, gifted, disabled, suicidal, and homicidal adolescent boys. No normal school would take him with his record of cutting, biting, bullying, and mutism. At eighteen, his schooldays were over, and he lived down in the finished basement, whose walls he'd covered with swastikas, then mandalas. He slept inside a tent and worked on chess problems, and he built model cars and classic planes, which he hung from the ceiling on fishing line. The floor was covered in towels and bath rugs. No one was allowed to clean, visit, or call down, but twice a week, when the dad brought the boy to Dr. Kowal (and took him out for lunch), the mother and maid slipped down there to open the windows and shake out the towels.

The boy never mentioned either woman, or the sister, who was away at college. He rarely mentioned anyone, even in his stories of babyhood. He was a lone pair of eyes and ears, and an especially sharp nose. He talked about days spent flat on his back in a white crib, inhaling his stinks, along with the baby oil and powder. He never cried, but kept his eyes fixed on the ceiling, where the crystal hanging from the window spelled out the colors of the spectrum. He was up night and day. When he was picked up, laid against the crib wall with his legs stuck out, he was given a bottle or rubber stopper for his mouth. Flat, he was secure, intact; upright, he was dizzy, nauseated, scared, and deafened by his helpers' noise. He had two helpers—the maid and his mother. His father never lifted him out, or even touched him, but spent many an hour peering down from the heights into the well of the crib, where Baby Louis lay in wait.

He never smiled, and didn't speak until he was three. He understood everything said to him, but he didn't bother to convert the babble. With his sharp eyes, he read the faces, and paid attention to tone. He could mimic their speech, when he talked, as strips of nonsense music. That should give you some idea, he told Dr. Kowal, of who I was.

He didn't want his accounts turned into something the doctor could sell, so he snatched the notebook out of his hands, clutching it, until Dr. Kowal promised just to listen, with his hands visible. Louis sat on one of the chairs with the doctor right beside him, so both of them could look at the spackled wall. On that wall, the story the patient was telling was blocked out: where the crib was, which window collected morning sun, and the tree backlit by a streetlamp.

Sometimes Louis held the doctor's hand. To signal that he needed extra support, he'd fling his hand, palm up, and bounce it on the chair's arm. "What do you think I'm saying?" he announced, the first time. Dr. Kowal didn't catch what it was, but he smiled at his patient. He'd learned that Louis liked a toothless smile. Teeth frightened him, but a bland curl of closed lips, with eyes open, was a prompt that evoked a corresponding flicker, where the boy's face seemed to crack with the effort.

Continuing to bounce the hand produced two reactions. First, Dr. Kowal held down the boy's arm by the wrist. Then, feeling the muscles like knots, he opened his own fleshy hand to clasp the boy's fingers. A minute later, after a deep sigh, Louis was asleep, with his head cocked back, mouth open.

Dr. Kowal wanted this patient to try something new, a blend of low-dose tricyclic, with a new SSRI. He had phoned the father, and they'd discussed its introduction. Louis ate once a day—a hamburger, a black-and-white frosted cookie, and golden ginger ale in a glass bottle with a pry-off cap. Whatever he needed to take that day was tucked into the burger, after it was fried. Louis looked for it, dug it out with a fingernail, and swallowed it with the ginger ale. It was the crackerjack prize. He would accept one pill a day, so ingesting a compound would take some urging. Perhaps, the capsules could be cracked and spilled into the ginger ale? No, Louis drank only from capped bottles that he opened himself.

He had taken to calling their back garden his yard, and he paced its borders for a half-hour twice a day, rain or shine, numbering his cycles and reverse-cycles. Once out of school, he no longer took the Sunday drive.

It was the only time his mother saw him. She stationed herself by the kitchen window. The maid watched from the second floor.

Dr. Kowal was looking out his own window, and he saw the latest Wolf car—a red Audi A3—take the spot left by Mr. Browning. It was the family's first foreign car. Louis himself had picked it out from a magazine.

This month, the boy was turning nineteen. He had grown three inches in the two years of treatment, but was still a stick figure.

Was he any better? The dad thought so, but he was now taking care of Louis's mother, who'd broken her hip on the cellar steps, when she'd tripped on a newly painted car, left there to dry. She'd thought to turn on the light, but the bulb had burned out. The boy had shown a flicker of concern, when father and son found her, lying on the steps next to the maid, who was applying ice. Why hadn't she called for help? She was going to, but then, they heard the car in the driveway. Louis slipped past the two bodies, and sat on the cellar floor. When his father asked him for help lifting the heavy woman, the boy came up from behind, digging his head into his mother's back and holding her shoulders. The three of them hauled poor Mrs. Wolf to the car, but Louis refused to go to the hospital. The mother was now on a walker, and Louis was willing, when his father was at work and before the maid arrived, to get her out of bed and into the bathroom. Sometimes the father would find them at night, sitting together watching reruns. It was a lucky accident, and yes, the boy *was* better. How else to explain the change?

Dr. Kowal found Louis in the waiting room, sitting by himself.

"He dropped me off."

"Good," Dr. Kowal said.

"Bad."

"Why bad?"

In the office, Louis sat down on the couch, brushing its nap in circles, first fast, then slow. He tapped his heels and toes; then, once more together, dropping on his back, with his knees up.

"Are you telling me we're beginning your analysis?" the doctor said, moving to his armchair.

"Not."

Dr. Kowal waited.

"Here's how I see it." The boy stopped. "Am I talking too loud?"

"No."

"I can't hear. Speak up!"

"I said no."

"Today, I woke up early. I could tell, because it was still dark." He stopped to stretch his neck left, right, and left again. "Someone was there. When my eyes got used to the dark, I saw them sitting at my desk. How long they'd been there, I don't know. I couldn't see a face. I got up and found the guy fast asleep, with his head on my desk. I could smell his hair. I didn't want to scare him, but what the hell was he doing there?"

"Tell me what you're thinking."

"I'm wondering if it was you."

Dr. Kowal waited.

"I know it wasn't. I know who it was, but for a second, I thought you'd snuck down there during the night just to check me out."

"Why?"

"Why?" the boy said. "How would I know? Something that couldn't wait till today. Till you had me here in your clutches!"

"What would that be?"

"I guess it was some idea you had about my future." The boy sighed. "If you think I have one."

"Do you think you have one?"

"What do *you* think?"

"When you got up and you thought it was me sitting at your desk, what was the feeling?"

"I thought what I always think—'coo coo!'"

"What do you think about your future, Louis? Can we talk about that?"

"I don't like it when you say my name."

"What was the thought?"

"Ask me something else."

The doctor waited.

"I didn't even kick you out."

"So, what happened?"

"I fell back to sleep and it was morning. I had to get up, and get Fatso out of bed. I got us something to eat, too."

"You mean your mother?"

Without answering, the boy got up to sit on his chair. "You stay where you are," he said. "I'm okay by myself."

For a minute, Louis sat; then, paced the room, sat down again, and soon the hour was up; but, before Dr. Kowal could announce the time, the patient said, "Is it okay if I come back tomorrow?"

"You can come the day after tomorrow for your regular time. Do you want an extra hour this week?"

"Ask my father." He paused. "No, I'll ask him. I don't think they have the dough for this, do you?"

Before Dr. Kowal could answer, the boy said, "I'd rather come here, than have you sneaking into the basement. You know what I mean?" He laughed. "I don't want to disappoint you."

"I'll see you Wednesday."

"Call me by my name. I can take it."

It was not his long day—that was Friday, when hospital rounds pushed his appointments into the evening—but he was tired. His last hour was reserved for his supervisees, a lawyer who'd gotten a doctorate in psychology, and was trying analytic training. But there was an hour before Abby Goff arrived in her yellow T-bird.

Stretching out on his couch, with a fresh tissue under his head, he tried to imagine what Louis Wolf saw as his future. The hoped-for relief from a simple advance in age had occurred, but it wasn't much. Work was needed, if the boy was to get any further. He was smart, imaginative, with the ability to reason, when inner needs didn't swamp him.

There was much to be said for the right friend or partner. And an outlet for the trapped energy. Marie Divine had found it in the hours of walking, and restless travel. He closed his eyes. One of his own favorite visions was the sight of her in her first street clothes. He remembered the thin wool pants, pink silky blouse and gray sweater, with black patent-leather pumps. Her hair hadn't grown out, but it was softer. In the habit, she looked wizened; in the johnnies and jackets, like a child. But, this was different. She invited him home for a family dinner, and to meet the brothers. It was then that he first heard the laugh that could split your eardrums. They all had it, even the mother. It still rattled him, because it was rare. She collected incongruities, odd phrases and scenes, she explained, until she was ready to burst out laughing, and she did burst. There were professional terms for these, and she would know what they were, but they didn't really apply. That in itself was a good sign.

The first time he proposed, when Marie was twenty, and living at home, she'd laughed in his face. Who would want to marry a nun and a basket case!

I don't think of you that way, was—of course—what he'd said. Well, I *do*, was her reply.

When she told Mrs. Divine about it, the old lady advised her daughter to pray; then, she offered her help. We want to see you settled, was what Mrs. Divine had said, when Dr. Kowal was there, drinking a highball in their parlor.

"I *am* settled," Marie said; then, laughed that shattering laugh: "I'm settled with you, and you're saddled with me!"

When the mother said she wasn't going to live forever, and what would "my girl" do all alone in a four-bedroom flat?

"That's the least of my problems," she'd said.

He waited a full year, after referring her to a colleague, then asked again at Christmastime, when the brothers were all home. He had a velvet box with a diamond solitaire of a bright, watery quality. It was a delicate ring, suited to the girl's thin, spidery hand. The priest brothers exulted at the sudden news; one ran out that minute for a case of champagne, which they chilled, two or three bottles at a time, over that holiday weekend, toasting each time their sister showed up with bare hands.

"Put it on, Sissy," they brayed. "Don't be a little ninny."

They sang sentimental songs, music-hall songs from the '20s. There was a turkey dinner with friends—all priests—from the seminary days. Once the news was public, how could the girl back out? The doctor was in love—couldn't she *see* that? was what the oldest one kept saying. Marie had reported it to him.

"Do you love me at all?" he'd said, a few weeks after their engagement. "You don't have to answer that," he always added, "if you don't want to."

"You haven't given me a chance," she said, and he was mortified. How small she could make him feel.

As a wife—even as a friend—she was not a strong presence. It was enough for those so ill to be present for themselves—was what he came to understand. And when exactly had he taken up her case again? Never officially, but his attention turned more and more to the resurgence of symptoms and signs.

"Do you still love me?" she started asking this past year. He was, by then, a training and supervising analyst, publishing cases and review articles, getting up before dawn to write. He wasn't sure she meant it as a joke.

There was a sharp knock, and he rose, checking his watch. He greeted Dr. Goff, and sat behind his desk, but he couldn't seem—try as he might—to keep his mind on the oral report of what Dr. Goff's patient had said, in four days' worth of sessions, and how Dr. Goff had replied.

His attention—instead of hovering and even—was sharp, and struck the spots in the dialogue, where his student had gone off track, saying too much, or the wrong kind of thing.

After each sentence, Dr. Goff swallowed, and her voice rose a notch. Dr. Kowal rubbed his face to smooth it. But, Dr.

Goff saw everything that was there on his face, and stopped reading, mid-page.

"No," he said. "Keep going. I was distracted."

But, the trainee, blushing to the hairline, had tears in her eyes. "I stink at this, don't I?" she said. "Why don't you just say so."

"I wasn't really listening, Abby. Go back to the beginning of day two—the Tuesday. Start over from there."

Instead, she'd closed the folder on a half year of bumbling, inconsistent work on a very sick old man. "If you wanted to destroy my confidence, you couldn't have found a better way of doing it," she said.

"I accept your criticism, and I apologize, but let's make use of our time together. You mustn't turn my lapses against yourself. You know that, Abby."

"I know that," she said, grimly.

"Let's get back to it."

"I don't think I can do more today. Can I just sit here a minute, Doctor Kowal? I hate coming here, you know that. Everything I do with my patient is dumb, even when I know it's the right thing. I feel programmed. And I sound like a robot. How can that help anybody?" She paused, glancing behind her. "And I hate coming *here*. You've got the world's shittiest office. It's gross. How can you ask sick people to come here, and get better, looking at these bare walls and this ghastly rug?"

Dr. Kowal sat back, closing his eyes. "I'm ready now to listen," he said. "Keep going."

"And, I feel even worse now. Why did I say all that to you? You were looking at me—and you admitted it—like I was dirt, an idiot. I knew you didn't like me, but do I deserve this?"

He opened his eyes, easing the muscles in the middle of his back. "Why are you so angry, Abby? What's on your mind?"

"I'm not going to talk to *you* about that!" she said.

"We can talk about whatever you want to talk about," he said.

"You're giving me that disgusted look again. Please stop," she said, opening the folder. "I'll see if I can go on. I'll try."

After his supervisee had read her full week's notes, and they'd connected the vague, halting exchange to the *terra cognita* of conflict and compromise, derivative urgings and suppressions, dream and wish, and the trainee's aggression was channeled into energetic probing and theorizing, she felt strong, well, and sturdy enough to continue with her first analytic case. She'd overstayed her hour, though, insisting on finishing what she'd started. This was not good supervision, but he let it go.

At times, even expert analysts sought the advice of a peer, but Dr. Kowal had never solicited another analyst's opinion, about patients or candidates, but this relationship was different. He tried to imagine what someone else would say. Dr. Goff had already dismissed three of the institute's senior analysts for her own treatment. She was an illustration, if one were needed, of analysis "interminable," having had decade-long, failed treatments, before deciding to become a psychologist, and then, an analyst herself. Why and how had she been accepted by his institute?

He knew why. Dr. Goff was the most intelligent and best-trained applicant they'd had in years. She was disciplined and eager, and his institute had its full share of neurotic (even borderline) individuals, smoothed out and shored up by the training. Some were capable enough, if they knew their blind spots, and picked their patients with care. Every profession had its misfits and mediocrities, but few attracted, as his did, the very people it was designed to help. And they tried—the institute leadership—not to be snobs, but ever to be strivers, aspirants, whose clay was shaped and re-shaped, but never set to hardness.

Tomorrow—it was too late today—he would call Ned Weaver, who'd assisted him in his course on contemporary theory. Dr. Weaver was the youngest of the institute trainers. He had the most diverse background: a doctorate in philosophy, the Peace Corps, a social-work degree, and involvement in three east-coast institutes, each with a different view on etiology and method. He was already supervising three out of the four new candidates, by their choice. Perhaps, Dr. Weaver could help. It could be an opportunity—not an insult, or sign of failure.

Driving home, shortly thereafter, he thought he heard a quaver in Hildegard's sustained note. Not a knock, more a burp or syncope. He pictured, as he always did on the silky homeward drive, the interlock, smoothed by oil, cooled by fans. This was a time when he could think about his own machinery, let it race for a moment.

Tucked into Hildegard, on her vigilant course, he cleared his mind completely, tuning the radio to his favorite signal.

There was nothing, of course, wrong with his car. It was old. He heard nothing now but its plaintive hum, a somewhat tuneless chant, as his own ego was replenished.

IV

Rella

I

HER FATHER DIDN'T die. Rex was still around, heartsick. For weeks on end, he'd be in a teeming capital, riding the elevator to a numbered room with a too-large bed and a window onto other windows. His heart, inside his dry-cleaned suit, ached for himself. Cinde, Lee, and Rella were members of his family, and he was married to Kween, mother of Cinde and Lee. Rella was his natural daughter, as we've always known, when we thought he'd absconded or was dead, or too sick to care. He *was* sick, he *was* sick, was his refrain.

His days were lonely and crowded, a familiar story for men of his class. He'd lost his taste for food, sucking on stinging candies since Kween had taken his cigarettes. (She still smoked and so did the two older girls, to keep the weight off and have something to hold, now that no one sewed.) He still liked clothes and wore his close to the body. His watch was smooth on his wrist, its links polished and beveled to a satin finish. When he looked down and saw this bracelet and black dial on a wrist that was strong and flexible, the outer rings of his life dissolved and he connected himself to himself in a satisfying loop. He liked to touch the metal skin. His own skin was white and the parts of his person that emerged from the suit holes and slashes were tanned, roughened by the sun.

On a trip to Rome, he had the task of bringing home presents for the four women he supported. Hats, maybe, or earrings, a special kind of purse for the partygoer, a book or print for the one with glasses. His wife only wore diamonds and he had a special arrangement with a broker in the district. She named the parts of her head, neck, wrist, and fingers that required the icy enhancements, and had earned them. She turned the diamonds yellow and it was Rella's job to clean them by lacing and clasping and poking them around and into her own body. The first Saturday of the month was diamond day, and what started out cloudy and jaundiced became white again on the girl's wrists, neck, fingers, and ears. She did not clean her stepsisters' jewels because her zests and acids had no effect on their blues, reds, yellows, and violets.

He was on the streets of Rome, the sun beating on his bare head. He loved cities, but only if he could cover their principal arteries with the soles of his shoes, and touch what he saw. He loved the crumbly grain of Rome, its walls and columns, fountains, palaces and towers. He liked the oily air and rancid water of the Tiber; but, each day, hotter than the one before, shortened his walks. He'd already collapsed in a crowd photographing the Trevi Fountain. They loosened his tie and sheltered his soaking head in his own linen jacket. They unfolded his legs and brought him warmish water to replenish his fluids. They fanned him with newspapers and, at last, he got up, leaning on the tie-maker, from whose store he had just emerged, when they spotted him swaying against the show window.

Rella was his ex-wife's only product. Sheila was a twin and Rella was meant to be a twin, but the first girl died before birth. Rella was never meant to be alone: was that it? Sheila was a banker's daughter and full of airs and expectations, almost worse, in that sense, than Kween, but he had a taste for grasping women, so long as he was part of their seeking ways. He had everything to give them: looks, character, wealth, security, and that typical male blindness, a sex-linked trait, but a weak one.

Rella was sixteen and he was thirty-five when Sheila, thirty-two, left their home. She went to visit Stella, her twin, and never came back. Their mother had dressed them alike from birth. They were educated side by side, came out together and were married in a double ceremony, presented to their husbands on either side of their father. Stella had lost her husband to drink, and moved back home. Five months later, Sheila moved back, too. In the trial, Sheila asked for nothing but her freedom, so he preserved everything intact for Kween and her two daughters, eighteen and nineteen. Rella had been a mother to her mother, and sometimes a sister, but never the sister that Stella had been. At first, the twins and the grandmother insisted on keeping Rella with them, as a partner for a threesome, but the adult twins, once burrowed back into their birth home, wanted only their mom. Rella looked like none of them, not even like her father. After a six-month try-out, a time, incidentally, when he had met Kween, Rella was flown home to her father. Kween had taken a job at the travel agency where he had booked a rare vacation trip, now that he had no family or responsibilities. There was a Mediterranean cruise modeled after Odysseus's return trip to Ithaca that had caught his eye, as Kween was catching it in her contoured, black suit. Yes, she told him, she was in mourning; it had been ten months since she'd lost her husband. He was in currencies and flying in and out of the third world with no protective immunizations to speak of. Both of his daughters, Cinde and Lee, looked like him—flat-faced with gem-bright eyes and unmatched ears, the right smaller than the left.

By the time Rella was flown to her father, he was more than in love. Everything about Kween was different from the last one. She was dark, big-boned with a luscious, earth smell like the dregs of a precious French wine. At the time, he didn't even notice the daughters. He had a daughter, but she was living with her mother's family. He said this several times to his new lover, but to her ears, it suggested if not death, then a final destination.

Day two in the ancient city was a foot-tour of the Roman Empire, the spotty terrain of ruin and rubble with the occasional intact memento. Rex was in white and sheltered by a straw hat, but still burned and sweated under the southern summer sun. He was German-Britannic, very fair and given to ordeals. Colosseum next to the Forum next to the Pantheon, whose round hall of ancient gods with eye open to the sky had become a circus of altars dedicated to the Christians martyred by Rome. The marble skin had been flayed for grafts onto the new church across the river named for the first martyr. He didn't want to go there where two things had become one, but his feet were taking him because he'd promised Kween and her two daughters, Vatican-blessed plunder.

At home, Kween was sitting with her head under a bullet-shaped hairdryer, bristles piercing her skull, a skunk odor circulating from skull to nose to mouth, and back. The nail woman was leaching varnish from her fingertips and now cutting into her cuticle with a pointed stick. Kween closed her eyes, but blazoned on the hot fleshy pads was her self-image, fried and desiccated. She looked up to see Cinde and Lee side by side, silver foil foliating their crowns, while blue bleach feathered their brown hair with gilt streaks, which was their happiness, for their skin, like their mother's, was dark and their hair, thick and wiry. The gold streaks would cue the viewer to the presence below of those deep-set eyes, like lightning bolts. Kween closed her eyes with satisfaction. They wouldn't get far, those two. Their paths were obstructed, as hers had been—but earlier, because her long limbs and trunk were lavished with every good thing in the way of female armament, while theirs was stunted by their father's contribution. Their legs, arms, and fingers were short, their trunks long and lean, their shoulders athletic, no necks to speak of. Kween looked at her fingernails, dipped now, each one, in pearl pink and alive with pain. Her hair was cooked and her eyes running from the fumes.

But, there was still one who could rush the finish line, even walking at a snail's pace. Snaillike, Rella could not be worn out or worn down by laws laid upon her by the senior women of the household. Snaillike, because equipped with a shell the points of their heels couldn't shatter or crack, although inside that shell, an unformed mass—Kween had seen it, or sensed it through the shell's tiny porthole. Inside that hole, a pair of eyes. No one but Kween knew she was in there. To Cinde and Lee, she was just so unremarkable, having none of their qualities: naïve, trusting, gentle, where they were canny, skeptical, heroic. Dark and robust, where she was colorless and weak. Their mother saw the hard shell, where they saw only the worm. That was youth: youth was feckless and optimistic.

Kween gathered her daughters together, their brown heads laced with golden snakes, new clothes on their backs, propped on steel-reinforced spikes. They were not chatterers, so the three departed the beauty parlor in a silent knot. In the car, three small phones were dug out of leather sacks. One was ringing. Cinde's friend, Mary, was at the end of the line. Mother had lit a cigarette and set the car in gear. Cinde was silent, but mother and daughter heard the intake of breath and held their own. With them, it was always listening. Words cost them and they didn't like paying. When Cinde closed up her machine and tucked it away, Kween's and Lee's eyes were wide open. Kween threw the butt out the window and was first through the intersection. "Tell," she said.

The doctors' ball, a triennial event of national renown, was to be quartered in their city, with all single, widowed, or divorced members of the Galen league given a lift and lodging. It was to be a masked ball with a fairy-tale theme, although the Galens (men only) were to be in work clothes, meaning knee-length white coats and tools—lights, sticks, probes, magnifiers, measurers—appropriate to rank. Any girl graduate of a four-year college, under six feet and a hundred sixty pounds, of childbearing age and no history of mental or chronic illness, would be considered for admission.

Marriage was still, after all these years, the finish line for college-educated females of good family. It was the delectable thing for unfranchised females, and the standard by which the girl population became of age; that is, citizens. You could marry any number of times and each marriage had no time limit, but men, once married, tended to remain tethered, or—if released—not to elect a second trial, so unmarried girls, like the three in Rella's family, were like a plague of rats.

Kween and Kween's daughters, informed and alert, continued home in tense silence. Their skulls hurt from the heat, the dyes, the abrading curlers, and yanking; their fingertips were raw and hot, their skins, underarms, and secret part, screamed from rough lyes and the force used to skin all their warm fur.

Rella was waiting. Early that morning, she had made their coffee and tea, toasted and buttered their bread, assembled the kit of pills for each: contraceptives and anti-depressants for the stepsisters, and for each, a powerful multivitamin; hormone replacement for Kween, calcium and an anti-seizure drug. Lee liked long-cooked oatmeal, Cinde liked cold flakes and an egg, and Kween, just the toast, coffee and a cigarette. Rella sometimes sat with them to hear their plans, or to fold the newspaper, section by section, as it was passed around. Still in high school, she rushed off after loading the dishwasher to catch the school bus.

Such a pretty thing as she was, attention was paid, both by peers and elders. Even those men, the principal, the clothier, and the stationer, who knew her father and should have desisted, schemed to cross her path, offer advice, and distract her with hall passes, handkerchiefs and paper. She was at home in the world, but preferred to be at home.

She awaited her family at the upstairs window, running down when she heard the car. Her stepmother, without so much as a word, put the car keys in her hands, but Rella lingered to hear what her sisters wanted so to tell her, before their mother silenced them. All she heard was the unit of time to expire before whatever it was that had excited them, took place. Like a hen, Kween hustled her chicks away, closing the door behind her, tempted, as always, to lock it.

Rella watched them, then drove the car into the garage, collecting purses and bags. A phone was ringing somewhere and Rella dumped out the purses to grab the silver square whose red light was pulsing. She pressed the connector and listened. After a pause and a crackle, she heard Dad, calling from Rome.

"Rella," he said, "is that you?"

But this portable one was patched to the home phone, whose ring had alerted Kween. "Hang up," she said.

"Dad?" Rella couldn't help saying.

Before the next command, Rella closed the machine. She was in the back seat, where all the purses lay empty and limp with their contents dumped on the pale leather. Which belonged to which? She sat back on the cool surface and closed her eyes, only then thinking to re-open and reconnect.

The stepsisters, Cinde and Lee, were holed up in their mother's room, perched on her couch. This Dad was not part of their world. He was their mother's, yes, but he was also, and—when on the premises, insisted upon being—Rella's.

Their mother called him "sweetheart," but to them, he was a fool. They made up stories, just to laugh. Their mother used him and then, when her own aging needs took a different course, kept him out of town. That was Sweetheart Kween was talking to, so the girls eased their backs and legs. They noted that the news of the day was not conveyed to him. He was encouraged to enjoy his copycat voyage and not worry about the folks at home. That's how she put it, "the folks at home," and they laughed to hear it, after she winked at them, their signal that the three of them added up to so much more than the two who were man and wife, or—the other pair. They'd cancelled Rella's papers on day one, right after the honeymoon. Rella had just been flown to them from her mother, and all that afternoon, Cinde and Lee had looked, tested, examined, and then rejected this other part of what they hadn't asked for.

She was young and small. She was single and they were double. At the door was the new bride and groom and sure enough, the fool carried their hefty mother over the threshold. When she was upright, the daughters made their announcement. There was someone here, who'd brought her suitcase and planned to stay. Who? Kween asked. She's in the kitchen! the daughters cried out. At first, Sweetheart didn't know who it could be who'd brought a suitcase and planned to stay. That moment of bewilderment gave Cinde and her sister their clue.

The fool went forth right after to the Mediterranean world, to those depots of his import-export trade, not to return for three long weeks. By the day the door closed behind him, the sisters had been through Rella's haul: three dresses, a sweater, underwear for a baby (panties, shirttail, petticoat, and four pairs of white socks), tennis shoes on her feet, and Mary Janes slipped into the silky runner of the suitcase; hairbrush, and a silver baby cup with a C on it. C for what? In sum, nothing. They sat on the bed in the spare bedroom (the maid's room, if they'd had one) and watched the wretch unpack her rags and deposit them in the paper dresser and rusty cabinet.

When she sat down next to them, they moved away. She was a cheerful person, but laden with another atmosphere that both sisters craved, even before they knew what it was. It kept them inert on the bed while Rella told them her story without casting blame on the villains—the negligent mother or Sweetheart, who thought remarriage was the answer and had picked their mother as its fulfilment. To call him a fool, which they did, was no judgment; it was no insult: it was who he was. Rella did not see this. Blindness was not exactly what her atmosphere was, but it was related.

At first, they were smiles and girlish conspiracies: they told their story and Rella swallowed it. They saw it sink in, increasing the density of that atmosphere. She patted them both on their long backs, squeezing herself in between to use both hands. Their father was dead; her father would be their father, if they'd accept him in exchange for offering Rella four things: mother, two grown sisters, and a home.

Hearing this, Lee ran out of the room crying, but Cinde, the smart one, stayed around just to see. This was no bargain. Then, their mother was at the door, clapping her hands for attention. Rella, Cinde reported, had made Lee cry, which, in a sense, was true.

Another truth was—as Kween and her elder daughter knew—that Lee had been the Rella before they had a Rella, and Cinde, the Rella, before Lee arrived. That's how it worked. The two sisters, long free, waited until their mother signed off. She made further calls to flesh out the ball prospect. By afternoon's end, she had the promise of four invitations, not the three asked for, because tokens were to be sent out in pairs or quadruples but not in primes or odds. That was the way the Galens worked. Medicine and superstition went together with pomp and mummery. No matter. The party of three squealed with delight.

Upon that note, Rella broke the connection from her post in the car.

She wanted nothing to do with marriage. Family meant something, as did father, mother and sister, but husband, wife, and their sign: marriage, meant little. Her mother and father had married, as had father and Kween, but nothing she had seen gave value to this elective affinity, lawful in some places and holy in others, but sensible only in the rear view, as the child saw its link to two strangers, whose private relation answered to an urge. Rella was a thinker. She had time. Cinde and Lee wanted out, and their mother wanted them out. This was the mystery to which the doctors' ball was the solution.

Her father, a lonely person, married twice, was wandering. Marriage had driven him out. It had driven Rella's mother home, so tired she needed to refuel like a baby. And there was

Rella.

She gathered up purses and bags. Divide it up later. It was Rella's first flash of rebellion.

II

The stepsisters were not fat or skinny, nor were they as ugly as you thought. They weren't as well endowed as their mother: their strength was in their bones and muscles, not in pockets of pretty fat. They had some college, the driver's license, could hold their liquor, and they were ready to marry. It was fun to stay home, watch TV, and shop for clothes, to eat and to sleep. Downtown, where workers went, did not appeal to them. They had tried simple summer employment (folding camisoles, licking envelopes) but never for long. Lee called home to cry; Cinde blew up a dress size. Home they went. They were their mother's daughters and their father was a "good provider." His work took him far away, lending money to backward countries until, in one of them, he caught a bad cold that got worse. The insurance policy was the comfort left to his widow and orphans. But not enough comfort, so mother went out again, for the sake of herself and them, and now, they were to go out, too. It was time.

The Galen Ball was ideal. Each Galen had a hand to offer. Some of them were old, true, and none was young, and they were not kind, but they kept out of the house for most of the day, and their sins were venial.

Dress was crucial, so the sisters took Rella with them to the shops. Mother was no help at all. She favored a lot of skin and tottery heels, but their skin—around the shoulders and back—was greenish-gold in tone and rough as concrete. Rella thought to drape their solid uppers in Venetian lace and loose Mongolian lamb over dresses of rain-gray silk. Their mother would be pleased to see them so well packaged. Rella knew just where to stop—at plain pumps and jewelry that burned colorless. How did she know so well how to convert these meaty horses into light and smoke?

The trip was so successful that the sisters offered Rella something from the sale table. She still wore the garments her mother had bought her. They were cut from whole cloth, so they lasted even when hems and sleeves were let down, but they seemed too youthful for the swan that Rella was becoming. Why did their fool of a mother have to marry the father of a swan?

The sale table was a twisted mass of color, but Rella ferreted out a white frock, a velvet column with a scorch mark on the single shoulder, which could be covered. But, extras—no! the sisters said. No shoes, no jewels, no stockings, underfixtures, no shawl, and no shrug. And be quick about it. The sisters were eager to move on to Alexander's, to dine on crown roast and saddle of ram. The ball was a week away; Rella's father, the fool, due home the day before. They had bought her the vanilla dress in a moment of weakness, but had no intention of releasing her on the Galens. (She was too young, and their mother had already flushed the extra ticket to the underground stream.) Rella hugged her parcel close, but was also laden with everything of theirs. The dress in its antique style had trained her eyes inward on a fresh scene. In the scene, she was dancing barefoot with her hair released from its plaits, which Kween so delighted in braiding—sometimes so tight, her face flattened and eyes stretched into a satyr's mask. It was hard to breathe. The hair was rebraided weekly. Once a month, she was circled and bound and poked with her stepmother's loot in diamonds. They started out yellow, but by day's end were like flowing water, although ashy streaks were left on the flesh.

In a week's time, with the hair's natural growth, the pigtails relaxed, and Rella's face returned to high relief. But the hair was never released, and its triune web was woven with a long disused formula.

The sisters were chopping their meat. They liked to take

their meat and sides and mix and mortar them into a savory
pudding. It made Rella sick to see. Her head ached from the
thought of having a woman's dress. She had no appetite, but
the sisters had ordered her coffee and a doughnut, which left a
halo on her napkin.

"Use your knife and fork," Lee ordered.

But the waiter had left only a teaspoon of a different matter
and pattern from anything on the table.

The sisters were filling themselves with everything they
needed when an elderly man appeared. "Don't I know you from
somewhere?" he said, peering into all three faces.

The sisters wracked their brains for the link between their
plain street address and the prospect the man seemed to offer.
He wore a decoration on his lapel, a pin on a ribbon with initials
S.P.Q.R. He unpinned it and dropped it onto Rella's napkin.
Before he'd even turned his back, Cinde had palmed it.

"Who the hell was that?" she charged, closing the lips of her
purse around this treasure.

"Don't ask me!" her blood sister said.

"I wasn't talking to you."

"I know and I don't know," said Rella, "or maybe I can't
remember."

"Fool!" they both said.

The episode and its backlash made Rella cry. Her tears wet
the doughnut, seeping into its grit and oil. The doughnut was
not just a doughnut. Inside was a tooth-cracking ring, boiled
in the batter. When Rella dunked it in her coffee, they saw it
emerge, free of crud.

It was a crude thing, but compelling. The sisters craved it,
but held back.

Rella dried the dripping hoop on her napkin and slipped it
on her arm. She saw at once a braid and initials: C.L.R., before
pulling down her sleeve.

That the bracelet was a natural thing, there could be no
doubt, but it was also handmade in an age when stone and only

stone was there to be worked. Her father would know its time, its make, and the tool that had scratched out the monogram. He could attach a value, and the pathway it traveled to arrive here at Alexander's. As their cab glided down the alley, with the sisters in back, Rella saw the black and gold neon sign.

The sisters were not pleased, and the strange medal was left in the pit of Cinde's bag. They were there for the first enchantment, and they didn't like it. Even their mother, home alone gazing out the window, was anxious.

But their mother had no words to comfort them. She tore open the bag of dresses and wraps, sniffing at what she saw. She'd been outmanned, and not for the first time. Rella spirited away her own bag. "Where do you think you're going?" Kween said.

Rella had a minute before they'd come after her, so restless they were and so quick to turn on each other. She rolled up her sleeve, and there it was, the hoop. In the lamplight, there was a link, a tiny whorl, pierced by a pin. Held against the light, she could see a sparkle in the dead and unreflecting surface. The stone cuff must belong to something else.

III

Father was just one of his many names. His daughter's name was Rella, a short form of Regina, a satellite of the root Rex. His now wife went by Kween, but her real name was Khan. To Cinde and Lee, whose names were shards, he was Stepfather and, like the priests of Rome, had authority, but no fleshly link to his filiae. As he trudged across the scorched table of the Vatican plaza, he felt the play, so terrible in Rome, of vicious, buried gods. Martyrs manned the roof, pricking the sky, but who knew for how long. One had been revived and had four states: dead, alive, mortal, and immortal. His father was a double-crosser. The mansion up ahead opened its arms. There was no earth here, no plant, only platter. Rex rose up the staircase and was instantly swallowed. It was lifeless in here, wrought in hellish ways. The reigning Caesar was mostly kept hidden. He was not a real father, although he called himself one. He was handled as a god, fiercely hoarded by his minions, smothered in heavy robes and crushing hats. Rex was coming to call on him.

And stayed no one knows how long. He may still be there, rooted and helpless. Someone was dispatched with the plunder: a bracelet, postcard franked by the idol, and a rosary. Freed, finally, of his duties, he was held, forever lulled by the waves of the two worlds.

IV

The day of the Galen ball dawned perfect as an egg. There was much to do, when suddenly, a knock at the door. A box came in. In it, beads of pink quartz and a dog-eared postcard. Rella deposited the box of gifts on the breakfast table. Tired from a night of dreams and wakeful agitation, Kween pitched the card, unread, at Rella's throat. A corner struck and quivered there. The beads were whirled and whipped that same way, breaking the skin at the temple, making a map of bruise and blood, then slithering to the floor, spreading at fifty-nine angles. The day's rage was unleashed, but it could grow.

"Lookit," said Lee, pointing at the rosy decoration on Rella's ivory mug, "the mark of Cain."

"A brand," the stepmother muttered, "of her own G.D. father."

Cinde seemed unsatisfied with either curse, watching as Rella collected the beads, rolling and ricocheting. Breakfast lay roiling in stomach pits, contributing its sour part.

When her father failed her on the day preceding, Rella had despaired. It suggested permanent exile and a new loss. The postcard said, under its ancient stamp, the usual thing: wish you were here. There was a color shot of a monument like a wedding cake, with layers all the same size. It looked familiar.

That day was spent in an orgy of grooming. Hair was washed, dried, brushed, parted, and fluffed. The heavy locks of Cinde coiled like snakes around her shoulders. The hair was hot and strong smelling. The gold, laid on at the beauty parlor, had rusted. Lee's mat foamed at the neck like a sea sponge. All four women labored to cut back the growths.

With the help of a sharp razor, the girls' faces emerged through the threatening clouds. Rella thought to shave each skull, turning the live fur into a brocade of laurel and vine.

And then, for the dresses.

All that had flowed and floated on hangers now clung, fused to the body, matter into matter. The hand arranging stopped in flight seeing the dresses cleave and tighten. Pigment and polychrome were applied. Eyes hollowed out into holes.

Kween mother was speechless. No wind or brace of rain could alter the work that was not nature. As her girls resolved into final form, Kween and Rella gazed. The pair still smoothed, simplified.

Without so much as a second glance at her ruined altar, Kween fled.

Through the opened door, Rella could see the parade of silent Galens. Meanwhile, the rose beads, collected in the ashtray, were boiling into a fine gauze.

So, she, Rella, stripped out of her togs and drew on the scorched sheath. She wound the gauze around her swan neck, letting loose each braided helix. There were three tickets of entry, and it was her lonely course to start anew.

Strong Boy

Two MONTHS AGO, I rode up the elevator to meet my maker. He lived on the thirteenth floor in a duplex apartment with his queen, Margaret. They had two cats, a day maid, and cook. They were childless, except for me, and I hadn't lived with them since the winter of '25, when a blackout turned the mister murderous, and the missus was the only one he could stand. We bumped into each other in the dark. I was five and moved all the way down to my aunt's house on the mezzanine level. I snuck out before the lights came on. They'd trip over me lying prone or standing up, and my nerves were never the same.

In the mezzanine were Aunt Alice and Uncle Bill, my cousins Eddie, Mary, Isabel, and little Hamlet. Another runt would make no difference, or so I thought, as I hauled down a diaper bag with my blanket and pillow, and two sets of overalls, a jersey, and baby shoes on my feet. They had to take me in, when I mentioned we were family, although the two in the penthouse paid a visit to the bottom only once a year, on Easter Saturday, for a highball, and some one-sided talk.

I was an accident is what I heard, but they all had a different version. Mother was in her fifties and had had a brace of miscarriages. Dad was sixty, but looked ninety, with his pure white hair and horseshoe back. His head was at my level, but I had a better deal, because he had to twist his and, sometimes, toppled over. I looked down until, "Don't you be looking down on me, squirt!" is what I heard. "Peace," I said, and I hauled him up with my good arm. The bad one had been twisted in my delivery, or deliverance, as I heard someone call it. Mother had everything wrong with her, and getting out in one piece, no laughing matter.

Getting in, of course, was the accident. Here's what I heard from Aunt Alice: on a train trip to Miami, Dad's back only a half or quarter moon, they'd booked a Pullman, locked the door, and couldn't get it open for love or money. There was nothing else to do, and all they had to eat was a two-layer box of chocolates from the New Haven RR (Dad was the under-chief), and a quart of Wild Turkey. Mother was a nerveless wonder, who'd never met a person she didn't like, or made a decision she regretted, including marrying her cousin, Adalbert. She still had her black silk pajamas with one pink stork running up the pant leg, and a little pink cord looping around the collar and under the buttons. You can imagine how cute they were on my beautiful mother, with her platinum-blond pageboy, and black-cat glasses. But, they were bored, and he was beside himself with rage. Heads would roll, but before that, my mother had him dead to rights, and the train pulled out of the station, with two turned into three—his miracle, Da, as I called him, or Sir—and whisky into water, for they had to gargle, with a mouthful of tooth powder and a mouse on their tongues. Da says "fur," I say mouse; Mother Margaret says, "if you don't pay attention, it'll go away," which is what she always said.

So, she grew a belly on top of a belly, hardly noticeable, since I was the product of spirits and cocktail olives, petit fours and cream cheese on date bread—so small, I might have snuck in, and no one notice, but it was full summer and they were at the beach house playing gin rummy with the maiden aunts who lived next door. Mags (as they called her) had a belly ache that wouldn't go away, no matter how many Tums she sucked, or cups of black tea with honey, so she called it a day and retired with a sleeping pill, then another, until I was born in the dead of the night, squealing, until Da found me with his foot (he always wore socks to bed, even in summer), thinking it was the cat.

But no, by morning they could see it wasn't, and the old

doctor, who lived across the bay, putt-putted over to cut the cord, and to see if I was still alive.

Margaret was feeling kind of punk, and that's all she remembered, but the maiden aunts converted their knitting that day to my booties and capes, hats and sweaters. I still have them. The maid was using them for dusters, but I whisked them away. What would I do with these filthy rags but start a figurine collection with broken teacups, and my talent for making something out of nothing,

So, that year, even before my first birthday, I was something to reckon with, and each of them blamed the other. "Dammit to hell, Mag. Nobody told me this could lead to that," he said, pointing to me, a clod sitting under the mahogany table, peeking through the holes in the lace cloth. "Don't you talk to me that way, you!" Mother returned, but both were looking at me, seeing how I might bear it, the full load. I already had—I heard them say—a guilty look on my face, born with it.

But, I stuck it out for four more years with nothing but time on my hands, so I took up what hobbies I could: cards, *Racing Form*, listening to the fights and *Amos 'n' Andy*, and doing the puzzles in the funnies. I taught myself to read and write, just by keeping my yap shut, while Margaret wrote her thank-you cards for the baby showers she had for every miscarriage, because I instigated the program of turning the nighttime into the right time, "Tea for Two," and "O, Sweet Mystery of Life," but Margaret had a bad cooker, and all the baby cakes fell flat, and two or three of these messes made Da hesitant. We were often in the big bed together, side by side, because I was a crybaby, plus slick as a weasel, sliding out from under a pileup. Sometimes, they didn't even know I was there, until I put my little hand out to tickle or pinch. Then, whammo, out I'd be, hanging onto the tufts of the chenille spread, waiting for the clout that would send me flying, scared silly, just enough to put me to sleep on top of the clothes hamper, or hugging the base of the privy, on that little rug.

Da would cry. It wasn't his fault, and everyone always blamed him. The waterworks would get us all going, until Margaret thought to heat up the coffee and pour out the schnapps, and happy days were here again. That's why I loved them: their comeback was quicksilver.

That was part one of my short but happy life. Second, was life in the mezzanine, brawling with the Talbots and eating up my share of American chop suey and hambeans, never enough to go around, so first to hit the three chairs gobbled it up, whatever it was. The ones who poked around and were still planked in front of the floor-model Victor, were losers-weepers, with a piece of white bread and a lick of oleo, if we had it; sometimes, just the white bread, the kind that never went stale, just shrunk into tiles. At eight, I went out on my own, delivering the paper door to door—hiding it in the bushes for the cheaps who wouldn't drop the extra nickel in my weekly envelope. I sent myself to school every morning—and not the sister school the Talbots went to, but my own elementary, fifteen blocks from the apartment. I found it on one of my rambles. I was out first in the a.m., and not back until dark. What did I do with myself? the Talbots liked to know. Mostly, I didn't give them the time of day, but little Hamlet begged. He was a few years younger, a little bit of a thing, with buckteeth and hardly any hair. (He pulled it out at night, once he'd worn away holes in the blanket, by rubbing. You could hear it—one thumb in his mouth, the other twirling his baby fine hair, until he had none.) His bed—which was mine, too—was snaky with hair. We were all nervous Nellies, and the nights were long and broken with screams and coughs, crying, moaning, and talking a blue streak—each Talbot had a way, and sometimes more than one. We were bleary-eyed, pale, with black circles around our eyes. One of the girls was cross-eyed, and the other had one leg longer, and a gimp. (No one thought to spring for a lift for the short leg—who had the cash?)

Once I was down, the penthouse Markles cut me every time—not so much as a how-do from the mister—no surprise, really, given his character; or the missus—for whom the sight of me, spitting image of the high-hat McGoons, who'd dropped her as soon as she'd married Da, was a knife through the eye. And I was handsome—gleaming white choppers (when I grew the second set—the first were rotten), head of wavy black hair, and a mugful of freckles. I wore my rags proud, like Da, even though they never saw the inside of the wringer-washer. I was a looker, as vain as the day was long.

The whole neighborhood was in love with me, old and young. Billy Boy, they'd say, I've got a nice piece of marble cake for you, or some Boston baked beans, my favorite. The girls wore out their shoe leather traipsing up and down the blacktop, waiting for me to land, with my news bag and a grin. I was young, but made up for it with savvy and the gift of the gab. The girls trailed behind as I trooped to third grade, and the principal waited outside the door, bell in hand. "Good day, William. Good morning to you." "Same to you, Miss O'Callahan," I shouted, and winked, as I passed in review, last to arrive, first to leave.

They would be saying the pledge, as I appeared, to catch another wink from Miss Coughlin. They were all maiden ladies, and liked it that way.

I sat in the front, and had the charge of beating the erasers, sending up a choking cloud, so Miss Coughlin could race over and hammer my back, stroking me, even giving me a little pinch. I had the charge of the supply closet, and passed out the gum erasers and fat pencils. I liked the smell of glue, of wax, and of raw paper, and stayed in there, with the door shut, as long as I could, or until: "Where is my Billy Markle?" I heard. "Where, O where is my Billy?" A unison rose up to greet me, as I emerged, girls squealing, boys pounding their desks and feet.

I was good at all of it, and liked the attention, the paper stars, and seeing my name on the honor roll, with a red-ribbon bow; taking home a promotion card with "is" underlined, and "is not" crossed out. That's how I did it.

The worm turned in grade four, when my makers hustled me, one fine day—maid on one side, cook on the other—to the train station with a suitcase of new skivvies and a pint-sized suit. I was remanded to a hick town, shaking like a leaf, and yes, bawling like a baby, where the boarding school doors opened and slammed shut. This wasn't the high life of the Markles, or the bedlam of the Talbots. I didn't wear a striped pajama, or lug a ball on my ankle, but pushed around and organized, morn to night, forced to bunk with a crowd of toughs and ninnies, and nothing in between. One of my front teeth was knocked out, first hour, for gassing an older boy, a foot taller. Everything about me stood out: the only Roman among the barbarians, with teachers who knew no more than a baby. I wrote home to Auntie Alice, but they snatched my letters, punishing me for milksopping, by making me track the rim of the pitch fifty times in my boxers and saddle shoes. I couldn't sleep for the snoring and weeping, the howls and nightmaring, bullies by day, nurslings by night. I used my best weapon: silence. I applied it everywhere, earning the respect of the other mutes. They formed an honor guard, and walked me everywhere. Alone, we were nothing; together, we were an action, pure and dumb.

This lasted five years and, from a sunny boy, I became a full-meat male, with a head hard as a turnip and hair clipped to the bone. I had four tattoos: Ganesh the elephant, a model T, a peanut, and the shroud of Turin. I ran the school from my headquarters near the brazier, where we burned what was offered, pinched, or forfeited: suits of clothes, hymnbooks, chairs, desks, book bags and bed kits. We torched the goods at night. "Burn!" and it burned. I was sprung in ninth grade, straight to reform school, with not so much as a cruise past the old apartment. By then, I was a cast out, for neither Markles nor Talbots would claim to know a bum and jailbird like me.

And bully for them—I'd have done the same.

Overnight, a loner. I read the Webster's dictionary, *Kidnapped,* and *The Five Little Peppers and How They Grew,* and every day, made something out of nothing. This was my gift. I was a boy in a million, a strong boy, by trade; and, once on the loose, picked up for jobs way above my station. Wherever it was, I rose to the top—weaving rope mattresses, driving a trolley, reading for the blind, spinning the wheel of chance. I could do whatnot with my hands, and I did it all: driver's licenses—good anywhere—breeding hounds, cracking safes, running numbers, and dealing cards. In my spare time, I floated overseas as a stowaway on the White Star Line.

Aboard, I met Queen Anne, working the game table, and singing for her supper. I was eighteen, she was fifty, if she was a day, christened Anne McQueeney—the stage name, a flip away. She was a pearl, and pearl colored, bathing in a tin tub of canned milk, lavender seeds, lanolin, and beach sand. I scrubbed her back with a brush, shampooed her hair in the sink. She was a bottle blonde. She paid me a fin a week for upkeep, including feet and hands, and a slick of pure petroleum jelly. She was like a mother to me, but also my baby girl. I ironed her evening dresses (black, blue-black, and midnight black), and shined up her platform shoes. She was a midget, and her feet were permanently arched. She pranced on her toes. We met on the gangway, scurrying in with the rats, at the zero hour; she, with a vanity case full of rouge, toilet water, and a rhinestone choker; me, with a zoot suit—picked up on 53rd, where I heard about the passage. I was a messenger for the Herald Agency. She was the talent, understudy to the lounge singer, a chippie who worked the below-decks club, where the lights never stayed on in the gassy sinkhole of rotten fish and seaweed. I'll never get the smell out of my nose. Our cribs were down there in the slosh, but glad rags were kept above sea level, for the niceness of it. It was the job of a lifetime, and where I met my Mary.

For a time, Queen Anne, all bathed and primped, tiptoed

nightly out of the hold for her singsong. The chippie was down for the count—arsenic or rat poison; sometimes, she went for herself, or was done in by dime-a-dancers, crew, and even the cabin boys. I was the bouncer, and sat by the snuggery door, gaffer in hand. It might have been White Star, but below decks, another story. Even the crew avoided the crawl space, just above the engines. It was pitch dark in there, a few candles and a fire in the grotto, which was also a drain. No piano or accordion, just clapping hands, and tapping feet, smoking, belching, guzzling, and spitting, with always some business going on in the back, under the tarps and rusty cables. In the gloom, all you could see was the Queen Anne puss, over a flashlight, ardent, hurting, awful. She knew a ditty, "The Rag-Tag Gypsies," the sisters had taught her, and a show tune, "Over There," and she could belt them out. We all felt good, our lips wet with dram, and our hearts open to the past, where the memories were stashed, even if we were only, like me, a decade or two above zero. The crooning went on for hours, as the mugs slid table to floor, rolling away, rolling back, in a rhythm we all came to love.

As the candles went out, we slept. We dreamed, and when the ship's horn blasted, we rolled out, ready for what came.

My Mary was the ladies' maid, cute as a button, who snuck down to inquire. News had reached the upper decks of the hot club in steerage, and the nobs wanted in, so Miss Mary's mistress, a dame with a brace of greyhounds and a trunkful of furs, sent her down. My Mary was fifteen, tiny, but with a southpaw and a lip that folks could sense before they ducked. Her livery shone in the dark and smelled of camphor. She waved a torch right in my face, calling me Buster.

Soon, she was slipping down in the dead of night, with the dogs and the old dame dolled up and hung with her gauds. They had their own barrel, and a butler with his tray of Boodles and Indian tonic. They were from the other side, on a return trip from the colonies, where the boss had a summer cottage. First, they added to the gaieties, Queen Anne singing her heart

out, and the fires raging—we must have burned every stick
of furniture that wasn't bolted down, but then, the old puss
wanted to sing herself, and had a voice worse than a crow, and
the habit of running a tune front to back, over and over, driving
everyone out in spooling and spinning rage. Mary was the only
claque, and it hurt to see. You could tell, even in the murk, the
squalor, that it hurt. We bucked her up, but she soon stopped
dropping by, and I had to sneak up the service stairs for a peck
on the cheek, or a bite and a scratch. Still, I was out of my head
by the time we hit Southampton.

Sullen, we watched, as off they trotted, the human cargo,
the officers and crew. Left behind, the below-decks, waiting
for the turnabout. The surprise to come was sight of my Mary,
stampeding up the gangway with a paper valise, and an old
muskrat coat, collar popped up to her nose, and cloche bonnet
pulled over the eyes. You had to laugh, but not for long.

Docking stateside that winter, we hired out as maid and
butler, cook and driver, companion and man's man, char and
window-washer, scribe and barber, nurse and ashman, whatever
the traffic would bear. Bella and Boy we were, and rented a cubby
down in the Battery for the weeks of day labor. We preferred
live-in, sucking the fat of the land, and able to do all for our
folks. We were born to it. We liked to do for them, fawn, butter
them up, and be proud. We learned all the ways and means of
the top drawer. To smooth their feathers, settle their hash, and
butter their peas, we were rag and polish, sandpaper and steel
wool. They were the nutmeat and we the shell. We fortified the
tenders, tenderizing them to start with, because every family,
rich or poor, is roughage, and rough goes to rough, but for a
team like ours, steady, awake, and menial.

But, my Mary always sprung up the grades to housekeeper,
with a key ring to attic and cellar, hidey-holes and lock-up.
She jingled and sang, ordered, poked, and checked. A Mary
household was quiet as the moon, smooth as cream cheese. But,

what would happen was the usual backbite: the betters would sniff about, get the lay of the land, and start to feel in the way, unwanted, and left out, and next thing you know, Mary was pounding the pavement, with me right behind her.

Which brought me here, and sent her packing overseas. Such was what we were stuck with, forever on the high road, with nothing ever tucked away, or left over. I foundered for five or six minutes, then headed west to the lonesome plains, and pushed out to the sea; this time, the other way. War came, and war went. For a while, it was the end of everything, and then, the start of something big. Homeport was where I landed, the city on the hill. I was twenty, if I was a day, but no flies on me, so they all knew me on sight, and called me by name. Half the cousinage were pushing up daisies, and the other half, spavined, addled, soured, tanked, or on their uppers. The Markles still resided on 13-14, Mister and Missus, happy in love for the rest of their days, unlike their "get," guttered like a candle, on a first Friday in Lent, the feast of St. Louie the Leech. I'd made those first Fridays, offering myself and my day's works to the Sacred Heart and his queen. I touched my heart with a finger, just as he did. So these first Fridays were my time with him, where he lived, in a small but perfect home, on his slab, or his gilded cage, a bull's eye in the spangling monstrance; like me, he was made for something different, and we became thick as thieves. They had to sweep me out with a broom, or swat the feather duster in my face. "Time to go home, Billy Boy," were the sacristan's six last words.

So, home I went, and up to 13-14, knocking on destiny's door for the first time since the day I left them. I knocked, and I hammered away with both fists. I spied an eye in the eyehole, and placed my eye to meet that eye. "Is it you?" I heard him say, and then, my name. The gate swung open, and there he was, who made me what I am, was, and will be. I kissed his mug, and dropped at their feet my truck: medals, scapulars, rosaries made of seed and shell, holy cards, daily missal, the Rule of

St. Isaac, and the niblets, tokens, icons, totems, candles, and incense sachets, spoons, and cups and cruets. I'd walked it all over in a wagon from my crib under the freeway.

"Come, all ye faithful," I said, and in I went, but the parlor stunk like a funeral home of dripping tallow and fleshy, white flowers. "Hail, Holy Queen," I said to the female, and "King of Kings," to him, but words failed them. "Own up!" I said. "See this!" I said, pointing to my heart with a finger. Deny me three times, they couldn't.

My string of days had played itself to the last bead. My battered heart and lung, my flipper arm, and the skimpy cloth that was my covering were returned to my maker, worthless goods. I was not going in the usual way, but like the desert sands, hollowing in one spot, piled up in another. Or pulling a thread that turns a muffler into a snarly mess. It was given to me be taken as I had come, by accident. And to close my eyes under my maker's.

The Sensitives

THE SENSITIVES WERE a family of five: Jack, Alice, and their three children: Gemma and the twins, Alessandra and Benigno. Jack worked at the stables and was–unofficially–a gambler; Alice had been a stationer and now a housewife, as pleasant a woman as you'd hope to meet with her dark eyes and a toothy smile. The elder girl took after her grandparents and was almost worn out with the effort of pleasing two such different generations, at war fifty percent of the time. The twins were in love with each other.

For a long time, Gemma was like a second mother to the twins, especially after Alice went back to work at the stationer's, bored to tears by housework. Gemma was domestic to her fingertips and sewed all the twins' clothing, knitted their blankets and sweaters, and hand-laundered the family linen. She especially liked to iron, which she did in the cellar with her bare feet on sheets of fresh newspaper. If her hands were busy, her heart was light and her head clear of mental knots.

The twins took their sister, and everything else, for granted. They wore their handmade clothes for the roughest play and balled them up at night. They chewed the linens still warm from the iron and spat on the meat pies, but not on the fruit. Badness was for them a sport, and no one saw what they did because they'd been born only half alive and their issue contained the family's only boy.

The grandparents, Gepetto and Sancta Maria, lived over the post office in the center of town, which consisted of church, baby school, alimentation, beer bar and stationer-press-cigar. Of the family Sensitive, the one they most abhorred was the missus, who'd thieved their best and only boy, Giacomo, fresh from the priest high school, and an idiot. Grandmother Sancta could see this skirt from her kitchen window, at first an insult to the eyes, but lately giving her something to do for the dull hours of the day, and a target for the fury building up in her broomstick frame for forty or fifty years. She was the maddest person in town, which was one reason her husband drank from morning till night. Gepetto started the day with cold beer bought fresh from the bar; wine for lunch came in a hose from the neighbor vintner; and–at exactly three o'clock–an anisette with water; gin and tonic with his English neighbors over a game of bocce; more wine with dinner and a nightful of apple brandy, barely conscious of his Sancta Maria, for whom the day was a bag to be filled with scenes preserved for the day when life might offer less rich occasions for sin. Through the night these bags silently bled their contents and, by morning, Gepetto caught a glimpse from the sleeping mound beside him of his springtime bride. It was a moment of clarity before his empty bag was swollen full of liquor.

During the day, when no school, the twins came by to see what was up and what they could get just by asking. Boy and girl, they hardened themselves to the assault of oaths, screams, and speech hot as oil on a fire, which their nonna had ready for them. They divided this stream, Sandra taking the first blast—there before they even crossed the threshold—and Nino absorbing the moiety, or what came after the nonna had filled their stomachs with bread soup and wine mixed with water. The nonna liked to cuff them, too, if and when their half-baked looks or broken speech derived from whom the nonna thought unworthy to give her grandchildren. They were so tough and mulish that this was no hardship, where their sister would cry for a month if so much as a high-speed word grazed the glassed-in baby bath she lived in. The nonna coveted the love of this Gemma, but the girl paid only feast-day visits and the obligatory once-a-week pranzo, an ordeal of snubs, slights, oaths and insults, slopped soup, odd smells, burps, clattery dishes and the repellant sensation of touching the nonna's sinkful of dishwater, cold and floating a bar of greasy hand soap. Arrows of wrath crisscrossed the table until the grandmother and daughter-in-law were separated by grandfather and son, passing between them the earthenware pitcher of farmer-wine at twenty proof. The twins enjoyed the scene, each taking a side and slugging it out later on the gravel, flinging gravel nuts.

"Stay home next time!" Jack said to his wife, "if you can't keep a civil tongue in your head." But Alice at home, or on the street, or in the press-tobacco-paper was a different creature, dark-eyed with a dazzling, movie-star smile. And Alice didn't want to stay home, or eat her solitary lunch at the beer bar. She had a right to a place at her mother-in-law's table, along with her three children and the man to whom she'd given everything she had, and—in the old days—used the teeth on him (the "snappers," he called them) whenever and wherever he wanted them used. Alice loved family, which was why she'd married into an Italian one, when her origin was so many degrees of latitude north. The beauty part was Jack, although a pure Sensitivo, had no national signs. Where his father was black, Jack was white; where his mother was red, Jack was yellow; where her nose was crooked, his was straight; where his teeth were rotten, and mostly gone, Jack's were worth the expense and attention of a city dentist. Jack, like his daughter, Gemma, had come from who-knows-where, but he, like her, had still landed under the branches of the family tree.

Gemma Sensitive was growing into a tall girl with an hourglass shape. Her hands were large and capable, and never ornamented although her father had offered his oldest daughter birthdays rings and bracelets. Inasmuch as Gemma's mother loved family life, Gemma didn't, although she worked twice as hard at housekeeping, and was glad when her mother returned to tending the store. One day, when her feet were blacker from standing on too-fresh newspaper and her basket was nearly full of smooth hankies, undershirts and underdrawers—for she ironed everything, even the twins' woolly socks—Gemma looked through the cellar window and saw her grandmother's face. Gemma heard the thumps of clogged feet coming down the steps to the earth floor that was the Sensitive's cellar. Gemma held her breath. She held the iron mid-air.

"Poverina," she heard before she saw her nonna's face, all bright eyes and purple cheeks.

Nonna was holding open a bag full of cherries from her own orchard, but why, when the cherries ripened all summer in unceasing plenitude, did she think her granddaughter wanted or needed a bagful just then, while she was ironing? Here's what she heard: Carlino, a first cousin once removed, son of Carlone, the grandfather's oldest brother, was home from the States where he was studying the chemistry of killer diseases. Was that the whole of it? No, Gemma's cousin, whom she'd known only as a neighbor boy, had come home as handsome as a statue, taking after a side of the family that had slept since the days when the country was reunited. So, then why was this nonna saying "poverina" to Gemma, who went back to the shirt she was ironing. Honoring all the family seniority was hard work and had to be spaced out.

The grandmother explained. Their Carlino had come home engaged to an American. It wasn't right, but it had happened.

Gemma looked up. The grandmother's joy had imploded and on her face was the usual vicious mania. Who but an Anglo, like another one she knew, would have preyed upon her nephew, tied up tight like all Sensitivo men by the women who fed their mouths.

"Go home now, Nonna," her granddaughter was saying. "It's time for you to go home."

"Is that all you have to say?" the nonna said, still holding open her bag.

"Thanks for thinking of me," the girl said.

"Be patient. Wait and see," the grandmother said, but Gemma had seen enough to know that waiting and seeing brought nothing good.

Gemma reported the news to her mother, sitting with her feet up and a glass of minerals. Alice knew exactly who this Carlino was, a boy who'd put no less than an ocean between himself and the Sensitivos and left it that way for going on eight years. The news was enlightening: it meant the nonna had left over from her work of cutting off branches of the family tree enough good will to cultivate this new growth. Alice, though, wanted her children in the world and not used as graft for the Sensitivos. Still, there was something to be said for crossing the ancient stock with yet another alien and wayward growth.

By then, the twins were home, and their father, who'd heard the news relayed by his own gentle drunk of a father. What no one knew but he was that Carlino was the nonno's natural son and Jack's bastard brother. This was yet a new cross for Jack to bear: the upright being how his father had skunked his mother with a daughter-in-law; the cross piece, the fact that now his mother wanted to marry her granddaughter with her uncle. Jack requisitioned a couple of liters from the beer bar and sent the boy twin to get it, which meant the twin girl, screaming in rage, had to go, too.

A day later, Gemma Sensitivo met Carlino Sensitivo on the piazza. Carlino was recovering something old, and lost these eight years, of waking himself up with several scalding drops of black coffee. He bought himself a pack of cigarettes and smoked one, caught between the scientist who knew he was sucking the finger of death and the local who was drawing the breath of life. Gemma spotted him standing at the beer bar. She was riven by his male sweetness, speaking to her as in a dream. She entered the bar, a first, and saluted the newcomer, more at home than the native-born habitant. It was the easy way he canted his weight onto one leg and propped his elbow on the bar top. The barman nodded toward the signorina, his cousin, and Carlino opened his mouth to show the twin someone else's dazzling smile, all lips and several dozen calibrated white teeth.

Miss Sensitivo, up to then just a housewife, felt instantly at ease.

"And your name is?" he said in an American accent with no trace of dialect.

"Jame-a," she said with her accent pure and narrow, rooted on five blocks of their town. She heard his voice and felt a satisfaction known only when she'd taken the damp cloth off the basket of clothes to be ironed, or when the hot iron sliced up the inseam of her father's Sunday pants, his only black ones, with wool dyed at the origin, shortly after being shorn off their own Dalkey lamb, who ferried down with her mother's worldly goods from the North Sea.

"Come again?" he said. "Jame?"

"A," she said. "Gemma."

And already, as simple as that, they were talking in a place Gemma had never before visited, a place that was home to her grandpa and home away from home to her own father.

The new boy ordered a third coffee and pushed the cup, with the baby teaspoon, to Gemma, or Jame, as he called her.

The barman opened his eyes onto a third entering his bar, normally empty until the hose arrived with the day's wine. It was the carina Americana he'd seen coming out of the church early that morning. It was still dark, and a damp wind was blowing yesterday's dust and wastepaper round and round the square.

Into the bar this carina came, taking her place at the young man's other side.

"Jame, this is Sal," Carlino said.

"Sel?"

"Sal. Sally."

"Sellee."

Sally so took for granted the Italian boy from whom she'd accepted a baguette ring of chemically built stones that she was spending her time here in Lotto learning the language and paying her respects to the Protestant god she neglected at home. She was fonder of him now when it was just the two of them here in this lonely place. She could fulfill her duty in their

Catholic church, where Protestants had visiting privileges when they were so far away from their own wooden cottages with clear windows and clean altars. The Protestant god, related to this ancient one, went everywhere and that was his right.

Everything that Gemma could see about this Sellee was different. For that reason, Gemma was glad she'd come, although she'd left the twins with no cow milk heated in a pan with a melted bar of candy, no sharpened pencils, no runny noses swabbed and coated with grease, no clean clothes laid out in piles. Their mother went out early to the stationery store, their father to the stables, so the twins made off to the nonni, where they found their grandmother lodged in her window, overlooking the square. She had nothing they needed, so off they went again in yesterday's clothes and empty stomachs to the beer bar, a place they'd made their second home.

Sally's first thought, upon seeing these pipsqueaks, was that they must be Jame's. And sure enough, up they ran, to pound their fists on Jame's ample hips and sides until she was off her chair and had one in each hand, hoisted off the ground, so embarrassing it was to have the American couple see these rotten children (for that's what they were and she saw it in an instant). She saluted her cousin and his friend and promised to meet them again, speaking the dialect that had never come so easy, now when she could see herself reflected in their eyes: a contadina with a basket of grapes on her head, just like the one on the raisin box they knew so well. (Gemma had never seen this box; what she saw in their eyes was raw admiration, curiosity, even appetite.)

Off she went to scold the twins and ship them off to school in yesterday's clothes and no breakfast either, excepting the metal can of succo d'arancia, which no one would give to a cat. Alice kept a few cans around to remind her of what she left behind, a national food so poor and sickening that she'd made a career in stationery so as not to spend all day gorging on the bean and bread soup, unctuous dairy supplements, and greasy meats from dangerous pigs with horns. For Gemma, these cans were what was ever ready when there was no time to boil milk or melt a candy bar. Now the twins had only each other to turn to, and they did, holding grubby hands as they were driven off to school by the angry, shaking finger of their older sister.

Gemma spent the day in thought, wearing it like a cloud cover into one room and out another. Alice came home at noon, said the Angelus on foot, and found her oldest girl watching her from the front window. The stove was cold, the rooms shuttered against the night, the feather mattresses like uncooked puddings on the beds.

A stream of oaths piled up behind Alice's gritted teeth, but stopped there and cooled because this was no sturdy signorina rifling the stock at the stationery store; this was her Gemma. Why was she standing there so, stopped in the course of her routine, her rings of labor and rest?

"Gemma?" she said, taking the girl's cool hand in her own ink-stained one.

"What?"

"Tell me what happened. What's wrong?"

"Why are you asking me that?" said Gemma, turning her back to her mother, and her face to the stove. "Oh, I see," she added. "Who I am is what you need."

Alice was puzzled by this answer. The kitchen cabinets, though, were replete with bread and local produce so she made her own repast and offered a bite of her sandwich to Gemma, still standing there, calculating something. Funny how this change tempered even the air.

"Aren't you still mine in some way, and owe me something in return?" she thought to say.

"Cooking, cleaning, washing, and ironing?" she shot back.

The speed and pith of that reply were not pleasing. But Alice had no other key in reserve to open this sullen daughter like a can of sardines, so she went back to work and, gathering up her wrath, stored it, available for later use. She had learned from her well-loathed mother-in-law the art of brooding on her anger to make the rotten egg that could be thrown or cooked. Gemma was a chip off this mother-in-law's block. It had taken sixteen years to mature, but the nonna had known from the moment of the girl's difficult birth. That left Alice with nothing but the rotten twins. Still, she wondered what had happened to the little housewife, up to now so content just to work and breathe?

Later that day, she saw come through the stationer's door, with the Irish bell ringing overhead, part of what it had to be. Here in person was this Americana who'd stolen the nonna's favorite nephew. Almost six feet tall and blonde as an ear of corn, the girl was pointing at a stack of letter paper that could be folded to make its own envelope. With her finger, she traced in the air a question mark. Alice Sensitivo drew back her lips to release the rows of teeth and deliver some Italian words so closely tooled end to end that only a fool wouldn't have laughed in her face, if she expected to do business that way.

Sure enough, the American, as glorious and clean as she was (compared to these natives who lived in caves with no air or light), was frozen to the spot, and no Carl nearby to contend with this insolent salesperson. Sally stared at the madwoman, whose lips were now sealed. Then, she opened her purse and the little purse inside the purse to show her some native money in big bills. Alice saw the bills and shook her head no. She told the girl to get out of her store in a dialect rare and succinct, never so well said, and all for Gemma.

The girl backed out of the store, corrected. But for what? Her mother, a Californian, had said, don't go, stay here where you belong, but the Italian boy had an answer for this. "It's the origin of everything, and you might even like it." Sally had given him the point for argument, and off they'd gone with her daddy paying the freight. Sally came from nothing but money and a love marriage, so happiness was hers to seek. She had had a good beginning of day school, board school, skill camp, and five years of college. There was nothing between her and the next

step but her own sweet will, and she spun the open numbers
like a croupier: be a model, go to art school, engagement with a
complex network of activities, events, and consequences; stay at
home and drink, overeat, starve, or pill pop. Then, she ran into
Carl swimming in the automatic pools. They were each in a lane
swimming against a machine-made tide, he on his back, she on
her side, getting nowhere.

From that point, California and Lotto had eyes only for each
other, and hands and lips and parts that fit one into the other.
It was an old game but with a fresh accent: his, which to her
ears sounded like a joke made in her grandpop's homemade
basement bar with knotty pine walls and LPs of Mario Lanza
and Ezio Pinza. But, being who he was, Carl had to bring his
intended to where he came from. "You'll like them," he said,
forgetting, or choosing to forget, what he knew. Now she knew
and it was the first check she'd received in twenty-two years of
fortified living. She wasn't a stupid girl, just preserved pest-free
and no predators. She and Carl were staying in a pensione, a
nice one, where they had an American breakfast of wheat and
corn, but she didn't go there. She threaded her way through
the stone streets with walls protecting gravel lawns and stone
houses. One street led to another, but not directly, and the
signage was designed to fool and trick. Soon she was standing
outside a stone door, looking up to watch a feather bed shoot
out the window. She could see hands flipping the mound of
feathers in their envelope. A few feathers, escaping through a
hole, floated down to the gravel.

And then the whole head came out the window. It was Jame.

***

The Sensitivo family was in a state of unrest, and even the
teachers at the baby school knew something was up when their
tormentors arrived late with dirty clothes on their backs and no
books or sharpened pencils. "Would someone please lend the

Sensitivo children a pencil?" This was said, and more than once, but hooray for the chance to show these Sensitivos exactly what was thought of them. "Well, sit there, then," the teacher said, "and do mental arithmetic." She had a couple of extras, fat ones with no erasers, for childhood was a time when mistakes are legible, there for everyone to see, and to be corrected in a vivid way, enough to last a lifetime. The girl twin hung her head, and the boy sucked his thumb. They were going back the fast way to an earlier and safer time.

***

The grandmother had shut her window, pulled her curtain, and locked her shutters when she saw what she saw that morning—a design meant to puzzle. The girl Gemma had been sprung like an arrow into the square and quivering there. Lost but now found was Carlino, in the beer bar. Then, trailing and twirling into place like a lunar moth was the American girl, whose hair was white from the sun and whose skin was the color of pasta. Soon, all three were in the bar with old Tommaso serving whatever he had. Then—and why oh why was this day so different?—the twins came along and were sucked into where everyone else was. "Get over there fast," she hissed at the nonno, stripping his legs of their night pants, thirsty, but first things first. The first thing that morning was waking to find the old lady gone, dressed and stationed at her open window. "Sancta Maria," he said, but softly, using a tone put away twenty or thirty years ago. But she wasn't listening and her face was quiet: no lighting had as yet struck to fire up the day's sights and sounds.

The nonno went out to enquire. First to the bar, where he got the story, then to the press-tobacco-paper where he got something more, possibly a loose end, then home to where his Giacomo kept his family in a loose tangle of ill-sorted members. Twins at school, Mama at work, Giacco with the horses or taking the numbers. At home, he found whom he expected, sitting at

the table across from the beauty who'd crossed the sea with his
bastard. The nonno didn't knock; it wasn't his custom, but he
never visited either—women's work. And there was no chair
for him at the table where there was a slice of everything edible
in the house. "What's going on?" he said to his granddaughter.
"Can you please tell me?"

But to talk in their common language shut out the blonde,
whom he already liked, and his English was limited to the
words he'd used when his son married whom Sancta called the
outlander. He liked the outlander's language. It was more like
a tool, and its face wasn't an animal face with unpredictability
built into it, even in his own native mouth. Being who she was,
Alice soon ceased to use the capable tool she'd brought with
her and picked up a crapulous dialect at the stationer's. He
knew the words for family members, time and weather, good
morning, good night, and a few common illnesses. "I'll just sit
here and listen," he said to Gemma, realizing only then that his
granddaughter, who stayed at home, had no English at all. So
what were they doing?

It was then that he saw the notepad from the stationer's whose
every page—because he snatched it up—had a cartoon drawing
in two different styles. It was like two languages working as
one, because even he could identify the objects rendered in the
distinctive hands. Mother, father, baby on one page; mother,
father, three babies on another. And here was the schoolhouse
and the church, and mother and father, stick figures on one
page, and in a conjugated ball on another.

He wanted to speed up this story, so he flipped to the last
page, but Gemma snatched the notebook from his hands and
hurt him. She got up and poured him wine from last night's
supply, but he didn't want wine. He wanted what they were
drinking. They were drinking a warm, pale mixture with no
smell. He refused to ask for it, but he was staying.

If he was staying, they were going, Gemma said in the
language she shared with her nonno, stabbing him with it. He

stared at this creature, now more her mother than her gentle father. No one had ever looked at Gemma with meaning in their eyes. There was no need to. She belonged to them by virtue of blood, but more by the way she clung to the house and tended it in their interest. What they didn't know—and what she didn't know until the meaning glance was directed her way—was that their interest was second and the house always came first. As the nonno continued to look at her, Gemma took stock. The things she'd been telling the golden princess through drawings was a fable except for the page with the house containing each of its street-facing windows, a closed door, two chimneys, a border of flowers and flowering trees, gravel path and gravel lawn, and the satisfying two-meter wall built at the beginning of time to belt in the house.

But here, looking so hard, was this old man with his claim. She pondered the claim. He had produced one son, Giacco, and through that line, he was arresting Gemma in her design, putting himself and his claim before everything else. "Just put me first," it was saying in its idiom.

The golden principessa was looking, too, and learning what she could from the tangling glances. Where she came from, people connected along the edges like electrical wiring or plumbing pipes. You could feel your lights go off and on, and a draining sensation or flooding, but it was hands off and purely instrumental. That's why the sex was so good: none of it was used up in collaterals. She liked what she was seeing. It pleased her eyes, even though the old man's look was like a weather sky: thundery, windy, black with shreds of blue, and muscling clouds. She could watch it forever, but her eyes slipped off target to gather data from the other face. The other face was clicking its transformations like slides in a projector. Perhaps this was something not meant for other eyes. Too late. She had seen.

The rest of the day was routine, or so it seemed. Twins came home, tired and cranky and less satisfied with what they could get, and quicker to turn on each other. Giacco had won seventy-to-one that day in a carriage race, something he didn't really care for, but nothing else was running. Alice brought home her solemn face, chastened by something she'd done that day that was shameful, the kind of thing the nonna would do, baring her teeth and streaming her words into a single missile. All she wanted to do was take her Gemma's two large hands and bury her face in them.

The fiancés were united in a bond forged of some matter that had its own secret source. And the nonna was back at her window, glaring at the empty square with the moon tipping bitter liquid onto the beer bar's glass of neon blue.

Sleeping Beauty

DESIREE WAS A roly-poly idealist. She was twelve when her mother turned to her and said: "They're going to hurt you, and hurt you bad." All Desiree heard was the word, "you," because it was a rare coin in her mother's treasury. How come? was back talk, so Desiree swallowed it down, and spun the sentence in her own air space: they're going to hurt me, and hurt me bad. Hurt me. Hurt me, and hurt me bad.

She could hardly stop the rolling, rolling in and rolling out; the words were lost to the music, or torment, but also a lullaby, a wish that her mother had made tantalizing.

But, a seed was inside the chant, and Desiree soon picked it out and ate it. The seed made its home in fertile ground, and grew into a fur. It felt like a fire, but she knew it was a fur. It was white, and she could sometimes hear it. When she opened her mouth, a piece would fly out: different shapes and sizes. She stored the remnants in the closet, under a pile of outgrown dresses and cast-offs. There was always more.

Maybe it would gel and become a cat, or spin and buckle for a sweater. For now, she wasn't choked or mortified, just a little puffier than usual. And, her mother started calling her Puffy.

It was a lark to be alive, but don't get used to it, her mother said. Life was a fuse already lit, and she showed Puffy the snuffed match kept in her pocket.

They both wore aprons, but mother's was the one with pockets.

Puffy woke up one morning and took her apron off. It was hot with the fur multiplying its hairs hour by hour. She rolled up the apron and put it with the remnants under the outgrown dresses and cast-offs.

First thing her mother said, pointing, was: "Where'd you put it?"

"I forget," Puffy said, and "it fell off," and "it's too small for me," and "I didn't like it. I want one like yours."

The difference between the mother and daughter aprons was the mother's had a top tied around her neck, and Puffy's, just a covering for the lap, tied around the waist.

The fur was boiling inside her that day.

The mother took her apron off and hung it around Puffy's neck. "Now, give me yours," she said, adding: "Why do you make me do these things to you?" Puffy fetched the apron, and her mother tied it round her daughter's full waist, pinching her.

With the aprons on, Desiree went to school. Her friend, Adele, saw the extra apron, and yanked it off. "Who did this to you! No, don't tell me," she said, putting a hand against Desiree's explaining mouth. "You're a fool to wear it. Even wearing *one*," she said, flipping its skirt, "you're a fool. But, two!"

Adele balled up the apron, and was going to toss it in the brazier, when Desiree coughed up a ball of white fur. Adele shot out a hand to catch it, but it dispersed at the touch of flesh, and floated free in the breeze, like dandelion hair.

"What's that about?" Adele demanded; but, then, the school bell rang, and lines were formed. Because of the eternal apron, Desiree went to the back, allowing six feet between herself and the last and least-desired girlie, as Desiree was always that, plus one. The little creature ahead was a hunchback, so when Desiree coughed up a second ball, the fluff fell on the flat back and stuck there, like a beautiful snowfall, until the girl threw out a scrawny arm to dust it off.

Dusting and general housework were what Desiree did during school hours. She whacked the cobwebs with her broom, swept up and down the aisles, and wiped the dust around the ABCs chalked on the board. Adele still had the big apron, and was sitting on it. She was mad, and knew exactly why. And was seething, and the seething could be heard in the aisles alongside, and by the heads of the one in front, and the one in back. The front raised a hand: "Teacher, Adele's spitting on me."

"Me, too," the one across the way said.

"I can feel it, too," said the one behind.

"What's that on your chair?" said the teacher, walking to the site of conflict, and tugging at the string as hard as she could. And, of course, the tie or string came off, and dangled like a dead snake. The teacher, giving Adele a dirty look, took the snake to the board to dangle it in front of Desiree's round eyes. "Is this one of yours, four-eyes?" she said, for Desiree wore glasses, too, and her eyes were tearing from dust and fluff.

The teacher strung the limp string around Desiree's sweaty neck, tying in front like a bow. "Now, go," she said, "and for your penance, stay in the latrine for forty-five minutes. Then, go up to the principal's office, so he can call your mother; then, go home, and stay there. No coming back until today week."

Desiree listened, but didn't get what "today week" meant, and pondered it. She raised her eyes to where Adele was sitting, shaking her head, and her fist. Later that day, Adele spent forty-five minutes in the latrine. By then, Desiree was home, taking questions about the missing apron, actually the same question, but each time, louder. "You're a stupid, stupid, stupid, and I hate you. Dry up and float away," she added, which caused Desiree to cough, and sure enough, a bolt of fur shot out, striking the mother in the eye. There it dispersed, like dandelion fluff, but more yellow than white.

At first, speechless, and then diverted by dashing the eye with a fistful of cold water; then, looking at the redness in the mirror, crying a little, and lying down with a cool cloth over her face, brought by Desiree, soaked and soaked again in a basin of ice water; then, the mother reared up and grabbed Desiree by the collar of her school blouse: "Do that again and I'll kill you dead." And, then, with a swollen eye, she fell asleep. Desiree watched at her side, stroking the mother's powerful arms, and kissing her hand, honoraria she could only offer when her mother was unconscious, or dead to the world, as she put it.

She was struck by the changing color of the eye, half open, when the cooling cloth was whisked away. It was reddish blue and sparkly, unlike the green murk of the other. The eyelashes had turned white. It was its own thing, and no match, but when the mother slapped off the cloth, freshly cooled in the basin, she rose; and, in the mirror, saw a wrathful face, and said nothing. Did she see it? The new eye was bigger, and Desiree wondered what it could see.

She was dragged off by the hair to the kitchen, because it was time for the mother to cook the mess, and she didn't like being alone. "Now, sit there, and don't let me hear a peep," she said, pushing the chunky idealist so tight into the table that her hands were caught by the razory rim. Tears formed, but the mother was busy with her pots, banging them, and running scalding water for the mess, which also took a rotten egg, a can of sardine fish, with the key thrown in as seasoning, some bluish meat, and seed potatoes, hard, dented and grubby, with some vinegar and spirits. Flame rose from all the burners and the huge pot squatted on them all, spewing from its mouth a foul smoke.

This was the night for specials, but, because of delinquency, Desiree was spoon-fed Monday-Wednesday-Friday, instead of Tuesday-Thursday cream of wheat, seasoned with eggshells and carrot tops. "Eat up," she said, the kitchen reeking, because the pot boiled until the solids burned. The gunk was spread on splintery board, to be eaten with a metal-edge ruler. The mother served herself fruit Jell-O with a candy umbrella stuck on top.

"Now, tell me what happened today that sent you home so early, my girl," the mother said, as gel cubes slid down her parched throat. The mother was always hot and dry, while Desiree was cool and moist: things stuck to her, that the mother had to scrub off with a scouring pad, leaving the girl's skin a beautiful pearl pink, when it wasn't gashed and red.

After slicing a crust of the mess; then, breaking it with her hands, before the mother took a fork to smack them ("Use your ruler, like I told you"), Desiree opened her mouth to answer, but was struck by a memory, like a dream unfolding. She remembered a baby girl, perfect in every way, wrapped in sky-blue fuzz, being handed to a pair of hands, veiny and creamy white. When the hands tightened, the baby extruded its liquids and solids, down and up and all around. That day, the bundle babe was wrapped in newspapers and set out to dry in the sun; and later, the rain, the dark night, and sparkling clear morning.

"Spit it out!" the mother said, and the dream popped. Nothing left but table and chairs.

Desiree forgot the question, and mumbled the usual formula, something Adele taught her.

"What'd you say to me, you little nothing!"

But, the mother paused to parse the mumble, which spilled out, puffed with fur.

"And, what's that?" With this, the mother fisted the puff, and opened her palm under Desiree's nose, ramming it into her mouth; but, instead of getting the new thing in, out came another ball of fluff, expiring in the air, dispersing like dandelion hairs, full gold.

"You're a hateful girl," the mother said. "And I wash my hands of you," she added, getting up to rinse off the gold fluff that was turning her hands black and blue.

"Now, see what you've done!" she screamed. "Get out of my sight."

Desiree went to the wishing well, the bathroom basin where things would drop and vanish into the underworld. Into this basin fell her tears and fur. The water spirited and spouted. A face appeared. It was the father, gone now so many years, and even eons. "Father, dear," Desiree said to the floating face.

"Yes, my child."

But now, that was the mother beating on the bathroom

door. "Let me in. Who are you talking to? Who told you, you could talk?"

And, in she flushed, and beat, beat, beat, the girl's head clunking on the sink, a well without water. "Now, wash your mouth out, and clean up this mess," she said, pointing to the drop of blood, so red and round in the pure balls of fluff.

Wednesday

Overnight, the overlooked fluffs banded together to make a baby sweater, softer than angora. This sweater was too small for Desiree, but she tried it anyway, as dawn pierced the dusty window, splintering and splaying magnificence on the sooty walls. Miraculously, the sweater expanded to fit the plump limbs and featureless trunk. The porker, as the boys called Desiree, was undeveloped, although she loved the word development, and asked herself: have I developed? closing her eyes with pleasure. What would the development bring? The sweater, a golden red, a rosy peach, a reddish coral, was snug. It was warm and alive, and it tucked and pressed until the featureless trunk was a map of rolling hills and tidy valleys; so, she took it right off, and off it came, dissolving into a dust, hanging at eye-level. With that, she closed her door. The mother rarely entered: the bedroom was scented with growth, and dense with ideas and fancies— heavier than air—but held in suspension. It was in there, where Adele came to visit, that Desiree had become the idealist. Adele could see it, but kept out of it.

Her mother's room was locked; and, on Tuesday, she was in there, making her peace with the eye, because she was stuck with it, a beauty spot, but off-balance. So, she took a dangling earring, the last present of the husband, one of a pair, its mate lost in a crack of the forest of possessions, old and new, and jamming every shell, box, cave, crater, and span in the locked room. Half of each pair was lost, or hopelessly snarled into chains, belts, strings. To balance the new eye, she fastened the earring to the favored ear, and shook it, savoring the tinkle. The room was full of things that rang and tinkled, buzzed, knocked and burbled, for the mother hated silence as much as being alone.

Balanced and firm on her feet in their tap shoes (so every step could be heard, and sometimes felt), she exited, locking the door with one of many keys. Breathless with excitement, for every day was battle day.

She met her daughter in the bathroom doorway, and pushed her in. "Gargle," she said, "and spit." An enema bag hung on the door, which Desiree covered the sight of with a ratty bathrobe. Her mother yanked off the disguise, and hung the rubbery pod and snake around the girl's moist neck. "It's your birthday," she said (it wasn't), "so, happy birthday."

In the mirror, Desiree saw the large, multi-colored eye, with white whiskers for lashes. Her mother saw her seeing, but set it aside as the first in a heap of nasties and faults.

To school, Desiree went, with the enema bag around her neck, knotted tight, with no breakfast or rousing drinks. Sent off without her glasses, so groping her way by following landmarks (a stop sign, pawnshop balls, Stop-Look-and-Listen, GIRLS, BOYS). In she drifted, through the gap in the fence, and was assaulted by an unheard-of silence. Sight of the rubber scarf and breastplate, plus the aprons, had turned the idealist into a martyr. But, furies were building under the cap of silence, and a rock was shied past Desiree's ear; then, a yo-yo, which bounced off the enema bag. Violence ceased, followed by a second heavy silence. Adele held up a referee's hand, and the school bell rang.

The teacher laughed herself sick, and was excused; the class turned over to the principal, the only man in the school, and a young one, inexperienced and naïve, overmatched by the schoolmarms, who rarely let him in, and used him as a boogeyman, until his character was assessed.

He walked in, with a goofy smile and clothes that didn't fit him. (He, too, had a mother.) First thing, he turned his back, and started writing what looked like a spelling lesson. All his

words were wrong—so wrong, even the dumbbells laughed.
But, everyone learned the wrong words. It was hard not to.
Every word he chalked was a loss, even to speech and important
signs, like dollar, cent, arrow, plus, minus, equals, dash, dot, and
to-be-continued. Their heads were spinning, as logic dropped
out. It was bad, and it was good, and the girl with two aprons
and the rubber comfort was forgotten in the bedlam.

Even after the school day was over, and every subject wrecked
(numbers, places, conduct, God and his creatures, sky and
matter), the children—for such they'd become—stared silent,
mouths agape, and hands limp. Only Adele could spot a faker,
and she marched out, pulling Desiree by the rubber cord. They
were free in the vacancy of the two schoolyards, where Adele
unknotted and untied the items, and wound them around her
own meaty elbow and hand, handing them back as tidy bundles.

Off they went to spend the day, wandering. It was the
happiest day in Desiree's life, but one: the day her daddy gave
her the umbrella, when she wanted to jump off the roof to see
if she could fly. She couldn't, and, as one thing led to another,
she never saw that daddy again, but new daddies arrived. The
first one died at her birth, or a few days after, as her mother
reported. "And do you know why?" There was a gap in the form
of causation, and the mother filled it in, making the only course
open to Fatty, as she was then called, the idealist vector, for who
would kill their daddy just with their own face? Idealism was
seeing it different, or better; reversing the sign, upsetting the
parties, which was what the teacher had done that day, but why?

That is what he didn't know, as he packed his schoolbag
with the rubbish he carried: reader, spelling chart, times
table—something had happened. He saw the two schoolgirls,
wandering, just as he was wandering, but that didn't help. They
saw him, too, and waved, because he had saved the day.

At home, the mother was gritting her teeth. The hairdresser
had dropped dead at sight of the eye. Rescue squad, police car,
chaos. Luckily, the mother had sunglasses; and, putting two and

two together, slapped them on. It was a killing glance, and she was familiar with looks that killed. Save it for later, she thought.

By the time Desiree had arrived at her doorstep, she rewound the items around her neck and waist, and the evening was peaceful. The right meal for that day served, because the mother had other things on her mind. They watched TV together, although Desiree never got her glasses back, so the screen was a glowing stamp of creamy moods and jumping lines.

That night, the mother locked them in, and went up to study the eye in candlelight, after unscrewing the lightbulbs in Desiree's room; closing the window, covering it with drapes and blinds, and turning up the radiator. "Maybe you'll lose some fat," she said, walking through what felt like a deep-pile rug, when there was no rug there. The rage she felt was almost equal to the curiosity, but the room was dark, and time short.

Thursday

Love walked in, with the principal at the door, carrying a bright bouquet of flora. They were generic flowers, so no name came to mind, even as the mother took the flowers, and looked them over. Yellow, they were yellow, and that was it. "What can I do for you?" she said to the man, tall and bone-thin; so young, that his face was smooth as a pebble. Desiree was still locked in her room, boiling hot, comatose and almost dead, so couldn't make the introductions.

"Does," he said, "a Miss Desiree—I forget her last name, but her best friend is Adele Spengler—live here? And," he continued, although he saw the mother's face blacken, and was just starting to notice the eye, "is she home? She's late for school. I'm here to pick her up. Your name, Ma'am?"

Now he was noticing the eye, and reams of analogies and precedents, from history, myth, religion and dream, flooded his mind. "How'd you get it?" he said.

"How'd I get what?"

"That peeper. Gorgeous," he said. "It looks like an oil stain gauded with sunlight on a black-tar street."

She didn't want to touch it, but felt the loving attention from this quack of a teacher's excuse for a man.

"Let me get the queen bee," she said, "and you can take her away. But, maybe you'd like some coffee and tea. I never let Desiree out of the house unfortified. She's sleeping in today."

And, truth be told, she was asleep, and no pounding or kicking, slapping or punching, rattling and shaking, screaming and tickling could rouse her—not even a glassful of water right in the face. So, the mother left her there and went to the stairs to yell down: "Come up, Sir, and give me a hand," but they tried and tried, and yet the sleeper stayed in dreamland.

"Tell you what I'll do," the principal said.

"I'll tell you what you'll do. You'll stay put, until this problem is solved."

But, the principal slipped out the door and vanished. When he arrived at school, first thing, he took Miss Spengler aside. "How do you wake a sleeper?" he said, winking and making a face, so she'd know which sleeper. He also pointed with his thumb at Desiree's desk.

Adele looked puzzled. Sleep was a new curse, or had it been self-induced?

The schoolmarms were looking for the principal, to threaten and punish infractors, so his time was up. "Tim," he said to Adele, shaking her hand. "Pleased to meet you. I saw you two on the street yesterday, wandering."

By that, Adele knew she couldn't count on this immature man, a schoolmarm's boy. She was on her own, and spent the day thinking and planning. Her mother was dead, so she was her own mother, and also mother to her brother and father. The ship was hers, but she had no authority over the Desiree household, with that fright of a mother. It was almost hopeless, this kind of case.

Meanwhile, the mother watched over the slumbering daughter; first, opening the shades, blinds, drapes and window to see a string of birds on the sill, serenading, twittering, and cleaning their feathers. It was enough to make you sick, but the commotion made Desiree's eyelids flutter, and all the birds flew in, and perched on the bed. "Get out, flies!" the mother said, punching the bed to make them jump, and out they flew.

Desiree was laughing, although eyes still shut.

Just as Adele was planning, the mother, too, made a plan. Enough was enough.

Friday

Desiree had been a love child, but the mother wasn't, and the first husband remained fond of his baby, even after the day and night in exile, wrapped in newspaper, and returned by a meddling neighbor. She was wet, frozen, and covered in print, when unwrapped like a flounder.

"She's covered in words," was the first sound out of the husband's morning mouth. He was a slow waker, fully awake only at night, but up on this day, because he sensed something awry. And, sure enough, there was no baby girl in the crib, a little hayrick lodged in the sewing room, where the wife, who'd forced the marriage with her father's shotgun, made their living running up union suits, and selling them overseas. The baby had its corner under the sewing machine, alongside the treadle, although she hadn't yet felt her mother's pumping foot.

When the paper was stripped off, the husband read the story imprinted on the tiny pink column. A photo was reversed on one of the arms. The story was about a family of cats, living in their own house, years after their protector had been carried off on a gurney. They had lived well and cleanly, once they'd dug a latrine in the unpaved basement. They were hunters and gatherers, all twenty of them. The husband made a plan, that day, to see the house, and bring the baby with him. There was a tussle, words and blows, and the husband's death, a month later, took place without ever setting foot on the cats' perfect lawn, mowed by an interfering, but cat-loving, neighbor. The story printed on the baby was the cause of death, but the coroner simply called it exposure, because the husband was rock-solid when picked up, and dead as the proverbial nail.

The love child's days were numbered, but harder to kill than the mother thought, or harder than the resources at hand. Babies are strong, and they have to be, and this Desiree was a superior baby, the offspring of a witch and a doctor, with aunts and godmothers to boot. One by one, the mother tricked the godmothers into death or exile, but the aunts held fast, looking the other way. They were the father's sisters, old maids, whose lives and savings were poured into Brother. They were fierce, and all their energy stored in the canteens carried on their backs, and in their purses. Even after the mother had stolen these canteens, the aunts had resources stockpiled, but they were tired, keeping Brother's only baby alive, through spells and medical interventions. They were all trained nurses, and rented rooms and flats a stone's throw away. In their medical bags were tinctures and potions, solvents and inks, pills and syrups. Whenever the baby was threatened by a carving knife or rusty nails, safety matches or acids and lye, the aunts were at the door with cookies. How did they know? They knew.

But, the aunts were tired out. They were old, and losing force. One of them got married and moved to Mexico, and another went to be her maid. Only one was left, and she was in a wheelchair, and hard of hearing.

Desiree was alive, true, but—unlike the cats—had nowhere to go.

Part of the story was still encrypted on her back, where she couldn't see it. No one knew it was there. Because of the work of the wheelchair-aunt, the baby survived, underfed, disciplined, weak-willed and tearful. But, a love child she was, and the aunt told her so. Adele guessed it.

Friday week
When Desiree was finally awake, more awake than she'd ever

been, she saw the mother lying beside her, watching her with the eye. She was holding her hand; but, was she holding it, or locking it down? The hand had no feeling at all, and could not release itself. When Desiree tried to yank it away, she saw her mother's glittery teeth, and the tongue stuck between them. The sight released a gasp, and a puff of fur flew out, touching the mother's nose, and sticking there. She looked, for a moment, like a rabbit, and Desiree laughed. Enraged, the mother dropped the hand in her fist lock, and hovered over the inert daughter's body. It was a thin body, because days of famine, with no school lunches or snacks at the Spengler's, or penny candy from the bums on the street to make up for the missing messes. "I won't cook for you," the mother had said, "no matter how much you beg me, and you won't cook for me." They spent their days watching TV, and slimming down. Desiree spent most of her days asleep, and the signs on the door from the truant officer accumulated, until some of them blew away.

Hearing the laugh, but not feeling the fluff that made her nose a rabbit's, the mother put the significant eye close to the daughter's. "Open up," she said, when Desiree closed her eyes.

"Open up," she said again. "And keep them open. Do you see what you've done?"

Desiree shook her head, and the fur, more of it, settled on the mother's cheeks and chin.

"Well, look again!"

Desiree was looking, and now the mother was covered in snow. "Mother," she said, or cried, "Mother?"

But, it was too late. She had said the word, and couldn't shove it back in. Choking only caused a blizzard of fur, of all colors and weights, and the mother was blanketed, but buzzing underneath like a mad bee.

It was time for Desiree to escape, and where to? And, she didn't want to go, for this was home, so licked off the fur what she could, the top layer, and combed off the rest with her fingers. Underneath, a new mother, bright and shiny.

And Adele at the door, banging. She tore up the stairs (the door was open, flaky with notices), and saw the new luminous creature. The floor was blanketed with fur and dried-up skin, but the mother was no longer mobile. She was a doll, and the two girls, Desiree and Adele, manipulating her limbs, got her sitting up, and walked her around the room.

"This is the salvation," Adele said to her friend, "although maybe not prime."

They walked the mother doll to her bedroom, but the door was locked, so they let her fold up there and, miraculously, she became paper. Someone else was working on this and, sure enough, the wheelchair-aunt was looking out her window into the hallway window of her sister-in-law, her niece's mother, the murderess. In her weak hands, a doll with pins protruding, and a noose around its neck. Now, she could die. Her work was finished; but, instead of croaking, and left there to rot, she booked a flight to Mexico to dwell there with the remains of the Hanover family, because that was the family name.

Saturday

And it was the day to return to school, which Desiree, with twigs for bones, yet still a full idealist, did. Walking, but not talking. She met the principal along the way. He'd fired the schoolmarms, and united the classes under his own pens, chalks, maps, and pointers. He would teach them, but only Desiree and Adele showed up. The classes had withered away, or grown up, because time expands and contracts in a free world.

He had learned his lesson. A=A, B=B. A word was a word, if he said so, and the girls nodded in unison, like twins. They were twins and they were orphans. The paper doll was boxed, and sent to the attic with other remains, and the girls lived with the cats, full of sadness forever after.

The seed matured. It was finished with fur, and took on its second phrase, dormancy. Under lock and key with the boxed paper doll was the edict, not quite cancelled, inactive for the nonce, yet still ringing in Desiree: they will hurt you and hurt you bad. The difference was that she never whispered it in Adele's ear, or let it rip in the classroom, where the family of three did their daily work. She kept it to herself for as long as she could, delivering it, at intervals, to herself, a token and a relic; a key, if she wanted to use it, that would open the gate of the past, which stretched to infinity, so keep it closed, I told her.

Mirella

I

MIRELLA ROSE AND found her dreams all crushed. The lemon that was the world was a brown rind stinking in the sand. A dog might come and lick it. There it sat half rolled on its ass, its luscious lips and sting turned to mush.

Hello! She reminded herself that today was Wednesday, a day reserved for the foreigners to come and learn their ancient household words at a tea prepared by Mirella, the source of these words: cake, doorbell, dishtowel. Lemon, they already knew, along with dog and cat and baby girl. Mirella was walking them through each room of the house. They were Anglican ladies with no feeling for home, but avid to know, once her doors were open, everything about Mirella's.

So Mirella strapped on her luxury gown and sat at the dressing table to squeeze out words for the tea drinkers. All English words had a funny sound in her ears: sink was one, rug and sandpaper others; even words like cream and feather and rain, that kissed across the open sea or white page, sounded like trash to her. Juicy was unpronounceable, but the tea drinkers loved to say it, when they described their trips to Mirella's home, her real home where the lemon now lay on the sand.

Today's words would be: lip, compact, balsam, and ten others as they came to her. By now her students could make childishly clumsy sentences with awkward forcings of noun and verb, and something always dangling that was their true meaning. Each new word was a pearl in these sloppy joes. This latter coupling had been given her just last week by the foreigners. They paid her in currency, but tipped with a tongue twister, a junky piece of slang or neology, left undefined.

When Mirella had written out her words on a sheet of paper, she took up her brush, and shook the curl papers out of her glossy locks. Looking in the mirror, she saw each curl distinct, a lazy loop of cultivation, for her hair was naturally straight and baby fine. Within the frame of silky gold was Mirella's face, still childish, pink from sleep, but etched in places by the turmoil of an emigre's life, which always adds two years for one, but is twice as meaningful. Her eyes were the dark blue of lower-middle Europe, and sad because her father's were; her nose was small and straight, and her mouth was—even without lipstick—a full-blown rose.

She resisted the urge to cry on her luxury gown, made to wrap a bride but not designed to send the bride so far away from home. It was bridal and maternal, it was girlish and mature, thin and warm, revealing and chaste. It was not pure white, but a white that absorbed accents from the world around it, now rosy white, now bluish, or shot with sea green, orchid, brown, and yellow. Its soft skin kindled the light and sent it warm to the eye. Soiling this robe and resigning it to the hands of experts was a crisis not meant to occur more than once in a lifetime. The robe traveled by container ship to Mirella's homeland and was unstitched, part from part, piece from piece, then steamed in glass and cooled on the snow, exposed to the sunlight and cold. Cribbled with wrinkles, the silk was stretched, cold-pressed, resewn, and hung by its hem in a dark room, laid with sweet grass. Packed up in velvet, the gown was shipped back, somewhat lighter, more absorbent and reflective, softer to the touch, yet closer to losing the will to cohere.

And thus was Mirella, this morning, gazing with mind's eye at the lemon of a world, wrapped in the once-washed robe. Robe was a word they were never going to get: it was hidden or at least shadowed by the commercial cover word: luxury. Luxury was an English word with a Latin radius, but referring in this country only to price, a number with a sign. Mirella meant to hold that word—robe—or withhold it, as these natives would say.

She rose from her vanity, closing her mind's eye to the lemon, easing around it so the tails of the robe hung free with no dangerous billow or furl, no contact, as they would say here. (All their drive stuttered over their words, causing an emphasis, where Mirella's countrymen spread their energy smoothly over their beloved words, each one laved with the tongue, pressed to the roof of the mouth, spun by the breath that was shared with the body's treasured elements.)

This was a kind of morning work and Mirella was relieved by it, wrapped in the warm but light clasp of her robe. The devilry was in the rest of the day. The kitchen was four walls stuffed with the fabrications of home: iron pots, thick crockery painted with designs, cloths, laces, and food in a hard-to-get-at state, food demanding the utmost effort of limb and imagination. A whole day could be spent tracking the food and walking it home, then to commence stirring, grinding, peeling, carving, mashing, rolling, seeding, boiling, searing, pouring, coating, ladling. Eating and drinking broke up these skeins of labor and were themselves labor, but labor expressed as a horse running, a goat bolting.

Mirella's husband, Salvatore, was sitting at the table, reading a cereal box and eating a bowl of dry flakes, drinking his milk through a straw. The machines of the kitchen were still, the air was damp. The quiet intolerable until Mirella opened her throat to pulse out the morning litany of greetings, questions, comments, and judgments. Salva didn't appear to be listening, but he came to life in this word freshet, shook himself loose from the night's bondage. He was called Al at work and his English was flat and perfect. He did mental work with his father's laboring hands. His day was automated and most of it spent on wheels: rolling in a car and around his desk on the chair's small rotors. His clothes felt rolled on and the electric razor had tiny cutting wheels. But the frame of his day was

Mirella in her luxury robe or in her wools, cottons, and silks bought in outdoor stalls three thousand miles away.

Salva's world was intact. He asked no more than to breathe the air, to roll, to eat morning, noon and night the easy-to-get-at food of this wondrous country. But he also liked the frame that his bride had made of their ranch house with its grass lawn and side house for the car. She took this frame and filled it with her dreams.

Today, though, the freshet didn't spring from her lips when Mirella's feet touched the threshold. She was so close, he could feel her breath on the top of his head, but no torrent of words that was a woman's greeting to her kitchen. It wasn't just silence, either. The mood without the torrent was severe, stiff: it shocked him and he stopped spooning the flakes into his mouth, but took a sip of milk, just in case.

Mirella passed him by and pulled out her battery of ironware.

"Not talking?" he said, feeling his way, starting in English. He spoke to the back of her head, where her golden hair was thickest and a little knotty from sleep. He repeated what he said in the other tongue, but neither evoked a response. Even the clank of metal on metal was muted.

"Beautiful robe," he said, his voice wavering as it strove to fill the sudden void.

In fifteen minutes, she had produced little cups of black coffee and pushed one toward him. He hadn't drunk coffee since he was a child and had forgotten what it tasted like, so black and gritty at the bottom of the thin cup. She drank one cup and poured another, spooning sugar with the baby teaspoon.

"Cheers," he said, tasting what was hot and vile, tarry and burned. There was nothing like it in the soft, sweet, bubbling food world where he'd made his home. He burned his tongue and soothed it with his milk. He could not catch his wife's blue eyes, downcast and smudged by yesterday's makeup.

"Not bad," he said, fool that he was. Let him roll away, and he did, hat and ruinous coat made from the slops of this country's

contempt for the tangible. She watched him with eyes boring
holes into his shoddy back. He was an amiable man, something
he learned here in the frame. He loved his days and he loved
his nights with their old-country accent and turgid tempo. In
his dreams he harmonized the differences, the carryover, the
remainder that refused to be consumed in the equation. By
morning, it was combusted and gone, and he was free to start
over. She had once loved this man, but what did that mean? He
was an export, and she was an exile.

II

The phone rang. Mirella waited till she heard it stop and start
again, and one more time, the signal to pick it up and speak as
loud and fast as she could. From that heady, drunken binge,
she sucked the gas, as these people might say, to fuel the day. It
was Mother and it was Father and they talked themselves dry,
voice over voice over voice, all on one stave. One of their own
had fathered this invention. Was "father" the right word? she
wondered, hanging up the phone, or was this more evidence
of the pace of the dissolving universe. Father was turning into
something else; it was diffusing; it was not just the man whose
stout plenitude, sameness and singularity kept her girlish feet
planted on solid ground, but it was his station and his orbit.

I am neither what I was, nor what I am. This was today's
headnote of pain and rather than let it ache unrequited, she
opened the door to the birdcage, after removing the cloth.
The bird, as always, was awake, its stern gaze meeting Mirella's
through the wire frame of its home. "Good morning," she said
and he returned the compliment, shifting weight over his feet.
The bird, colored to burst like flame in the rainforest, was called
Henry. He was a hundred years old, if anyone remembered his
age, and had three names. He was Henry to the doctor, now
defunct, whose grieving daughter sold him to Al. The Italian
couple was warned to let this name stand. The tea ladies knew

the other name for bird, but Henry was a bird, and not that other thing. There were no such Henries in Mirella's homeland. Dogs and cats, yes, but no domestic birds of this kind, so Henry had his own domain in Mirella's mind and she begrudged him nothing of it. He liked housework and followed Mirella into each room to observe its daily progress. Sometimes he helped, pulling a wrinkle clean, or fanning the paddles of the blinds till they lay flat. He was a heavy bird and preferred rest to exertion.

Birds are not sensitive, so Henry detected nothing of Mirella's mental wound. He had his language, she had hers, and they were both loners sharing a habitat. When Mirella, her dusting and vacuuming, polishing and sponging complete, sat down to finish her word list, Henry stepped into his cage to watch from there. As Mirella wrote, she whispered and whistled the words, unaware that Henry was learning them in this degraded form. His word list was growing, but he did not use this language, he stored it, just as he had stored the times table, the mysteries of the rosary, radio commercials, and the ticks of the clock from his last home. Now he had a foreign language, sticks and bones, because each word was garbled.

Rent money, insulation, ashtray, wax: these Mirella tried out in the air of the kitchen. Firedog, union suit. Now, she couldn't help it: she was laughing. Banana boat, fish and chips. The bird laughed. Neither of them had heard this sound before. Mirella stopped writing and Henry shifted foot to foot. Mirella needed one more word.

It was only then that she realized that she was starting from their lexicon and making up hers from its poor signal. The color drained from her face and even the lemon shrunk down to yellow foot and toes. Only then did she see that a drop from Salva's unfatted milk had made its way along the tabletop, along a wrinkle in the cloth, and was hanging from the edge, stretching its tongue to unite with the luxury robe's silvery lap. Time stood still. Mirella waited, Henry bit a bar of his cage, his tongue protruding like an animal from its shell, but then the drop resealed itself, a tensile ball, and there to stay until the cloth welcomed it back into its starched and lonely weft.

But no. Mirella was up. The sudden disturbance of the air broke the bond and the drop landed, a mere point of spit. She spread it with the toe of her slipper, resolving to put the luxury robe in cold storage, and there was the last word of the day, whatever it really meant and to whomever. She snaked the smooth skin off her shoulders and let it flow to the bed, pooling there in waves like gleaming mercury. She dressed herself in a tight gray suit, clear stockings and black pumps whose soles and heels still bore the cobbler's thumbprints. They were from a great foreign house and never, if they lived ten lifetimes, would the Protestants learn the names of the multitude of their intimate parts. She was ready.

III

The lemon lay on the small of its back braced on its knob. Next to it were the knife and silver plate with lace doily. Bowls of flowers here and there, stout and stalky, smoky and spiced. The water was boiling and the tea bag (because these ladies liked their tea weak) ready. On the table in the salon were a whole cake and a pineapple, candies wrapped in noisy paper, and an artillery of flatware, instruments the tea ladies still could not identify, because no shade of such words existed even in the roots of their language. They didn't use or touch these silver sticks, spears and tongues, but were content to eye them. One such implement was designed to pierce the thick hide and delicate vessels of the lemon crescents, but they used their fingers, even after being shown. Mirella liked to spoil them with lemons, four or five, all cut and splayed like the innards of a wet flower. That word was almost the same to them as to her, and once she heard theirs, hers sounded as if the fruit acid were gunked with sugar, so she used a different word, a generic.

Henry was perched on the back of a kitchen chair, poised to

see the preparations. Sometimes his curiosity, whetted by the strange energy of these days, led her to point to the cage and, by that, to force him in—and not just in, but covered, silenced, shamed. Their eyes met across the empty space and Henry showed his keeper a closed beak and half-closed eyes, then he buried his feathery head in his shoulder. That she understood, so he was left free, with an extra: she didn't close the kitchen door when the boiling water was poured into the pot to be placed on the spirit flame. She left the door open, not just ajar, for a pair of eyes to see but not be seen.

For here they were, the Anglican ladies in their hats and gloves, and Henry felt the excitement in his undercarriage: the voices so familiar when they begged permission to remit in his native tongue what they couldn't say in his keeper's. He watched out of the corner of his eye and kept his straight glance on the kitchen clock. He knew they came at three and stayed till five, and he resolved to stay awake.

IV

There were four tea ladies and all were present. They drove together in a ten-year-old sedan with plush seats, spotless inside and out. The boss was Ann Mary, single and majordomo at a small insurance firm. She sat in the front seat, driven by Catherine Mary, her married, baby sister. In the back were Mary Jo, a commercial artist by training, and Mary T., sister of their pastor and his homemaker these twenty years.

In rushed, with their coats and powdered faces, a turbulence of spices, flowers, smoke, and spirits. Mirella held her breath and offered her cheek, first this, then that. She would open a window in a trice if the bird began to cough. But no: the kitchen air resisted the cloud moving its way; its own air was denser, lying in sullen pockets, laden with oil, gristle, and acids, so the bird breathed freely out of its holes.

Every girl in her country was named Mary, so the surprise

of this quartet of Anglican Marys was a fresh joke to Mirella, every time good and whole, and getting her through the ordeal of hanging coats and dripping scarves and greetings crude and nervy. "You go too far," she'd said the first time, but the words were lost in the blunt force of Mirella's contracted face. They got it, yes, all four, older and younger, and learned to let the teacher speak first and guide them with a prompt they repeated, embarrassed, of course.

These Marys every time lost all their contours, not to mention their tribal pecking order, in the company of their language teacher, whom they dared not address by forename or in the second-person singular. She was, by rights, a foreigner in their polity, but in *her* home, they were scarcely human, let alone women, some married, some employed, some with children of their own and domains three times the size of this one. Some enjoyed the transition and arrival; one did not; one was grateful to have something to do on her every fourth Wednesday.

There were two couches in the teacher's salon with the tea set on a glass table in between. Ann Mary sat by herself, eye to eye with the Signora. Catherine Mary sat on a hassock and two Marys flanked the couches at each end. Tea, lemon, cookie; spoon, cake, cup. Doctor, lawyer; up, down, faraway, and they were off.

Written on a sheet of boudoir paper was the row of today's words, each one capable of propagating more. Mirella remembered how laughter filled her throat at the thought of transposing onto her native scale—not these rotten eggs and stinking fish, but the lies and deceits hidden in them. Try it, she said, and she did. First, she said their word, her mouth flowing with saliva. They repeated their own word, but one had acquired a foreign accent: the baby sister, who turned back her own word reshaped by Mirella's mouth and tongue. This was not new, but since they recited together, as four voices in unison, this time— distracted by a fifth voice coming from the kitchen—Catherine Mary skipped a beat and out, in syncopation, came the word now strange to all. The woman blushed in shame. She was the slowest, married for love, with a new baby every other year. Pregnant again, and sick, she attended against doctor's orders and only to chauffeur her sister.

Truth was, she had never learned her own language that well: it was a loose and unreliable appendage to her pretty face and comely figure. Married to an ethno-American, who called her Chichi, using a southern softness, and surrounded by children, five and under, she had slipped from under her sister's thumb, except for their monthly outing, whose design was for her to learn something and commemorate the stiffish family into which she'd been born, the runt. She liked everything and everybody, but lived fearful of commanding structures: family, the episcopacy, citizenship, mortality. Speech Lesson, which is what her husband called it, was a relief because she just sat there like a log or chittered like a monkey, with someone else to do the thinking and the transfer from that to words.

Her reseeded body, though, was becoming more receptive, so natural to hear and learn her own tongue a different way.

Mirella heard the bastardy. Her ear cupped it. The bird in the kitchen, thrilled to be included, repeated it, trying it out along a scale, one pitch close to theirs, all the way up to a screech only a pedigreed bird could force. But, alert to the silence surrounding his litany, he dropped to the floor and tracked westward to just under his cage, vaulting by stages to where he could reinsert and swing the door shut, close his eyes and bury his head. He was the animal and the guilt hit him first.

In the chamber of her skull, Mirella reviewed today and the parade of days since arriving by ship on this continent, whence she'd brought a husband, the language, and a gown. What had this gown been called? She called it forth to her mind's eye, but no title arrived with it. It was a bright mental image, a vision with no claim check.

The pregnant Anglican needed to use the restroom, and sought it with her eyes. "Prego?" she said, and Mirella pointed a finger toward the closet with sink and toilet called "lavette." With the embarrassment gone, Ann Mary and the teacher locked eyes and worked their way down the list: commanding officer and lieutenant, with the other Marys mustering in. The drill's increasing sharpness and speed caused the vision to fade. As it dissolved, Mirella found the key to the drawer where it was kept with other garments of its kind, and slipped it back in. The baby sister was back, her hands washed and dried and her pretty cheeks pinched for color. The comfort station had offered her, and the cells inside her, a moment of wordless bliss. Mother and baby, her sister said, and Mirella repeated it. Baby was a word, even in Mirella's stringent ear, whose A stretched to infinity. She said it with ease, tucking the long E tightly inside itself—not the way her countrymen would string it to the moon—but the B's were still off-kilter to the Anglicans' ears. "In our culture," the elder sister said, "we release our babies," but she meant our consonants, "after a quick embrace."

Henry, head buried in feathery shoulder, knew the word baby, although he'd never had any of what were called, in his species, chicks. Chick, he could say, and said it, but to them, it was just bird noise—not a song or a garbled word or a playful chirp—just an audition of head garbage. Could be digestive, if he'd been fed, which set Mirella to wondering: had he been? The morning had passed in an orderly sequence leading up to this, but no allowance had been made for the pea-grain he ate morning, noon, and night. He liked cake, so Mirella, breaking off a chunk from her own plate, gave it to the youngest pupil, mother-to-be. "Prego," she said, pointing with her head toward the kitchen.

The bird liked pretty girls. He'd known them here and there in his long life, and they liked him, too. He allowed a hand to penetrate his holding and to drop on the fouled newsprint the cake chunk. Sometimes he kicked these gratuities out of his holding, just to show them, but today was a meatless day; in fact, it was a fast day, so he welcomed the mite. A finger was stroking his sideburn, sliding down to his scarf and sweater and up to his chin. With one snap of his beak, he could amputate that digit, but living as he had been, with humans, these many decades, he played out his impulses in dreams, in conversation, in thought. In sum, he always took a minute before discharging. He grew and he came to know himself, and not just to know what he liked!

Such peacefulness pervaded that the loss (or exchange) of the thirteen-word singlets and a couple was felt not as minus but as plenitude. The words went back and forth, in one language and out the other, folded into utility sentences, or just left to fade in the air. Even the cells multiplied in peace, the struggle between parasite and host eased by the way one minute swam into the next in bilingual agape. After a while, the sludge (union suit, ashtray, rent money) was set aside for word-hearts: after baby came water, lion, sand; then vision, goddess, tuning; and after that, benefit, monk, symbol, but that turned it a different way and time was up.

The Marys were wrapped in coats and scarves with each a hat. The minor Marys always took in more from the lessons, because mute and undemanding. They would soon master all their teacher had allowed them to learn, and go beyond, because mastery would germinate by growing fruits, flowers and nuts, as union and reaction, synthesis and feedback sucked binding fluid from the deep well of the mind. Even the bird was sated and slept well that night.

That night, Mirella, clad in the robe, awaited the arrival of her mate. He'd had one of his frictionless days, riding like an air car through the stations of his adopted world. His work had cost him nothing and he reached his door fuller than he'd left it, augmented by the two smoothly fitted envelopes. He compressed himself a little as he shucked the world envelope for the house skin, but there she was upon the couch, shiny as a planet, lemon-yellow hair and cream dressing. He stepped

208

JEAN MCGARRY

inside, slowing and still slower, pushing at the air. The house had filled with dreams.

Narcissus

WHAT HE LEARNED from his father was to hold back, and he held back everything. His mother loved every driblet of fluid and solid, but received only from the outline, and mostly from the back, when her eyes were free to dart and roam. From the back, he was a boy of few moving parts, integrity was all, and that meant from the crown of his head to his heels, he was one piece. A certain stiffness went with it, and routine. Each day, he clothed himself—start to finish—with the same set of movements, unhurried, majestic in tempo.

His mere presence would lower the temperature in a room, as he entered, not soldierly, but imperious, eyes out, no part of him touching object or flesh. The air itself contracted, giving him a margin.

His mother dressed him from the earliest moment, when his baby legs uncurled and his little feet could bear the compression of leather and laces, in suits, a suit in appropriate color and fabric for each season. The baby clothes were professionally cleaned and preserved in the cedar chest, each item wrapped in tissue and tied with a ribbon. He was, from the earliest age, immaculate. Toilet trained before he could walk. He only needed to be shown where and when to relieve himself. "Don't hold back," his mother said, but he didn't understand, and to the distant day, release and evacuation were rare.

***

He listened for his father's feet, the smothered and regular beat of leather on concrete. He listened hard, and knew when to position himself under the bay window, training himself to trace backward all the way to the slam of the car door, every single footfall. There were twenty-eight, never twenty-seven or twenty-nine, but one through five were inaudible, until, by estimation (his eyes squeezed shut, as were his fists), he detected five, four, and imagined the first three, bobbing with each inaudible drop and roll. Was he acute enough to detect the rolling of heel to toe? He wouldn't allow himself to look, but caught his eyes tracking the gait when the shoes entered the kitchen, where he would run to stand next to his mother, or behind her. Don't look, he told himself, but he had, and now he knew his father's gait, inside or out, was the same.

***

He lined up his pencils in ranks, the colored pencils and the lead. He liked to use every bit of pencil and had a collection of brass jackets. When he couldn't scratch with them, he took a jackknife and decapitated the wood and shaved the rubber. These jackets he lined up on the windowsills, like bullets.

***

On Fridays, the family had fish (frozen cod cakes or cod sticks, breaded fluke or trout), French fries and frozen peas. On Saturday, a steak, and on Sunday, pot roast or baked chicken. Dinner was at six sharp, but ready at four thirty, because his mother used her afternoon, so long and boring, to cook. By dinnertime, a series of reheatings might result in soggy or burned meat, and the mother would absent herself in tears, leaving a pot of congealed corn or carrots on the stove, and the scorched pan in the oven for the family to serve itself. While scraping out the mashed potatoes, or prying the chops from the fiery pan where they had shrunk and stuck, they could hear the mother's choking sobs, saying not a work to her or each other. If ingredients were too far gone, the boy would slather sandwich bread with peanut butter, and his father would mix himself another drink, retiring to the den with his paper. The boy worried that his father was hungry, and hunger could lead to rage, so he would prepare a plate of Ritz crackers with German mustard, smears of Braunschweiger sausage, with a dill pickle. The father would snack while he read, and Terrence would quietly close his mother's door and step into his own room to sharpen and line up his pencils for the night's assignment. He would spread this work out, refreshing himself by a look out the window, or a walk downstairs to see what Western his father was watching, sit on the hassock for a minute or two, and return to the next segment (math problems, spelling, an act of a play, the Battle of Waterloo, diagramming a complex-compound sentence on graph paper). If the sentence veered too far into the edge, a fresh page and a redraft. Eventually, the mother would emerge, red-eyed and pale, and enter his room to drape her cool arms around his neck and rest her head on his. He continued to work. The three of them completed the evening—weekday or weekend—with a selection of family fare: a variety show, half-hour comedy or hour-long mystery, a documentary on war, or the West, or a foreign country. They all went to bed at the same time. His mother went first, he followed, and his father turned out the lights. A goodnight kiss was blown—sometimes only he heard it, because his father didn't want his wife to dawdle. Her whole life, he liked to say, was dawdling, but not when he was home!

***

He rode his bike, he drove with the family to the swim club; on holidays, the family went to a restaurant with starched tablecloths and napkins, and a room so dark, his mother sometimes fell asleep with her fork still in her hand. His father had two mixed drinks and talked to the waitress—always the same one, an old-timer—about defunct restaurants they both remembered, their menus, staff, and what year they went under. These were the times Terrence heard his father laugh. Even his mother would look alive, stop chewing or sipping, wake up, if she'd fallen off. His mother had a beautiful smile, a little wide and stretched, but beautiful, with her small, white teeth, and light blue eyes. He had her face, from the nose up, but his father's square build and thin mouth. His father did not answer questions, not even questions about whether he liked his meal.

***

When he was old enough to push the mower (barely), Terrence worked with his father outside their ranch house. They planted bushes and mulched the flowerbeds, fertilized the fruit trees and set out traps for small animals and invasive bugs. They worked all day Saturday. On Sunday, they drove with the mother to the Lutheran church for a service that lasted all morning. He heard nothing, although he was confirmed and memorized the routine. God the father, the son—not to mention the gangly windbag of a minister—were less real to him than the brass jackets of his pencils, or his father's weekday tread. This was the beginning of the treacherous time, when even these reliable things started to twist, invert, or mutate into dark blossoms.

***

He had already told a girl he loved her. He had pulled down her pants and stuck a hand down, then up her round-collared blouse. But when she cried, he drove her home, walking her up to the porch steps, but no farther. He lingered in the dark, watching the lights come on in the upstairs bedroom. He wiped his hands on the dewy grass and used his handkerchief to dry them. Then, he started to cry, but stopped, when he pulled up the clutch.

Her name—he couldn't always remember it, and had to run through the classroom roll to where her last name fell between Laughlin and Niffen. Her name was Merry, and he fell asleep that night with his fist nestled near his lips and his sheets soaked. He remade the bed, while it was still dark, and buried the slick sheet at the bottom of the hamper, then rethought, and hung it on the line, waiting till the end of the day to stuff it back in the hamper. His mother never looked out the back windows, and it wasn't a washday.

The next night, he chewed one of the metal jackets, to mark the event, until it was flattened, and laid a BB on it. Merry could only go out "with boys" on Saturday. Friday was Girl Scouts, Sunday was family night. She was not to go steady until sixteen, or later. Her father, whom Terrence had met for a handshake and offer of a smoke, had a body shop, and his hands were tarry, but he draped them around his daughter's shoulders, kissing her on the forehead. When she was released, and he led the way to his own father's car (a Buick of the latest model, with all the options), he couldn't speak until his heart stopped racing. Merry slid across the seat next to him. He'd asked her not to wear that stale perfume. He recognized it as coming from one of the glass jars on his mother's vanity. His mother received perfume for Christmas and her birthday, and she had them all.

Merry was to take everything, to extract from him, if necessary, all he held back. Her skinny, undeveloped body was his playground, but also his battlefield. He touched, he patted, stroked, sucked, poked, licked, bit, and pushed into her tight canal what his father termed the "member." No matter how cool the night, even frigid, he was soaked in his own sweat, but he wanted more, and drove the depleted girl to a sub shop on the other side of town to feed her and replenish her fluids, and his, and demand from her an account of persons of interest: her field-hockey coach, the math teacher, her brother's friends, Charlie and Ed, who dropped by the house and even ate supper there. Did they look at her, or dare to talk? Who else had she met, and why was her mother buying her such tight sweaters? How had the silky underpants gotten torn? To never wear the padded bra, and go back to the training bra that looked as if a scarf had been knotted and twisted around her chest. Then, they went back to park behind the Lutheran church, on its unlit parking lot. She had to be home at eleven, but starting out at seven or seven-thirty, he got what he needed until the next Saturday.

One Saturday, she had the flu, but he was allowed to sit by her bed and read the homework assignment, *Billy Budd*, and outline a new geometric proof. He was in the bed, touching her hot, gritty skin when her mother opened the door. "Get off her!" she said, and he was on his feet, smoothing his hair. "Get out of here now. Go home," she said. "What's the matter with you?" he heard her say to Merry, too sick to do more than whimper.

It was a weekday, and the father was still at the shop. Terrence had to think fast. He waited in the kitchen, listening to the sharp footfalls above his head. He emptied two ice trays into a plastic pitcher and carried it upstairs, handing it to Merry's mother, with a glass. The sick girl was already asleep, and even snoring. He saw her crusted lips and nose, the purple smudges under eyes. Her hair was damp at the roots. He lifted her up and signaled to the mother, who filled the glass and held it up to her lips. Then, he took his handkerchief and dipped it in the pitcher, tied up a few ice cubes, and laid the cloth on her forehead, while she rested against his arm.

When he returned to the kitchen, the mother had fixed them both a cup of tea, and offered some packaged cookies.

"I don't like that, you know," she said. "How can a person trust you, Terrence?"

He didn't answer right away. He drank his tea, refused the saucer of Oreos, and as the mother was opening the front door to release him, encased her in his strong, young arms, pressing a long, thoughtful kiss on her lips. She shook him hard, then they kissed again, and he left.

From then to the last year of high school, he had Merry on Saturday and the mother on Friday afternoon, when the girl was at practice. He favored the mother, because she was as hungry and exacting as he, and even on the day when the father arrived home early, his wife coolly called downstairs that she had such a headache, and would he run to the drugstore for some Alka Seltzer? There were two close calls that day, as the brother was already watching TV in the basement. "Is Merry at home?" Terrence yelled down the stairs, on his way out.

***

He took another girl to his prom, a beautiful daughter of a family friend, even though the family had no friends. She'd been a neighbor when Terrence was in first grade. Then, the father was sent overseas, returning in time for Barbara's senior year. She had a French accent, and clothes never seen in an American high school: sheaths of soft, stretchy fabric, high-heeled Mary Janes, and tights of puce, fuchsia, and violet, striped and dotted. She told him the names of all the colors in French and in English. She showed him the labels on her dresses and skirts. Her bra and panties were black, pink, and navy blue. He chewed on the silk panties, wrecked them, but she only laughed. She had a drawerful.

His mother wept as his father photographed the girl in a black satin, one-shoulder gown. He had found a madras cummerbund and tie, and they were set apart from the mob of jitterbuggers, and crowned king and queen. Merry did not attend, although her brother's friend had offered to take her. That night, she was having her period, was the word at the gym, decorated with golden cupids and red hearts (it was February 14), and not in the mood. No one believed it.

He didn't drink or smoke, so the mass of pain and punishment meted out upon the pileup on Rte. 44, as the caravan of seniors tore off for the after-party: arrests, expulsion, stripping of prizes and honors, demerits and marks on the transcript, along with injuries and death, was something for him to consider, as he was inducted that Monday to serve on the newly created honors board, and decided that day to make the law his career, although he was gifted in everything and had a perfect high-school record. When his father heard about the melee—a tragedy, the newspaper called it—he struck his son, a first, because Terrence refused to say whether he'd shared in the whisky found in the girls' washroom, one bottle smashed over the sinks. Like his father, Terrence had stopped answering questions, even when it was his father who asked them. He returned his father's gaze, cheek flaming and blood dripping down his chin, with one so malignant, that mother, father, and only child were up all night, trying to repair the damage. First, they had to stop the mother from attacking her husband; then, dose her. She lay on the couch while father and son "had it out," as they referred to it later, although very few words, and fewer blows, were exchanged. Terrence and his father went to an out-of-town showroom that weekend, and Terrence drove home in a used, cherry Triumph, with a rebuilt engine and black leather seats. The father liked to borrow it, but waited until Terrence offered. Once, he took his wife for a spin. She talked about it for days, and wanted to tell her son that he was the one to "blame" for "reigniting the torch" in a peaceful, but humdrum union. Terrence told her to go wash her mouth with soap, but he was grinning when he said it.

***

College passed without a ripple. There were four girlfriends, sailing and tennis, and solitary, controlled experiments with drugs: hash, mescaline, acid, and cocaine. Then, a year before earning his J.D., Astrid Bayh, a fifth-year graduate student in art history, strode into his life. She had eyed him at a reception for her father, ambassador to Japan, and traveling with an exhibit of screens and swords, making its first appearance on American soil. He was drunk, and his daughter spoke for him that night, from notes written by an aide. Between sentences (she was a skilled actress), she swept the room, until Terrence, or someone like him, was found in the crowd. This rarely happened, but it had become a sport and a stay against the tedium of assisting the alcoholic, or her mother, a poet and expert in Byzantine art. Bayh was, like Terrence, an only child, but, in her own family, she was first among equals.

Terrence, who'd attended because of a fleeting interest in maritime law, felt the gaze before he identified the eyes. His face, normally cool and moist, was irradiated. Blood rose and congested. Even his lips swelled. He licked them, for the heat was dry. Others noticed the salient from podium to standing room. A couple swiveled to look at the target of this probe, because everything about this speaker had struck the eye. She was six feet tall and heavy-boned, with a gleaming cap of reddish-black hair, and a hawk's profile. Her bright eyes— black, blue?—were magnified behind lenses that spangled in the lights. She wore a peacock-blue dress with tight sleeves that opened, and flowered over her hands; a neckline exposing skin so white it seemed frosted. She was built like an archaic Kora— massive and columnar.

When the speech was over, he squeezed past the clapping notables and flacks, and was met by an usher, who opened the enameled portal, then stopped him with a gloved hand. She was behind him, and then in front, blocking the door. Her hand was out to shake his, but "where do you think you're going?" is what she said. Her parents appeared on either side of him, and were introduced at the start of what was to be a long night.

To be chosen had never been his wish; neither was it to choose. He'd chanced upon law-school escorts and bedmates. Proximity on the campus, or in the eateries and bars, was always enough. There was a range of acceptability, and nothing lasted very long, just long enough. He was first in his class, clerking and editing, teaching himself how to cook, and day trading with the nest egg inherited from his mother's mother. This sum was in both their names, and the only secret kept between them and the brokerage house. He kept half in his own bank account; it was his working capital and his future. He'd doubled it, then lost half of the gain, and now played the market when he needed to, but when he played, he sat in front of the screen for the full trading day, rising pale and depleted in gain or in loss. He wanted to stop, but what would he put in its place?

The ambassadorial night was divided into three parts, two of them shared with the parents. There was a dinner of raw rarities, flown that day from the Siberian coast, and enough beer and sake to send the ambassador to his room with the help of two ushers. Prof. Bayh insisted on a tea ceremony, and the parties removed to the garden house for a lengthy protocol, resulting in grainy bowls of bitter tea. He didn't like tea, but he drank a bowl, listening to the plinking instrument and ceremonial babble. When Miss Bayh pushed her glasses onto her head, he saw that her eyes were green, fringed by sticky lashes. That piercing gaze was the power of the refracting lenses. He relaxed his neck and back, unused to sitting on his own legs. He could barely rise; and, half-buckled and groaning, was escorted to the embassy temple, and from there, Miss Bayh led him by elevator and tunnel to her car, a vintage Firebird.

And, away they went. She reached for his hand, which he yielded, closing it in her fist with its razory gems, set high in their prongs. "You're hurting me."

"Damn right I am," she replied, stopping short to jolt him.

"I'm getting out of the car at the next light," he said.

"Why don't you get out now?" she said, foot to the floor, then braking, slipping into a parking space, and unsnapping her belt. The reward was his.

They woke up in her bed, the highest he'd ever slept in. You had to jump to the ground. For a heavy girl, she was surprisingly

light and agile, finding in him unknown needs to satisfy in
quirky and original ways. When she began her day, washing
and combing, dressing in yesterday's dress, she applied layers,
sprays, lines, colors, and powders to a wide, pale face like a farm
girl's. When she finished, and turned to him, blankets pulled
up to his chin, the face was, once again, noble and serene, lit by
the spangling lenses.

She asked for the items on his day's agenda and got them,
telling him that, while the ambassador was in town, they would
dine with him and Prof. Bayh. He felt his brain swept clean of
reference points. He knew his day had qualities and quantities,
but he couldn't deliver these to this woman, whose name never
seemed to fit her—nor did any other. She satisfied him with
primacy and generality. She knew herself, and would come to
know him, but her contours and what was within them were
beyond him. For the moment!—he told himself, dressing after
her departure. His clothes were balled on the floor; they felt
damp. Slowly, as he drank the coffee left for him, he assembled
his day with the help of a calendar. He barely recognized his
own handwriting, but arrived, clothed and dry, at his first class.
He'd been raised a Lutheran and remembered a few hymns and
prayers which he turned over in his mind to relax and warm up.
By noon, he was himself. He called his mother and planned a
surprise home visit, starting that night.

***

As he entered, his mother, teary-eyed, wrapped her arms around
herself to keep her embrace brief, the way he liked it. She was
speechless. Although the university was only fifty miles away,
her son rarely came home, and when he did, there was a warning
and time to book the cleaning service, send out the rugs, and
buy a new appliance or chair, a "conversation piece," because,
although he liked sameness, he loved the beautiful things that
only he and she had the taste to choose. But, nothing was new,

JEAN MCGARRY

and an unaccustomed layer of dust and grime caught his eye, nearly turning him back.

She invited him to sit on the couch, but he raced up to his room, and fell on the bed. When she came to the door, he pointed to the shades, which she pulled; and to the door, which she closed. He released a long-held, belly breath, and slept.

In his long absence, something had happened. The father had been treated for cancer of the tongue, and the mother had lost gall bladder and one breast, which had been replaced, but was slightly larger than the real one, a deformity she exaggerated, letting it sour her native cheer and contentment. The sour note, first unperceived by the father, gradually eroded his crust of confidence. He didn't ask himself what was different "in the home," he just felt it, and carried it around like a rotten fruit, aware of a bad smell and something hard just inside the skin of the chest, sometimes at the temples. She was too insignificant to be the cause of an event that he was still graphing—when it came, went, and was most unendurable. He started adding an extra drink to his nightly ritual. He went to bed earlier, and some nights, right after supper. She spent the evenings, after he retired, standing in front of the full-length mirror, and turning slowly, side-to-side, trying new bras and different drapings of scarves. She started favoring the one side, upon which the new, nippleless mound was planted. Soon, the father was being treated for migraine headaches and sciatica. The mother thought her heart was affected by the larger, heavier breast.

When Terrence woke up, it was early evening, and he listened to the sound of his father's padding feet. This was inaudible from the bedroom, but Terrence had staked himself by the window, half-hidden by the drape, and tapped the regular footfalls, seized—before the father reached the door—by a thought of Astrid. This thought was like a fuse lit at the feet and firing his brain. He tapped on the window, and his father stopped dead.

***

Bayh had no trouble finding the house. Her mind was grooved with the minutes of the compass, and the swirling suburban roadways of his development were through-lines with no cul-de-sacs. She was there with the help of the law-school registry. She sat on the couch long enough to see her man free of his backing, a hunk of old cardboard, and now riddled with broken lines. The parents had little to say, and nothing to offer.

He moved the little he had (a screen, checkbook, and four suitcases of clothes and shoes) to her flat by week's end. The ambassador flew back to Tokyo, but Prof. Bayh stayed behind to direct her daughter's dissertation on the Empress Theodora. To Terrence's now idle gaze, they were one person, a body and shadow. Prof. Bayh had a permanent place in her daughter's stateside home.

The two heads were bent over images of mosaics in huge volumes that only the mother could borrow. The heads were aligned in Astrid's black-tiled kitchen, where they cooked feasts whose elements Terrence could only imagine: meats rank with smoky spices, bathed in sauces so rich, his stomach turned, just smelling them, or looking into a pot. The flat was alive with a weave of warring smells and bubbling fat. Seated at the table, Terrence's lips and tongue were assaulted at each of the receptors: sweet, sour, bitter, and salty. He was crazed by the food, but stultified, too—tense and drowsy. The meals were preceded by heavy, sweet drinks, and accompanied by three colors of wine.

He had never been so hungry, or so replete, so bloated or hollow. He was worked and working. Table talk was of Byzantine art, unless the father had issued an SOS, calling Mrs. Bayh to the phone, where she was hooked in for hours, and Astrid retired to her study, leaving Terrence to face the hot and savory dishes alone.

His way of dressing was altered: his simple trousers and pale shirts were torn into squares and used by the maid to dust the shelves and polish the tile floors. Astrid had her own clothes made by an out-of-town dressmaker, with a dress form for each of her clients: a roomful of mannequins, as Astrid told him, using herself to block the headless torsos facing south, north, east, and west in a chilly room, with names inked across a breast. There was a family member a tailor, and Astrid herself, with the professor's help, pinned a swath of thin leather around each leg and arm, mapping with silk neck to groin, front and back, until the fabrics were his measure. Tightly fitted wool pants with pinstripes, gray and black linen shirts, and hand-knitted sleeveless sweaters, along with military-looking jackets, were returned. Their construction took very little time, and Terrence went back to the classroom, mid-semester, in a new livery. His hair was thinner and lighter—more like down than human hair—and his face had a permanent glow—not a tan, but a luster darker than the skin of hands and feet. He'd never been happier than in those days of becoming and adaptation.

He was made for Bayh, as she told him as often as he needed to hear it. He was riddled with insecurities. He imagined himself with a heart like a dried fruit, where his blood stalled, and his brain like a dry bulb, its leafage dusting his eyes and stuffing his nose. His mouth was dry from interminable osculation. He barely slept for the demands placed on whatever of his could be held, scratched, bitten, sucked, and inserted. She also said he was one of a kind, but the phrase confused him. Was he one, or the kind? He checked his license to reconnect to his birth date and dimensions, and the fact that one eye was brown and the other blue. There'd be trouble, and eventual blindness, with the blue eye. It ran in the family as a recessive trait. No one was supposed to know, but Astrid, who loved the blue eye, gazing at it with her head rotated, so his view of her was off-center. They were as loving as they were adapting. One becoming something evermore fitted for the other.

***

The professor returned to her husband when he was hospitalized, after a car crash, with a broken back, crushed lungs, and ruptured spleen. The ambassador was driving his own car, and ran it into a cement stanchion in the pre-dawn dark. He was wearing his glasses and no seat belt, and lived for eight days. He was flown back in a military plane with his wife and dog. Astrid met them at the airport. The obsequies were held in a Shinto shrine. The American president and his wife, the secretary of state attended, along with the hierarchs from cognate or friendly embassies. Astrid wore deep mourning; her mother, a white kimono with fantastic birds and trees, stitched in green.

Terrence used the opportunity: grief and a string of ceremonies, to reflect. He was two months from commencement, a bondsman, but also more than he was. Adopting the Bayh order of things and of people placed him at a distance, and above his teachers and peers, but he knew this aura stopped at the boundary of his person and their dwelling. There was a moat of fear and respect—beyond that, just the ordinary world.

He had begun to find Astrid Bayh's attention repulsive: there was too much of it, and a monotonous evenness: all of his parts were the same to her, and conjugation was a long and elaborate ritual, always enacted step-wise, with evenly spaced bundles of passion, like beads on a string. His mate laced him like a vine, squeezing in sequence like a boa keyed to a metronome. Within this embrace, he was paralyzed, webbed in pleasure that was smooth and continuous. The only variable was a richer scent that ranged from blossom to vegetable to rotting meat to ambergris. At that point, he was usually asleep.

Their food had given him a sharper outline, strength in his chest, arms, and legs, but a thicker neck. When he looked in the mirror, he saw that his face was blurred. Already, the bad eye was growing a lace.

He packed a few of the remaining original clothes, and wore some, leaving by the back door.

Where to go? He'd never return to the ailing parents. If he

did, life would begin over again, with the father just a shred of
his former self, and the mother locked in misery. He had no
friends, and his only money was tied up in risky, untouchable
ventures.

There was nothing to do but walk. First, he walked to the
law school, circling each building. His feet and legs had grown
flaccid. Even the bones were rubbery from weeks of lassitude.
But, he was young, and the tissue and muscle fired with untried
nerves, and even in the simple walk, warp and weft, first a
mental picture, then a command, traced a lining around the
long bones. He walked blind for hours, circumnavigating the
buildings, starting with the one he knew best, which contained
the lecture hall, and faculty warrens. He started a count. Four
times clockwise around Blackwell, eight times counter. At a
certain point, where a portico opened onto a lawn, almost a
pitch, he shot off NNW, and ventured along a diagonal until
he reached a rubberized track, and ordered himself to find its
center, then thrilled himself with a run, two runs, until his eyes,
in the sharp air, ran with tears. He drove his oxygen-starved
body up the stairs of the bleachers, up one, and down another,
twenty-four times each, then lay in the risers, where he couldn't
be seen, and stared at the sky, bright and gauzy. He closed his
eyes; and when he opened them, he was somewhere he'd never
been before.

Silky tubes ran from a pale jar to his arms and left leg. Pads
that twitched were attached to his temples and back of his neck.
His feet were tied with towels, and his member, engorged, was
gloved and extended to drip into a vessel he couldn't see. He
heard ticking and buzzing, and when he opened his eyes, saw
two screens with green pulsing graphs. His condition and future
were written somewhere near the door, because the vestals,
flushing in and out, stopped to read before tapping on his hot,
taut skin, or recharging the batteries, and reinserting spikes in
his wrists and ankles: again, a burning fire went out. It was a
sign of life, he heard them say.

Even the air of his lungs refused his command. So, he used his eyes, 20/20 in the left; and with them, delivered blow upon blow to the air separating him from the vestals, one more invasive than the last. But, they wouldn't look or connect with the flames he was sending. He drew supplies from himself and projected, but these servants felt nothing, although he was still the object of their fondling, as he had been with Bayh, and at home, and since the day he emerged backward through his mother's gloomy canal into the glare.

Each of his lives had been laid on like a sacrament. What number was this?

***

He was too young to be skinned, gutted, burned and shipped across the river, although the faithful boatman was there, waiting, oar in hand. Too much of him had been held back and was still in store for his own use. Bayh, in her weeds, appeared in the doorway, the day before his release. He'd stayed awake for twenty-four hours to overhear the end of his story; what would be resolved, and what not. He smiled to think it so differed from what he'd imagined—planting his own feet and hammering a tattoo, heard by his own alert child. Emerging whole from the car each day and injecting himself like a slow-acting poison into the home, where his vestals were kept waiting. Bursting out again like a bristly flower.

His story was almost over. The lace in his eye matched even more fragile lace stretching from lungs to heart, from spine to cranium. This was a textile as fine as could be found on any X-ray, a beautiful gauze as subtle and elusive as a galaxy. He had made it over the years, and it grew now by geometric progression, faster than fast, impressive to the vestals, one for the books.

V

The System

THEY WERE NOT married, but they were part of a system. In it, a certain freedom; outside, nothing. One was built low to the ground, chopped-off black hair, glasses, round face; the other, tall and seedy, a tea-drinker and lover of ancient texts. Fatty lived in the present, patrolled the school with a raggedy hemline and clunky shoes. She was brilliant, and a fine singer, with easy reach to the high C.

Betty and Boris, we called them, thrilled to see their command, in old days when two women were too many for one house and one bed. Not enough of something, and too much of something else. They had their routines, and never shared an office or a lunch where people could see.

The nuns didn't seem to mind. How could they, living the way they did, in twos and threes with wedding rings and Jesus as their bridegroom? They looked the other way; the spiciness came from us, although they tried to thin it out with vinegar and water, a panful of Ivory flakes, and rafts of Modess ". . . because."

Because why? Just because. And, we were satisfied. The system made us strong.

There wasn't much room for speculation. There was fact: a joint car, and a house far enough away from campus, and from snoopy neighbors, to elude detection. For holidays with a religious note, each went home alone to a houseful of Catholic brothers and sisters, aunts and uncles, grandmas and kids. Boris was born with a face of crumbly plaster and a walleye. Even as a baby, never smiled, and grew her body into a barrel, whose hoops would last as long as she did. The "hand grenade," boys her age had called her, but they liked her. Everyone liked her, or was it fear? She had a mind of her own and an appetite—not just for food, which, in those days, was plentiful, coarse, and styled to fatten the best of the herd.

She was secretive and lived inside her head, stocked with whatever she could find to read. She also liked gaping into front windows, eavesdropping in rude cafes and diners, hiding in the card section of the drugstore to hear what people were demanding, with or without a doctor's order. Boris knew everything there was to know about the neighborhood, the parish, and the precinct by sixth grade, which she skipped. And, suddenly, in junior high, having no boys to pal around with, her view darkened, and she spent more time on her knees in front of Our Lady of Fatima. That was the name of her church. In some ways, she was a boy, forced to be a girl, with a widowed mother and older brother studying to be a priest—and more than a priest, because already in Rome. So, it was just mother and Boris at home. Her given name was Mary.

Betty was born into a family of eleven boys. She was the baby and, lugging her home in a taxi, her mother took a spill on the ice, cracked her skull, broke her arm, and baby blue, for she was a blue baby, the first to survive, caught a cold and lived her first year in the hospital, an asylum, really, for the blind, the deaf, the retarded, the crippled, the defective at birth, the injured, and the sick. As soon as Betty could put two and two together—early, because she was a genius—she was a baby to watch. The nuns wanted to keep her for their own, for many of the surviving inmates joined their order the first day they could do it, at age fourteen, by the bishop's special dispensation, because staff was needed, and vocations to that servile order rare, and because their motherhouse was in the far reaches of Canada, and no one had heard of them.

But, Betty's mother, never too hale and now off in different ways (always wore a hat, even in bed, and went to all the masses on Sunday, confessing her sins in each confessional box on Saturday), wanted her back, her only girl. But Betty was formed by her first birthday, and never bonded onto her mother, although they went everywhere together, Betty tied by a harness to her mother's wrist or shopping cart. She was even manacled to the back seat of the car, when the uncle offered his sister and a handful of her children, a Sunday drive.

Time passed, as it does, and the girls met in college. Betty was fifteen and Boris, sixteen, each alienated in a different way. Boris was all business, a math major, with a twenty-five-hour-a-week job at the doughnut shop, where they made doughnuts from dough that Boris learned to mix in the long nights alone and locked in, because in a dicey part of town: red-light, pool, card parlors, and Sons of Italy. Boris was sending part of her salary to Rome, so Billy could buy himself a silk chasuble as a newly fledged deacon, and saving part of it so Mother and she could sail to Rome for his ordination one year hence. She was double majoring in classics because the old stories appealed to her native valor and bossiness. She liked college no better than high school, but toed the line, even attending daily mass, although her faith was long gone, disappeared in grade seven, when she saw through the pretense of a One-True-Faith smacked onto every odd religion. That alone would have done it, but other things had intervened. Her best friend, Bruno, a German police dog, was beaten to death by neighbor toughs, all Catholics and one destined for the priesthood. Add to that the misery, the stupidity, the drunkenness, squalor, tedium of life everywhere but in God's house, a castle, a theater, a place that made no difference. People went in, and came out to business as usual. Her confessor told her to slow down, take it easy on herself, and on the slobs around her. That's what he said. She laughed—a rarity—and came back to chew the fat with Father Mike, soon to depart for the missions, but the damage was done, or enlightenment, which is how Boris saw it. Life was work, study, effort to crawl out of the hole fate had put her in, and she was digging from that moment on.

I need a single room, she told the admissions at Angels and Martyrs: I snore, sleepwalk, have insomnia, a weak heart from rheumatic fever, night terrors and 'mares, allergies, stomach trouble, and I have to use the bathroom a dozen times a night, and sleep with the light on. There was only one such room, a closet with no window, and Boris took it, and installed a lock on her own dime. Betty was on full scholarship to become a teacher, but no sooner arrived with a cardboard suitcase, when she changed course, standing in line to get a beanie, yellow and navy blue with the number '59. Four dollars she had (she had fifty, saved from babysitting and light housework), but not for a beanie. "You can't enroll without one," the proctor said. Standing right behind her, putting away the five she was ready to hand over, no questions asked, was Teresa, soon to become Betty's roommate and fast friend. She paid for two beanies with a ten, saying, "just take it. You can give it back later. Put it on your head," only noticing that Betty had three times the hair, untamed, curly like an unshorn sheep. "Here," she said, pulling a bobby pin from her own head with its curly blonde hair, so blonde it was almost white. She was hauling a red, round suitcase that matched her shoulder bag. "Teresa," she said, "but everyone calls me TT. My middle name is Tomassina. I'm Italian." With that, she pulled a gaping Betty, so tall and so thin, out of the line of matriculating freshman. "Pleased to meetcha."

Betty knew she was in love, but so unfamiliar was the sensation that what she experienced was choking suffocation, heartburn, cramps, and a spiking fever. Next thing, she was crying.

She stuck to TT like glue, but also like snaps, belt, and a zipper. She even pushed her single bed next to her savior's (that's the word she used), and held her hand at night, gripping it until TT said, "Take it easy, I'm not going anywhere." Didn't matter. Betty changed her major to French and Italian, where TT was, and already fluent. TT was a generous soul, sure, but there was more to it.

For two years, Betty and Boris cycled under the same roofs and in some of the same classrooms. All were required to take theology, church history, and needlework. They met at "Tea and Sherry" for a visiting archbishop, brother of the nun-president, Sister Joseph of Arimethea. "Wear your beanies," the proctor said, and poor Boris, as we called her, had chewed hers in night sweats, because it was wool, tasty, and sewed, not glued. She'd bitten off the button, and the topper came apart in four triangles, two yellow, two blue. She was saving the blue, but the yellow wedges were threadbare, ratty, you wouldn't give them to a dog. She still had them, stuck in a frame somewhere with feathers and trinkets, part of her love history with Betty, whom she met that night, hatless. The proctor pulled her out to ask: "Where is it, honey, where's your cover?" The nuns called it cover, which is what they called their own lids and cowls. Boris was a born liar, and practiced, too. "Lost it," she said, "gave it up for Lent." Shaking her head, the proctor forced her to pin a hankie to her head. When Boris asked why, since they weren't in church, the proctor put a finger over her lips. "Silence," she said. His Excellency had taken the podium.

And he had.

TT had lent Betty a set of clothes, because she had nothing but tents and shrouds. She was, that afternoon, clad in a bright, plaid pleated skirt that showed her knees over knee socks, a red cardigan, and gold scarf. TT had helped her part and braid the wild tresses, and then wrapped them around her head like a wondrous pinwheel or maze. All eyes were on the hair, upon which, the pristine beanie rested like a cherry atop a sundae. When Archbishop Peter Fogarty's eye scanned the room and spotted it, he laughed out loud, covering his mouth and turning bright red. Then, they all laughed, even the nuns. The ice was broken, and next thing, you know, Boris had planted herself in her paltry headgear next to Betty.

"Brethren," the archbishop was finally ready to say, "and sisters," he added, closing his eyes to remember where he was—and his script, which was always the same mummery, but delivered with different tones and ornaments, according to the sex, the age, the site, class, occasion, and the looks on their faces. "I come to deliver the word of God, the good news of the gospel, and the message from His Holiness in his encyclical on marriage, the family, the apostolate, and holy church." And every ear closed with the faces, opening only when, changing course, he disclosed instead the system, its articles and entry point, and what should come out at the end, because "we are not monkeys," he said.

This was a message meant to stay in Rome, in Vatican City with its color guard and special army and conveyances, a fortress and dark hole. But, out it came, because the arch had seen the headdress of a goddess, something from the other side of Rome, on a mortal and pasty-faced beanpole. He was distracted, inspired, some say, and spilled the beans.

"Brethren," he said, "listen up, whoever you are." Luckily, the sisterhood, a teaching order, had fled the room, except for the sister president. For those who had ears and the Latin to parse it, the system came through; for the rabblement, it was just a different kind of mumbo jumbo.

Betty, as we said, was in classics, and in possession of a secular dictionary, scribbled away on a blank page, because the arch was a fast talker and a mumbler. TT and Boris were all ears, too, when they saw the new girl taking notes with flaming ears and knocking knees.

Soon, they were drinking tea and sherry and had the holy man pushed into a corner, savagely and greedily sucking in his every word, but further about the system—if he knew it—was denied them. Meantime, the sisterhood, the black flock, had returned, and wanted their share of His Excellency; and so the trio, with Boris in the middle, departed and didn't show for the concelebrated mass the next day. Part of the three-day festival of the holy man's visit to Angels and Martyrs. Purpose: vocations. Peter Fogarty was making the rounds for the sake of a declining sisterhood.

"Do you smell a rat?" was the first thing out of Boris's mouth. The two didn't know her name, but they'd seen her squat form barreling around, and there was an occasional offering of doughnuts on a Sunday morning, when she took the subway home for a day of rest. Betty had put two and two together, as she was known to do, signaling to TT to listen up.

They shook their heads and opened their ears, and the system, point by point, poured in.

"That explains it," Betty said, but TT was still puzzled, because she was an only child from a mixed marriage, and her father a traveling salesman, a Protestant, who'd seen something of the world, and refused to convert, although agreed, by canon law, to raise his young in the faith. TT had kept her eyes fixed on him, when he was around, and before the heart attack took him away to wherever they go, the ones who hear the Word and deny it entry. In her grief, TT's mother lapsed, returning to the fold upon the girl's departure. So TT was, some would say, a free agent. "That explains what?" the girl said.

With that, Boris and Betty became a unit, with TT revolving around them, because, as they knew by heart, no one can catch up if they miss the steady drilling, day by day and week by week, all and everywhere, of the Word.

"Too late," Boris said to her new pal, Betty. But, they kept her on, as a cleansing breath of fresh air, there when they needed it.

***

Days passed. Other visitors darkened the doorstep of Angels and Martyrs. The young men of Troy, of the Catholic school there, full of bursting seed and gumption to spread it. They piled out of a bus, or dribbled out, because A&M was known as the "stoup," where the frumps and hens gunked the stone bowl in oily algae and furry moss, before being scooped out to collect again at the nunnery. The bus filled with dread and reluctance, spilling in rage, with forethoughts of mischief. They were, in fact, a scraggly, meatless bunch, overgrown altar boys, runts and rejects, fodder for the army and pay-your-way clerical schools, mean, luckless, belligerent and unripe.

No one met the bus. It was a first Friday, and the girls were still at a late-afternoon service; for, making nine of these shaved off ten or twenty years penal in Purgatory. The bargain, even for an old pagan like Boris, was worth it. Who knew the true outcome to the ancient question? No one they knew came back to tell, but rumors abounded, and the news wasn't good, no matter what the archbishop had said. The "cloth" were talking through their hats most of the time, whistling in the dark.

The trio, by then, went everywhere together, from the moment Boris rolled out of bed and trudged down the corridor to pound on their door. They rose when all were asleep, the black flock and the ninnies in their charge. In the dark, the trio made their rounds, tracking the length of the four-building campus, ending up under the statue of the BVM, source of the system, virgin, goddess, author of the divine, and its consort. That day, the day the first bus came, the statue, a cold gray and gritty stone, was covered in snow, and they boosted up TT to dust off her head and put a little color on her cheeks with a Crayola, kiss them, and whisper a word of praise and thanks; and then, TT jumped down. They liked to be around the BVM, all stiff and perfect, inert and impassive, but during the day, they stayed away. She was a magnet, and lines of force bled inward. You could feel it, if you weren't thinking or just lolling about, which most of the girls were. Not the trio—they stayed awake.

The boys flooded in, or wept in, for it was the end of the day, and a collation was laid for the purpose of regulated and patrolled mingling: deviled eggs dusted with fiery paprika, celery spears gorged with cream cheese and stinging capers, date-nut bread with bitter walnuts, blood-colored punch with floating splinters of ice, and daggers of mint.

The ungainly youths circled around, their fingers grubby with tobacco and smears of shoe polish. First in was Tubby, a mama's boy as round and sweet as a doughnut hole. With swift hand, he gobbled, and soon his mates had stuffed, burned, choked, and were slaked with draughts of the blood and water punch, and restored to infantine satiation, becoming, in short, a different breed. Full, on this collation that was better and finer than their grub, they made, as a body, for the rickety metal chairs, set out around a patch of beeswax floor that was the site for dancing, as the sister-servitor set the needle on the record, and the scratchy pulse of inane waltz tickled their ears and excited them. The girls, too. Music—any kind—was an intoxicant in this scanted and stinted tribe.

Tubby, pushed out by his mates, picked TT, just picked up her hand in wordless invitation or command, and the two made their way to the beeswax circle. "Get ready," he said, and TT responded in an Italian dialect that Tubby shook out of his ears, making a face, which made TT laugh, so he laughed, and an ease came over them, enough to shuffle into the box step and stay there, moving their legs in place, so not moving at all. Seeing it, the nun clapped her hands to command them, then shook her finger. The sisterhood was not stupid for being *hors de combat*, and they knew that standing in place—even marching in place—was too close for comfort. Things could happen, things that would lead to other things. But the couple stayed in their box, and the sister had naught to do but pull them apart. The music stopped first, and each of the pair headed out at cross-purposes, and the beeswax circle was once again empty.

Tubby was dispatched again, pushed out, and made the rounds of girls in sprigged frocks and velvet vests, silky dresses, twin sets, gored skirts. All shook their heads, and one actually pushed Tubs away, brushing her hands and sniffing them, flicking her fingers and reaching for a hankie to rub them clean of contact. Two choices were left, but Tubby returned to his side of the room, only to be driven back by the tide. He went for Betty, changed his mind, and went for Boris; changed his mind, and back to Betty. By then, the sister-custodian clapped her hands, pulled the needle off the vinyl, and chased the boys out of the room, herding them back to their bus, where they sat until out they all came again to start over. By then, the parlor was empty, so they sat on the chairs and waited for the bus driver to haul them home, never to return, with Tubby praised, mocked, vilified and scapegoated, when the priest-brothers back at Troy heard of the escapade, and grounded the bus boys, when the next college on their dance card was the delectable Tiffany School, charm and business, like an ice-cream shop of sweetness and delight.

***

The trio was left with much to ponder. Something had happened to break the bond, disturb the peace and plans. Wounds had been inflicted, along with shame and festering. For a while, nothing was said. Boris went back to work, TT and Betty resumed their communal life, but lifeless and pondering.

The custodial nun had a bee in her bonnet, and passed it on to her pal, the portress, who passed it on. The archbishop's sister was last to know, but first to act. She talked to God, preferring the father to the son, for this kind of interlocution. The three persons were men; even the bird was male, so something was lost in the message, which required much repetition, expansion, illustration, and compaction, nutshelling, but Sister President was a skilled rhetorician.

"Dearest," she said, kneeling in the front pew of the college chapel, looking straight at the altar and the tabernacle, where the son resided as bread. Over the altar in fresco was a supersized image of the father as an old man, opening his arms to enclose the son and the bird, one on top of the other in a spangle of golden rays. Sister lifted up her eyes to this large, manly figure in a white robe.

"Yes, my child," she said, because she did both voices.

"Here's the problem," and Sister President sat back down on the pew and crossed her legs.

The flock was dividing between the chosen and the rejects, or set-asides. This was nature, but God was still God, and he came first, or so she said, in her flattering tones. "You come first, but we're second, after your lady wife, whom we resemble, being virgins and mothers, staying out of the fray, as you, or thee, and your two confreres did since the beginning of time, and before.

"Not confreres," she said for him.

"Right, but let's not get into that. Think of the centuries wasted on that debate on who was who, who came first, and what linked the parts."

"Don't back talk me, Sister Sue. Don't tell me what to think."

The sister was breathless, talking so fast and so loud, and throwing her voice into registers too far apart. Her throat was parched, too, so she stepped into the sacristy for a sip of water, and decided to mix in a little wine, although the convent priests were misers, and bought the cheapest altar wine, a scandal, really, considering what it was used for. She took out a gold cup and drank a couple of glasses to calm herself for the dialogue to come.

Back in the pew, she started again, talking to number two, this time.

"Jesus," she said, "can you hear me from there?"

"Yes, my daughter," said the bread, channeled by the nun in a mumbly, yeasty voice.

"Now is the time for all good men," she said, "to come to the aid of the party. Remember that one?"

"Speak your part, and cut the comedy," said the bread.

"It's a cryin' shame," the nun said, dropping her face into her hands. "They're ready for harvest, these girls, and what's in it for them? It's bad if they're picked, and it's bad if they're not."

"Not my problem," said the bread, echoed by the old man and the twittering bird.

"That's what I thought you'd say."

So the sister, a little tipsy, dropped by to see the roommates, of whom the cute one, an Italian, was picked. She found the girl lying on her bed, reading something that she'd hidden under the pillow, when the black-clad creature—familiar, but not in this intimate context—darkened the doorway.

Betty was reading charts of verbs, with their chains of tenses and irregularities, at her most frustrated.

The nun sat down on Betty's bed and patted the place next to her. "Come sit by me, my lambs," she said, "I've got bad news."

The girls were glum. Not a word had been spoken since the evil day of choice, when the apple of discord was awarded to the cutie.

The nun understood. One benefit of marriage to Jesus was he's a polygamist and all are welcome to wear his ring and take his name, or one of his courtier's, mate's, or family, ancestor or precursor, martyr, angel, saint, his mother and her family, to their heart's content, all the same, no one left out. It was a good deal, it cost nothing. Your ducks were lined up for now and forever. Take it or leave it.

Which is what the sister told the roommates, a contract in hand—just a sample, because don't overdo it, or lay it on too thick, was the way things were done.

So, what do you think? she was about to say, when the Italian flopped back on her bed, pulling out the book tucked away from prying eyes. "See this," she said. *The Marriage Act,* read the yellow cover, and Betty covered her eyes, just as Boris was battering on the door.

"Mum's the word," said the nun—she didn't like Boris; few did. "To be continued. Can I borrow this?" she said, plucking the book from TT's fists.

"Give it back!"

"All in the fullness of time," said the nun. This was the kind of book, a handbook or glossary, that laid things out for the catechumens, those still outside, curious, but blocked from entry. "You don't need this. Hold your horses," said the nun, "and wait your turn," closing the door to the three. Boris was in, smelling a rat. "What's up?" she said.

A tear was opening between the original pair, Boris and Betty, because Tubby had balked at Betty, while he'd choked in the face of Boris, and these girls were not stupid. Plus, there was a third and that third linked tighter to Betty, so Boris was twice out, picked last, and left out.

The air was electric with desire and strife because the book had inflamed TT. One of those nasty bus boys had dropped it behind a bush and, from there, it circulated, made the rounds, and now the nuns'd have a crack at it, but they wouldn't get it, if TT barely did, because it was coated with science and tricked out with line drawings of tubes, globes, hoses, bottlenecks, drains, arrows, and waterspouts. The terms were dry, even bitter. But, TT was a born luster, and could read between the lines of the succulence within.

"See you," said Boris to the supine Italian; and drawing Betty by the arm, the two took a turn around the campus, avoiding—a first!—the BVM. Why? They didn't know why, but something was different. What was clockwise was now counter. They left the campus, tramping into town and onward until they landed in front of the doughnut shop, where the air was sweet with fat and dough, glaze, chocolate, and jelly. "I'm treating," said Boris, and in they went. The wife of the baker was there, biting her nails. She was their age, but married five years with five brats.

"What's eating you?" was the first thing out of her mouth, spotting the assistant on an off day. "Have a doughnut?" she said. "Who's your friend?" She offered a tray of rejects; each had something wrong: misshapen, no hole, burned, bald, yesterday's, exploded, too flat, leaden, raw, gunky, crumbly, sodden.

"No thanks," said Boris. "I've got cash. Show me the glory

holes, the five-in-ones, the two-sided, the crowns and castles."

And she did. And Boris paid for three, offering the slattern wife her pick. Boris had learned from her insult, and Betty was first to notice the change.

"Okay," said Boris. "We've eaten our fill, and the baker's off-site, so tell us, Monty, what it's like, the marriage bed. A bed of roses, or something else? Speak up."

"Why are you asking me?" was the first out of her mouth, still chewing, but one thing they already knew was this: even here, married to the boss, was no free lunch because look at the size of her—a pick-up stick—and working in a doughnut shop. Didn't she like doughnuts?

She did. Of course, she did, Monty said, but how many can you eat in one day, and they saved the rejects for the babies, sopped in milk, or straight up. This was point one.

A dreamy look came into the baker's wife's eyes, not quite the same color, which is why he'd married her, Boris suspected. You could never get bored looking at that face with one eye a clear spring and the other mud. It divided her in two and made her seem a system complete in itself.

"Tell us the story," said Betty, sitting on the bench for those awaiting a fresh batch. The smell could knock you out; and Betty, almost as skinny as the wife, was lightheaded.

"And don't skip the good parts," said Boris, licking her fingers.

Monty leaned on the counter, scratching her head with a pencil, adjusting her white cap, and organizing her waistband and apron strings.

"I didn't go to college like you girls," she said. "I wasn't what you'd call college material, and neither was Mr. Hook."

"Why do you call him mister?"

"That's my way. My Mam called my Pa mister every day of his life, no matter what."

"And no-matter-what means?"

"Drunk or on the wagon, making it or on the skids, playing

the horses or bringing home the bacon, here today or gone tomorrow, he was always mister, Mister Tar, his name was. And he called her the missus, when he called her anything."

The friends were not encouraged by this.

"Did you have a nice wedding?"

"Beautiful."

"Meaning a cake, throw the bouquet, white dress, dancing at the K of C, or what?" said Betty, the dreamer.

"Sort of," said the wife, dabbing her eyes with the apron.

"Why the waterworks?" said Boris.

"I had to get married with little Mickey on the way, so plain as plain can be. Collation in the backyard of tea and doughnuts and lemonade, and a trip to Niagara for just the two of us, overnight and on the train. I still remember it, the best day of my life. I had a box of chocolates on my lap, and Mr. Hook ate every one. He loves chocolates, and these were good ones, not seconds."

"And after little Mickey, the other four. Why?" said Boris.

"One thing leads to another," said the baker's wife with a smirk.

"That's what we're here for. What's the thing that leads to the other things? Can you say it in a way that we'll get it, and not speak in tongues?" said Boris.

Mrs. Hook blushed to her hairline. "You don't want to know," she said. And then, "Wait your turn."

They'd heard that before, but they didn't want to wait, so Boris started pacing, and Betty biting her nails.

"Well," said Boris. "Let's start with brass tacks. Is it worth it?"

"Is it worth what?"

Boris looked at Betty, and Betty looked back. Here was the heart of the matter. Worth what? They'd been told by the nuns the four good things: death, judgment, heaven, and hell, but weren't buying it, or not yet. They were calculating because isn't youth calculation? Gimme this, but none of that. Were they young? Had they ever been? Boris was a calculator. Betty was still bathing in the waters of charity, TT's, but those waters were drying up by the raw sight of injustice. Was it her fault that she was tall and stringy with a hair mass like a Medusa's? Or, Boris's—that she was a little mountain with a bulldog's mug? Was this destiny, this piece of rotten luck? Or, was it—seen upside-down, or inside-out—a piece of good luck? That's where the system came in, although Boris still knew only its outline. Betty had the guts of it.

"Talk to the rooster," the baker's wife said, and she was speaking in tongues, because this slipped out without her knowing, or even grasping.

The duo grabbed at it. "Talk to the rooster," they said. But did they know why? Boris's sire was dead, as was Betty's. No rooster came to the campus that wasn't ordained, dried, and pickled in his boyhood chastity, or the runts who'd never come back. And how would they find one, and get it to crow?

But, in turning tail, they were stymied by the baker's wife, who had a million other things she wanted to tell them.

Household: the chairs and tables she bought on installment, curtains and curtain rods, braided rugs, things, things, and things, because the kids broke a lot of things and wrecked others, so the stream of things went in two directions, and where to put them, and what it was like to dust them, and wipe them, and brush them, and spot-clean. The torment of it, and the fiery joy of having and keeping. But she was expecting again, too bad. Before she could rewind to talk about washing the clothes and hanging them on the line, and hanging the cups on hooks, and shaking the rugs, Betty and Boris were out the door, slipping out as a customer walked in, a truck driver, who ordered a baker's dozen, jelly. Here was a rooster, a fine bantam, and Monty's face lit up. "Come back, girls," she said. "This is Mr. Hook's brother, Angelo Hook. Shake hands."

The duo shook the trucker's hand, first one, then the other, and looked into his face. This dodo bird would tell them nothing they didn't already know. They needed a wise cock, but Monty was already saying: "Stay a minute. Cool your heels. Ange, tell these girls if it's worth it, and worth what."

"Huh?"

"Do I have to spell it out, you big lug?" said Monty, punching her brother-in-law in the arm.

That gave him the hint, so he punched her back, nearly toppling her.

"Is it worth it," he repeated in a dreamy voice, deep and husky, "and worth what? Geez," he said, "What can I say? What else is there?"

He was still a bachelor, but he'd been around. He broke out in a sweat, he laughed, cleared his throat a dozen times, and whistled; "Was it ever!" were his last words.

As they walked out, Betty and Boris were silent. What did they know now that they didn't know before? One thing they knew—who'd ever jump in the sack with that Palooka. And yet . . .

Just saying it gave them an idea. It mattered to pick or be picked by the right one, and where was the right one? Where did you find him in an all-girls' school? The bussed-in Trojans were not to their taste. Not enough manliness. They laughed to use the word, but use it they did. And the trucker, he was cooked, but made of shoddy stuff, and they knew shoddy because they'd been born to it, and were not only plain and ugly, depending on the day and whether there was enough hot water to shampoo the mops, but plenty shoddy. Nothing they had was good except their headpieces. So, even though they were shoddy, and knew it by sight, they were aiming higher, if they aimed at all, so the field of dreams suddenly shrunk down to nothing.

Was it true?

Manliness was something to be tested, but who would do it? Who was up to it? Who had the goods? They nominated TT, who'd nominated herself, and who was fuming and boiling from the contents of the yellow book, purloined by the convent, and would they get it back?

Boris and Betty, drained, deflated, returned to campus, each to her own lair, and face down on their canoes, dreaming, hoping, offering up a day of prayer and sacrifice to the baby Jesus, just for a lick or taste. TT, sitting up straight, had her own idea.

Manliness

She boarded the bus the next Friday bound for St. Sebastian, the pincushion martyr, where the boys of Boston enrolled, sons of doctors and lawyers, different—better? TT wore her cutest rig—a felt skirt with a poodle on it, pretty pumps, a pink sweater with a cut-down neckline she cloaked under a velvet cape. Betty and Boris loaded themselves in the back, dressed worse than usual because they were the scientist and TT, the rat. TT had her own ideas, and planned to dodge them as soon as her dancing feet hit the ground. The bus filled with eau de cologne and powdery smells, the stink of drying nail polish and hair spray, and something else the duo inhaled with interest. They got it, but didn't partake of it. It excited them, and they grabbed for each other's hands, squeezing and letting go, and things only got worse as the bus, full of feminine flavors gone wild, hit the Mass Pike, and off-ramped to the woods of St. Sebastian's.

The air was thick with sighs and gulps of air. The bus driver laughed. He was a grandfather, but he remembered.

Off-loading, the posses wavered and wobbled. No collation, but straight in the darkening dusk to the gym, a dance floor and amplified tunes, jazz and jitterbug, tango and samba. The Bostons had snuck in their own LPs, and locked the sound room behind them. Two fathers were on duty, but Jesuits, who'd seen everything, left the boys to themselves, go to peace.

TT stood by a pillar with tilted head and a three-quarters pose, so the suitors could see her in the round. She slipped off the cape and arranged her lips in a pout studied in *Photoplay*. Her lips were chapped and puffy from biting and licking. Her front teeth protruded and made the lips even fuller. They were a perfect bow. She had large, glossy eyes, a bit popped, and she'd ringed them in black, larding the lashes with midnight blue mascara. Her eyebrows nearly met over the Roman nose. Her eyes were like fiery pools, netted in vines, and her lips overripe plums, stinging from the cheap lipstick. She'd rouged and powdered her cheeks. The face presented at an angle was a mask of inexhaustible vitality. Every male eye was gripped—even the priests', before they left the field.

"Oh my!" Betty had said, when she saw the project complete in the dorm's laboratory light. "Yikes!" said Boris, as the makeup started to settle, harden, and perfect.

TT had found a pillar far from the beam of athletic light, and side lit by a rosy exit sign. Under the warlike face was a cute body in trendy togs, items these boys would recognize as part of teendom.

Four males ambled over in a loose line, but in pecking order, headed by a golfer and tennis star whose banker father supplied the corridor with scotch, beer, and cigarettes.

He stood before this binary marvel (cute teen and Fury), and plucked her hand from the skirt pocket, where the poodle was stitched in powder-puff pink.

"Put it back," she said. (Betty and Boris were stationed behind the pillar, covering their chortling yaps.)

"Are you talking to me?" said the lad.

"Stand down."

Here was a linebacker with a big rack of meat for shoulders. TT pulled out a hand to touch the meat, and squeeze it. It wasn't fully cooked, but almost. She sniffed the boy's face and neck, and measured the meaty wrist with her own skimpy paw. Two of hers for one of his.

Placing one mitt around her waist and ducking under the
other, she arranged him for the dance floor, for the meeting of
her body with his, "testing," she said.

And so it went, and after testing each, TT picked her sample
by a different measure, because she'd spotted through an open
window the slender, purposeful key the male hid between his
thighs. What it unlocked, she wasn't sure, and it was a crude-
looking gadget, so nothing too fancy or elaborate. Through
zippers and over layers of cloth, she took the measure.

Then, retreated to consult with the scientists. They went
to the soda and cookies room, where the herd stood around
ready to doctor the drinks with spirits, but the rough beasts
shouldered off these invaders with their shiny flasks.

Part two was trying it out, and part two unfolded after
refreshments were taken.

TT filled up on a bubbly drink and a handful of ladyfingers.
"Take and eat," Boris said, but no one laughed, or finished
the line. Fortified, TT smoothed her felt skirt and tightened
her sash. She jiggled, head to toe, like a soaking wet dog. The
dancing lads had skinned out the door. TT entered and selected
number three, a rufous with a stocky build and saddle shoes. A
45 was spinning on the turntable, rockabilly, we now know, had
found its way into the air space. The boy was a Billy, and after
he and TT had danced a little, the three-minute hustle heel, toe,
and twirl, TT led him to the school chapel, open, dimly lit, and
fertilized with frankincense, a ripe and germy place. The altar
steps were padded by a thick rug, so TT rolled on him, hitting
the altar rail at the bottom. In that half-crib, she unpacked the
key and studied it in the red glow of the lamp. It was small, it
was big. When he stripped her of her garments, peeling off her
stockings to suck on a garter, big it grew, strong as marble. It
was red and alive. The Billy's eyes had rolled back in his head.

He was gone, but the machine was awake, geared to cool the
marble, conk it, then fire it, until it was just another grub. The
machine rolled over TT, delving and drilling on TT's delicate

trellis of bones. What can it be? she asked herself, as she was torpedoed.

"Get offa me now," she said to the panting lad, who flopped over on his back. "Get dressed, march!" she said, watching as he hauled his spent body into his clothes, and scuffled out on untied saddle shoes, stopping to stick his hand in the holy-water font and make the cross. Was he now a man?

And was he manly? the duo wanted to know, when TT shook herself loose. Boris laughed. The pretty skirt was twisted around with the zipper in front.

"Spit it out," Betty said.

The rufous was in the boy's room, gazing at the sinner his mother was sure he'd be, if given half a chance. Did he look any different? Patting down his hair, he made his way to the statue of St. Sebastian, spotted in red like him, by the hundred darts piercing his skin.

"Father, forgive me," the boy said, "for it wasn't my fault."

Sebastian, eyes raised to heaven, was as mute as he'd always been. He was just, after all, a plaster replica of a story. The rufous waited. His mates were looking for him, but didn't think to look there. Something had happened, something good, and they were first to sniff it out.

The Jesuit fathers returned, eventually, to the scene, feeling no pain. Entering the gym through the locker room, they spotted, behind a pillar, three girls huddled together, troublemakers, hiding something. The fathers made their way over, to be met by a scowl, and a stuck-out tongue.

"Father," said one Jesuit to the other.

"Yes, Father?"

"Do something."

"Tell me, Father, what should I do?"

"Where've you been all this time!" Boris said.

Sainthood

TT was escorted to the bus, a friend on each side, with the other girls traipsing behind, as the boys watched in silence from the barred windows of the gym. The wheels were turning. "Up you go, Alley-oop," Boris said, speeding TT up the steps and pressing her into a seat, covering her shivering shoulders with the velvet cape.

Oftentimes, and en route to an extracurricular, the girls of Angels and Martyrs were urged to offer up their prayers for the conversion of the Jews. But, this time, they set the petition aside. Some one of theirs had passed through to the other side. "Let us pray," Betty said, but was it too late?

They stripped the Italian and washed her up, dabbing her with Jean Nate. They shrouded her in her nightie, a grandmother craft, a white sack that covered her, hem to throat, wrist to yoke; wound her Italian hair in spoolies, surrounding it with a net.

"Sleep now, my dear," said Betty to the lamb, so peaceful now in her sleep.

"Death, judgment, heaven, and hell," grumbled Betty. "Why does it have to be that way?"

They were talking over the still body.

Boris retired to her single room, kissing Betty on both cheeks, and shaking her hand. "I'll sleep on it," she said. "Keep an eye on our queen bee."

The System

So, where do we come in, we others? By the time we arrived on the scene, a couple of decades later, Betty and Boris were settled into place: Betty taught classics, and Boris physics. We were all going to be married, the sooner the better, and we had no ears to hear, so what did we need of either? But to keep them busy, we all took a course called: the science of life, with ancient texts from the golden and silver ages, skipping over the middle two thousand years, then jumping to the latest thing. The in-between is, as you know, the Christian era, and we'd had enough of it. The race had gone downhill and we were just nitwits. We waited upon their wisdom and they gave us what they had: nostrums, ambients, wherewithal, authority, expansion, and exploration in the two eras: way back then, and now. We knew about relativity and the circulation of the blood, the nitrogen cycle and black holes. We knew the ins and outs of the Trojan War and aftermath, and the way the gods aggravated men and women, but not kids. Good thing, because that's what we were—kids, yet under the tutelage of Doctors Betty and Boris.

One day, August 1, our arrival on campus and day one, we were addressed in a hall of windows and beeswax floor by the nut-brown crone arrayed in the colors of a bluebird. This glowing but decrepit critter, leaped onto the podium and stared at us.

"Devils," she said, and we laughed, but it wasn't all that funny. A chorus rose in the rafters of piped music—plainchant, anthems, unisons, and counterpoint.

"Devils," she bellowed into her mike, and the music stopped, but something echoed in the hall's wooden shell. We strained to hear it, because we were starting out, and nothing so odd would befall us again. The version of the system we heard, though, was only a crib, a digest, all dried up and neutralized. That's what time will do—even in the small-time, small world we live in.

Betty and Boris and the black-robed faculty were in the front rows, belted off from the rest of us. They were holding a tea party in the hour after, for the new girls, us. We sallied into the refectory, silent and brooding, already stamped, but with a weak antigen.

Betty was pouring coffee, and Boris tea. Half of us were chattering, the rest at sea. We had lost something, and we didn't know quite what.

The crone in bird blues alighted in the doorway, and took the table's place of honor.

I know you've guessed it by now, the art of the system: Stop here, the crone said, rest here, like with like, and fatten yourselves on time.

It was raining that first of August and we carried this frail melody into the grayish, overgrown world. It was the system, devised by the Christian era, but never grasped: a tribal suicide, but with its own fluency and inner springs.

Goodbye for now to Betty and Boris, but see them on their own chosen path, away from us, always away, but never far.

MICHAL AJVAZ, *The Golden Age.*
The Other City.
PIERRE ALBERT-BIROT, *Grabinoulor.*
YUZ ALESHKOVSKY, *Kangaroo.*
FELIPE ALFAU, *Chromos.*
Locos.
JOE AMATO, *Samuel Taylor's Last Night.*
IVAN ÂNGELO, *The Celebration.*
The Tower of Glass.
ANTÓNIO LOBO ANTUNES, *Knowledge of Hell.*
The Splendor of Portugal.
ALAIN ARIAS-MISSON, *Theatre of Incest.*
JOHN ASHBERY & JAMES SCHUYLER, *A Nest of Ninnies.*
ROBERT ASHLEY, *Perfect Lives.*
GABRIELA AVIGUR-ROTEM, *Heatwave and Crazy Birds.*
DJUNA BARNES, *Ladies Almanack.*
Ryder.
JOHN BARTH, *Letters.*
Sabbatical.
DONALD BARTHELME, *The King.*
Paradise.
SVETISLAV BASARA, *Chinese Letter.*
MIQUEL BAUÇÀ, *The Siege in the Room.*
RENÉ BELLETTO, *Dying.*
MAREK BIENCZYK, *Transparency.*
ANDREI BITOV, *Pushkin House.*
ANDREJ BLATNIK, *You Do Understand.*
Law of Desire.
LOUIS PAUL BOON, *Chapel Road.*
My Little War.
Summer in Termuren.
ROGER BOYLAN, *Killoyle.*
IGNÁCIO DE LOYOLA BRANDÃO, *Anonymous Celebrity.*
Zero.
BONNIE BREMSER, *Troia: Mexican Memoirs.*
CHRISTINE BROOKE-ROSE, *Amalgamemnon.*
BRIGID BROPHY, *In Transit.*
The Prancing Novelist.

GERALD L. BRUNS, *Modern Poetry and the Idea of Language.*
GABRIELLE BURTON, *Heartbreak Hotel.*
MICHEL BUTOR, *Degrees.*
Mobile.
G. CABRERA INFANTE, *Infante's Inferno.*
Three Trapped Tigers.
JULIETA CAMPOS, *The Fear of Losing Eurydice.*
ANNE CARSON, *Eros the Bittersweet.*
ORLY CASTEL-BLOOM, *Dolly City.*
LOUIS-FERDINAND CÉLINE, *North.*
Conversations with Professor Y.
London Bridge.
MARIE CHAIX, *The Laurels of Lake Constance.*
HUGO CHARTERIS, *The Tide Is Right.*
ERIC CHEVILLARD, *Demolishing Nisard.*
The Author and Me.
MARC CHOLODENKO, *Mordechai Schamz.*
JOSHUA COHEN, *Witz.*
EMILY HOLMES COLEMAN, *The Shutter of Snow.*
ERIC CHEVILLARD, *The Author and Me.*
ROBERT COOVER, *A Night at the Movies.*
STANLEY CRAWFORD, *Log of the S.S. The Mrs Unguentine.*
Some Instructions to My Wife.
RENÉ CREVEL, *Putting My Foot in It.*
RALPH CUSACK, *Cadenza.*
NICHOLAS DELBANCO, *Sherbrookes.*
The Count of Concord.
NIGEL DENNIS, *Cards of Identity.*
PETER DIMOCK, *A Short Rhetoric for Leaving the Family.*
ARIEL DORFMAN, *Konfidenz.*
COLEMAN DOWELL, *Island People.*
Too Much Flesh and Jabez.
ARKADII DRAGOMOSHCHENKO, *Dust.*
RIKKI DUCORNET, *Phosphor in Dreamland.*
The Complete Butcher's Tales.

RIKKI DUCORNET (cont.), *The Jade Cabinet.*
The Fountains of Neptune.
WILLIAM EASTLAKE, *The Bamboo Bed.*
Castle Keep.
Lyric of the Circle Heart.
JEAN ECHENOZ, *Chopin's Move.*
STANLEY ELKIN, *A Bad Man.*
Criers and Kibitzers, Kibitzers and Criers.
The Dick Gibson Show.
The Franchiser.
The Living End.
Mrs. Ted Bliss.
FRANÇOIS EMMANUEL, *Invitation to a Voyage.*
PAUL EMOND, *The Dance of a Sham.*
SALVADOR ESPRIU, *Ariadne in the Grotesque Labyrinth.*
LESLIE A. FIEDLER, *Love and Death in the American Novel.*
JUAN FILLOY, *Op Oloop.*
ANDY FITCH, *Pop Poetics.*
GUSTAVE FLAUBERT, *Bouvard and Pécuchet.*
KASS FLEISHER, *Talking out of School.*
JON FOSSE, *Aliss at the Fire.*
Melancholy.
FORD MADOX FORD, *The March of Literature.*
MAX FRISCH, *I'm Not Stiller.*
Man in the Holocene.
CARLOS FUENTES, *Christopher Unborn.*
Distant Relations.
Terra Nostra.
Where the Air Is Clear.
TAKEHIKO FUKUNAGA, *Flowers of Grass.*
WILLIAM GADDIS, JR., *The Recognitions.*
JANICE GALLOWAY, *Foreign Parts.*
The Trick Is to Keep Breathing.
WILLIAM H. GASS, *Life Sentences.*
The Tunnel.
The World Within the Word.
Willie Masters' Lonesome Wife.
GÉRARD GAVARRY, *Hoppla! 1 2 3.*

ETIENNE GILSON, *The Arts of the Beautiful.*
Forms and Substances in the Arts.
C. S. GISCOMBE, *Giscome Road.*
Here.
DOUGLAS GLOVER, *Bad News of the Heart.*
WITOLD GOMBROWICZ, *A Kind of Testament.*
PAULO EMÍLIO SALES GOMES, *P's Three Women.*
GEORGI GOSPODINOV, *Natural Novel.*
JUAN GOYTISOLO, *Count Julian.*
Juan the Landless.
Makbara.
Marks of Identity.
HENRY GREEN, *Blindness.*
Concluding.
Doting.
Nothing.
JACK GREEN, *Fire the Bastards!*
JIŘÍ GRUŠA, *The Questionnaire.*
MELA HARTWIG, *Am I a Redundant Human Being?*
JOHN HAWKES, *The Passion Artist.*
Whistlejacket.
ELIZABETH HEIGHWAY, ED., *Contemporary Georgian Fiction.*
AIDAN HIGGINS, *Balcony of Europe.*
Blind Man's Bluff.
Bornholm Night-Ferry.
Langrishe, Go Down.
Scenes from a Receding Past.
KEIZO HINO, *Isle of Dreams.*
KAZUSHI HOSAKA, *Plainsong.*
ALDOUS HUXLEY, *Antic Hay.*
Point Counter Point.
Those Barren Leaves.
Time Must Have a Stop.
NAOYUKI II, *The Shadow of a Blue Cat.*
DRAGO JANČAR, *The Tree with No Name.*
MIKHEIL JAVAKHISHVILI, *Kvachi.*
GERT JONKE, *The Distant Sound.*
Homage to Czerny.
The System of Vienna.

JACQUES JOUET, *Mountain R.*
Savage.
Upstaged.
MIEKO KANAI, *The Word Book.*
YORAM KANIUK, *Life on Sandpaper.*
ZURAB KARUMIDZE, *Dagny.*
JOHN KELLY, *From Out of the City.*
HUGH KENNER, *Flaubert, Joyce and Beckett: The Stoic Comedians.*
Joyce's Voices.
DANILO KIŠ, *The Attic.*
The Lute and the Scars.
Psalm 44.
A Tomb for Boris Davidovich.
ANITA KONKKA, *A Fool's Paradise.*
GEORGE KONRÁD, *The City Builder.*
TADEUSZ KONWICKI, *A Minor Apocalypse.*
The Polish Complex.
ANNA KORDZAIA-SAMADASHVILI, *Me, Margarita.*
MENIS KOUMANDAREAS, *Koula.*
ELAINE KRAF, *The Princess of 72nd Street.*
JIM KRUSOE, *Iceland.*
AYSE KULIN, *Farewell: A Mansion in Occupied Istanbul.*
EMILIO LASCANO TEGUI, *On Elegance While Sleeping.*
ERIC LAURRENT, *Do Not Touch.*
VIOLETTE LEDUC, *La Bâtarde.*
EDOUARD LEVÉ, *Autoportrait.*
Newspaper.
Suicide.
Works.
MARIO LEVI, *Istanbul Was a Fairy Tale.*
DEBORAH LEVY, *Billy and Girl.*
JOSÉ LEZAMA LIMA, *Paradiso.*
ROSA LIKSOM, *Dark Paradise.*
OSMAN LINS, *Avalovara.*
The Queen of the Prisons of Greece.
FLORIAN LIPUŠ, *The Errors of Young Tjaž.*
GORDON LISH, *Peru.*
ALF MACLOCHLAINN, *Out of Focus.*
Past Habitual.

The Corpus in the Library.
RON LOEWINSOHN, *Magnetic Field(s).*
YURI LOTMAN, *Non-Memoirs.*
D. KEITH MANO, *Take Five.*
MINA LOY, *Stories and Essays of Mina Loy.*
MICHELINE AHARONIAN MARCOM, *A Brief History of Yes.*
The Mirror in the Well.
BEN MARCUS, *The Age of Wire and String.*
WALLACE MARKFIELD, *Teitlebaum's Window.*
DAVID MARKSON, *Reader's Block.*
Wittgenstein's Mistress.
CAROLE MASO, *AVA.*
HISAKI MATSUURA, *Triangle.*
LADISLAV MATEJKA & KRYSTYNA POMORSKA, EDS., *Readings in Russian Poetics: Formalist & Structuralist Views.*
HARRY MATHEWS, *Cigarettes.*
The Conversions.
The Human Country.
The Journalist.
My Life in CIA.
Singular Pleasures.
The Sinking of the Odradek Stadium.
Tlooth.
HISAKI MATSUURA, *Triangle.*
DONAL MCLAUGHLIN, *beheading the virgin mary, and other stories.*
JOSEPH MCELROY, *Night Soul and Other Stories.*
ABDELWAHAB MEDDEB, *Talismano.*
GERHARD MEIER, *Isle of the Dead.*
HERMAN MELVILLE, *The Confidence-Man.*
AMANDA MICHALOPOULOU, *I'd Like.*
STEVEN MILLHAUSER, *The Barnum Museum.*
In the Penny Arcade.
RALPH J. MILLS, JR., *Essays on Poetry.*
MOMUS, *The Book of Jokes.*
CHRISTINE MONTALBETTI, *The Origin of Man.*
Western.

RAYMOND ROUSSEL, *Impressions of Africa.*

VEDRANA RUDAN, *Night.*

PABLO M. RUIZ, *Four Cold Chapters on the Possibility of Literature.*

GERMAN SADULAEV, *The Maya Pill.*

TOMAŽ ŠALAMUN, *Soy Realidad.*

LYDIE SALVAYRE, *The Company of Ghosts.*
The Lecture.
The Power of Flies.

LUIS RAFAEL SÁNCHEZ, *Macho Camacho's Beat.*

SEVERO SARDUY, *Cobra & Maitreya.*

NATHALIE SARRAUTE, *Do You Hear Them?*
Martereau.
The Planetarium.

STIG SÆTERBAKKEN, *Siamese.*
Self-Control.
Through the Night.

ARNO SCHMIDT, *Collected Novellas.*
Collected Stories.
Nobodaddy's Children.
Two Novels.

ASAF SCHURR, *Motti.*

GAIL SCOTT, *My Paris.*

DAMION SEARLS, *What We Were Doing and Where We Were Going.*

JUNE AKERS SEESE,
Is This What Other Women Feel Too?

BERNARD SHARE, *Inish.*
Transit.

VIKTOR SHKLOVSKY, *Bowstring.*
Literature and Cinematography.
Theory of Prose.
Third Factory.
Zoo, or Letters Not about Love.

PIERRE SINIAC, *The Collaborators.*

KJERSTI A. SKOMSVOLD,
The Faster I Walk, the Smaller I Am.

JOSEF ŠKVORECKÝ, *The Engineer of Human Souls.*

GILBERT SORRENTINO, *Aberration of Starlight.*
Blue Pastoral.
Crystal Vision.

Imaginative Qualities of Actual Things.
Mulligan Stew. Red the Fiend.
Steelwork.
Under the Shadow.

MARKO SOSIČ, *Ballerina, Ballerina.*

ANDRZEJ STASIUK, *Dukla.*
Fado.

GERTRUDE STEIN, *The Making of Americans.*
A Novel of Thank You.

LARS SVENDSEN, *A Philosophy of Evil.*

PIOTR SZEWC, *Annihilation.*

GONÇALO M. TAVARES, *A Man: Klaus Klump.*
Jerusalem.
Learning to Pray in the Age of Technique.

LUCIAN DAN TEODOROVICI,
Our Circus Presents...

NIKANOR TERATOLOGEN, *Assisted Living.*

STEFAN THEMERSON, *Hobson's Island.*
The Mystery of the Sardine.
Tom Harris.

TAEKO TOMIOKA, *Building Waves.*

JOHN TOOMEY, *Sleepwalker.*

DUMITRU TSEPENEAG, *Hotel Europa.*
The Necessary Marriage.
Pigeon Post.
Vain Art of the Fugue.

ESTHER TUSQUETS, *Stranded.*

DUBRAVKA UGRESIC, *Lend Me Your Character.*
Thank You for Not Reading.

TOR ULVEN, *Replacement.*

MATI UNT, *Brecht at Night.*
Diary of a Blood Donor.
Things in the Night.

ÁLVARO URIBE & OLIVIA SEARS, EDS.,
Best of Contemporary Mexican Fiction.

ELOY URROZ, *Friction.*
The Obstacles.

LUISA VALENZUELA, *Dark Desires and the Others.*
He Who Searches.

PAUL VERHAEGHEN, *Omega Minor.*

BORIS VIAN, *Heartsnatcher.*

LLORENÇ VILLALONGA, *The Dolls'*
Room.

TOOMAS VINT, *An Unending Landscape.*

ORNELA VORPSI, *The Country Where No*
One Ever Dies.

AUSTRYN WAINHOUSE, *Hedyphagetica.*

CURTIS WHITE, *America's Magic*
Mountain.
The Idea of Home.
Memories of My Father Watching TV.
Requiem.

DIANE WILLIAMS,
Excitability: Selected Stories.
Romancer Erector.

DOUGLAS WOOLF, *Wall to Wall.*
Ya! & John-Juan.

JAY WRIGHT, *Polynomials and Pollen.*
The Presentable Art of Reading Absence.

PHILIP WYLIE, *Generation of Vipers.*

MARGUERITE YOUNG, *Angel in the*
Forest.
Miss MacIntosh, My Darling.

REYOUNG, *Unbabbling.*

VLADO ŽABOT, *The Succubus.*

ZORAN ŽIVKOVIĆ , *Hidden Camera.*

LOUIS ZUKOFSKY, *Collected Fiction.*

VITOMIL ZUPAN, *Minuet for Guitar.*

SCOTT ZWIREN, *God Head.*

AND MORE . . .